Promised Valley War

RON FRITSCH

For Lee Ann, David, and my family

ISBN: 0615567290
ISBN-13: 978-0615567297

Front cover photograph © iStockphoto.com/Brett Charlton

Back cover photograph © John Moll

For information address:

Asymmetric Worlds
1657 West Winona Street
Chicago, IL 60640-2707

www.promisedvalley.com

Notes

A **character list** appears at the end of this novel, beginning on page 239.

The "**tellers**" referred to in the Promised Valley series of novels perform several functions. They remember and retell their ancestors' stories. They preside at full-moon and change-of-season holidays, as well as at mating ceremonies and funerals. In place of the king, they hear and decide disputes among the people. They are mostly persons who "go with" members of their own gender.

The "**valley people**" are prehistoric farmers who live in an especially fertile valley. They believe the gods had long ago promised it to them in return for their good behavior and obedience.

The "**hill people**" are the hunters who roam the mostly barren hills beyond the mountains surrounding the valley. They believe the gods promised the valley—with the abundance of prey in its mountain-side forests, lake, and river—to them.

The "**town people**" are the valley people who live on a river bluff and run the kingdom under the direction of the king, the chief warrior, and the first teller.

The **"river people"** live in a seacoast kingdom south of the promised valley and travel up and down the river on rafts to trade with the valley people.

Chapter 1

It began in the last sunlight of a summer day on the eastern side of the mountains at sunrise pass. Shadows were long and tapering like the claws of a raptor, a hawk the size of a god perhaps, grasping the earth and the humans living upon it as if they were helpless prey.

According to his people's laws, Blue Sky was in forbidden territory. But one day the previous spring he'd decided the prohibition needn't apply to him. And after the rebellion his sister, Rose Leaf, the prince, Morning Sun, and he'd led earlier that year, not even the king could disagree with him on that point.

Blue Sky was in the ravine below his people's mountain guard post. If he encountered any kind of trouble with hill people there, he'd be on his own. None of his people could come to his rescue. He'd told the guards on duty he was going to see Wandering Star, the enemy who'd become his companion—contrary to the laws of both his people and the hill people.

Approaching Wandering Star's tent on the bank of the brook beyond the thicket, and no longer within sight of the guard post, Blue Sky saw a man's shadow poking out from a clump of bushes.

Blue Sky wondered if Wandering Star had hoped to amuse himself by leaping out at his unwitting farmer friend and giving him a damned good scare.

When Blue Sky, Rose Leaf, and Morning Sun were children, they enjoyed frightening one another, often pretending they were hill people, hunters drawn to the valley by their unnatural and evil desire to roast a farmer child over a fire like a kid, lamb, or calf. Blue Sky and Rose Leaf agreed the best-tasting child of them all would be the valley people's prince, Morning Sun.

Except for their royal family and their officials, who occupied a bluff-top town, most of Blue Sky's people were settled in farming villages in the valley their gods had promised them. They raised, cared for, and used for their own purposes cattle, sheep, and goats their ancestors had tamed. In their fields and orchards they grew wheat, barley, clover, lentils, apples, grapes, and other plants their ancestors had learned to cultivate to provide regular and generous supplies of sustenance for themselves and their livestock.

1

Wandering Star's people roamed the mostly barren hills on the other side of the mountains surrounding the valley. His people's able-bodied men and older boys hunted animals running wild and free. Their women, old men, and children gathered plants they happened upon, which likewise grew wild and free. The stories of their ancestors and gods had convinced them that farming was unnatural, evil, and forbidden.

Stopping to peer around a tall shrub toward the source of the shadow, Blue Sky saw his childhood fears revived. The man casting the shadow wasn't Wandering Star. Like all the hill men other than Wandering Star, this stranger had a beard and dark curly hair falling to his shoulders.

He turned and saw Blue Sky, who already had his spear aimed at the hill man's belly.

Although the hill man had his own spear, it was pointed at the ground, uselessly.

If Blue Sky had wished to do so, he could've killed the hill man, then and there.

But the hill man might've had comrades lurking nearby in the shadows. Hearing the hill man's screams, they could've come running and easily overwhelmed and killed Blue Sky.

The hill man was leaving himself vulnerable, keeping the tip of his spear near the ground.

The valley people's warriors learned in their coming-of-age training that if an adversary in such a situation made even the slightest motion to raise his spear, they should instantly impale him.

Maybe the hill people had a similar rule. Blue Sky hadn't thought to ask Wandering Star about that.

Blue Sky suddenly realized who the man was: the lead hunter in the ravine the previous autumn, the hill man who'd initially disregarded Wandering Star's warning cries not to take his hunting party any higher up the mountainside and risk death at the hands of the farmers.

Then the man looked up at the farmers' guard post and saw Blue Sky and his equally brave or foolish comrade, Spring Rain, ready for bloody battle all by themselves, but still holding back their arrows when they easily could've let them fly.

2

The hill man turned his companions around, giving up the deer they'd trapped in a thicket. He made Blue Sky and Spring Rain heroes in the eyes of their comrades and people—even though they knew they weren't and objected to the undeserved praise.

Now the lead hunter was staring at Blue Sky again, this time a spear-length away.

Blue Sky couldn't help but wonder if the man also recognized him.

"Leave the ravine," Blue Sky said, quietly, using the hill people's words he'd learned from Wandering Star, motioning in the direction of the lower entrance to the ravine.

The hill man backed away from Blue Sky, dragging the tip of his spear along the ground.

After he reached a safe distance, he picked up his spear, turned, and gracefully ran away.

Sprinting along the brook, he nevertheless startled Wandering Star, who'd been sitting at his fire preparing an evening meal. He was waiting for his farmer companion, Blue Sky, who'd defied his people's gods and laws, gone with an enemy hill man every chance he got, and become his friend and lover.

Wandering Star stood up and watched the intruder leap over the brook and rush from the ravine.

*****

"He was back there, hiding in the bushes," Blue Sky said, pointing with his spear. "He was staring at you. I surprised him when I came along. I could've killed him, but I didn't. I let him go."

Wandering Star frowned.

"He was the leader of the hunters who came here last autumn," Blue Sky said.

Wandering Star nodded. "My people call him Long Arm."

"What was he doing here?"

Wandering Star's scowl deepened.

"Are he and his comrades looking for game?" Blue Sky asked.

"Maybe. But if they are, they didn't let me know."

"Would they usually let you know?"

"Yes," Wandering Star replied, clenching his teeth.

3

He and Blue Sky sat down on the flattened log he used for a bench.

Wandering Star had chosen to shave off his beard, as all the valley men did, and cut his hair the length Blue Sky had his, with just a few curls covering the upper parts of his forehead, ears, and neck. The valley people wondered why Wandering Star's people hadn't punished him for doing what the farmers did. He said his people had no law governing beards and hair length.

Neither did the valley people. After the recent rebellion, all the older boys and men among the farmers started letting their hair grow to the length Blue Sky grew his. So did the older boys and younger men among the court people, including the prince, and the younger tellers. The men who still refused to let their curls, often gray now, cover any part of their foreheads, necks, or ears were the older men among the court people and the tellers—those who'd opposed the rebellion.

The tellers—who were almost all of the men who went with men, and some of the women who went with women, and had no children to raise—remembered and retold the people the stories and laws their gods and ancestors had handed down to them. Blue Sky was spending his encampment year in the mountains, after coming of age, with the apprentice tellers on sunrise pass.

Staring at the lower end of the ravine, Wandering Star assured Blue Sky that Long Arm hadn't come for the same reason Blue Sky had.

Long Arm and his mate had seven living children, five others having died in their infancy. But Long Arm and his brothers and cousins were among the best hunters his people had. Despite their many children, they never worried about starvation, even at the end of a harsh winter.

"I don't know why he was here," Wandering Star said. "I have no idea why he didn't tell me he was in the area. I can't imagine why he'd be interested in what I'm doing."

"He didn't seem surprised," Blue Sky said, "when I spoke your language."

Wandering Star, still scowling, turned to look at Blue Sky.

"That's the last thing," he said, "I wanted to hear you say."

4

*****

Early the next evening, Solemn Promise, the hut-mate of the prince in the encampment for the court people's sons on the other side of the great canyon at sunrise pass, approached the hut Spring Rain and Blue Sky shared in the apprentice tellers' encampment. Many Numbers, who'd come up to the pass to spend the full-moon holiday with Spring Rain, his mate, was with them at the table they kept outside the back door facing the forest. As he always did when the three of them prepared a meal together, he was giving Spring Rain and Blue Sky meticulous instructions.

Solemn Promise had accompanied Morning Sun and Rose Leaf on some of their visits to the apprentice tellers' encampment, but he'd never come on his own.

"Morning Sun had guard duty this afternoon and evening," he said as soon as he was within earshot.

Even the prince took his turn on guard duty during a full-moon holiday. When he did, Rose Leaf usually spent the time with Blue Sky, Spring Rain, and Many Numbers. They were expecting her to join them for wine, the supper they were working on, and all the gossip she and Many Numbers had lent their ears to in the valley since the last full moon.

"The prince," Solemn Promise added, referring to the man he shared a hut with, "didn't show up for it."

Many Numbers, Spring Rain, and Blue Sky laid down their blades, bowls, and spoons. They couldn't imagine Morning Sun skipping guard duty. He always loudly insisted upon doing what every other guard in his encampment did. He was thankful, he told his comrades, his mother and the court people weren't close by during his encampment year to remind him of his many princely prerogatives. He would've considered it especially shameful not to show up for guard duty.

"Why didn't he?" Blue Sky asked.

Solemn Promise was trembling. Heavily sweating, too.

Spring Rain handed him a cup of water.

"Nobody knows," Solemn Promise replied. "That's why I'm here. We went to the clearing. Neither Morning Sun nor Rose Leaf

5

was there. They weren't with the women, either. We've searched all through the forest, yelling for them. We can't find them anywhere."

Blue Sky, Spring Rain, and Many Numbers stared at their visitor.

"We were hoping they were here," Solemn Promise said.

"They're not here," Blue Sky told him. "We haven't seen them all day."

They promptly sought out all the others in the apprentice tellers' encampment, asking if they'd seen Morning Sun or Rose Leaf that day. None of them had.

The rules of the valley people's army were clear in a case such as this. They were required to send a messenger to the town at once.

"I'll go now," Many Numbers said.

"I'll go with you," Solemn Promise said.

They decided to walk all night and all the next day. They'd stop only once to sleep. They planned to reach East Land's village late in the afternoon of the second day.

They'd pass through Blue Sky's village to break the news to his parents, Gentle Brook and Green Field, who'd held themselves out to be Rose Leaf's mother and father throughout her childhood.

Then Many Numbers and Solemn Promise would proceed to the town. There they'd inform the king and the queen that the prince and the woman he was to marry that autumn were missing.

*****

Blue Sky hadn't stayed with his hill-man companion the previous night. Wandering Star wanted to look for Long Arm and find out why he'd been in the ravine, and he didn't wish to wait until morning to do it.

After Many Numbers and Solemn Promise left sunrise pass, Blue Sky went down the ravine to the brook. Wandering Star, though, wasn't in any of the places Blue Sky usually found him. His campfire had gone out.

Blue Sky decided to wait for him. He stayed all that night in his lover's tent, fitfully falling asleep and dreaming Wandering Star had returned and was lying next to him, their naked bodies curled together.

6

Blue Sky woke several times with a start, horrified to find himself fully clothed and alone.

Sunrise came. Wandering Star still hadn't returned.

Blue Sky hadn't previously imagined how dark a dawn, even one dazzling his eyes with its brightness, could seem.

*****

Upon learning that Wandering Star as well as Morning Sun and Rose Leaf had disappeared, all of Blue Sky's comrades except Spring Rain carefully avoided him.

Blue Sky couldn't hold their silence against them. He could see they were afraid opening their mouths to speak to him would only reveal fears they had no wish to confirm or confront.

Dawn came four more days, and Wandering Star hadn't yet returned to his campsite.

And Morning Sun and Rose Leaf were still missing.

Whether the gods had anything to do with it or not, the world in which Blue Sky lived began to make no sense to him.

*****

The rebellion had ended early that summer, when the king, Tall Oak, and the people agreed that Morning Sun could mate with Rose Leaf even though she wasn't Blue Sky's sister or the daughter of Green Field and Gentle Brook but was in fact the hill people's princess. After that, Blue Sky had often brought Wandering Star up the ravine to the apprentice tellers' encampment. Tall Oak had told Wandering Star he was free, if he wished, to live among the valley people.

One full-moon holiday some of the apprentice tellers invited Wandering Star to wrestle with them. His people's rules for the game were different from the valley people's, which required the winner to hold the loser flat on his back until the official counted to ten. The hill people's rules required the loser to voice surrender, admitting he couldn't take any more punishment.

Wandering Star decided he preferred the valley people's rules over his people's, which sometimes left a stubborn or foolish loser with a serious and permanent injury.

Noon Breeze, though, insisted he wanted to fight by the hill people's rules. It was the courteous thing to do, he claimed, with a guest. Besides, he said, it sounded like fun.

Wandering Star reluctantly agreed to fight him, following his people's rules.

Blue Sky assumed he did it only to shut Noon Breeze up.

Because of their size difference, Wandering Star, who was almost as tall as Blue Sky but more slender and sinewy like Spring Rain and Many Numbers, easily pinned Noon Breeze, who was short and scrawny. Wandering Star held him down well past the time when valley officials would've declared the contest over and Wandering Star the winner.

But Noon Breeze wasn't about to give up. Even though Wandering Star dug his knees into his shoulders and resorted to slapping him, as his people's wrestlers often had to do with their most recalcitrant opponents, Noon Breeze refused to beg for his suffering to end.

"Okay," Wandering Star said, "I give up. I can't take any more of this. You win."

Noon Breeze threw his arms around Wandering Star, who was attempting to stand up.

"You don't have to get off me," Noon Breeze said, "just because you lost."

"You either let him get off you," Blue Sky said to Noon Breeze, as their comrades snickered, "or you'll wrestle me under the hill people's rules. And I won't give up before you do."

Noon Breeze reluctantly released Wandering Star and scowled at Blue Sky.

"Who appointed you chief warrior?" he asked.

Another time Wandering Star had accompanied Blue Sky, Many Numbers, and Spring Rain to see Rose Leaf and Morning Sun in the forest clearing where they'd built their cloistered hut.

The hosts and their guests sat on flattened logs in the late afternoon sun drinking wine.

Wandering Star drank, too. He'd been afraid to drink with Blue Sky at first, mindful of the trouble wine had caused his people in the last war. But he soon realized a moderate dose of it caused him no harm, especially toward the end of the day, after there was no more work to be done, and they could take pleasure in other things.

Rose Leaf asked him if the hill people knew whether she, their king's only child, lived.

"No, they don't," Wandering Star replied.

"My mother, Thistle Dew, doesn't know whether her daughter is alive or dead?"

"No, she doesn't."

Rose Leaf sighed. "I wish my mother could be told I'm living with the farmers. I wish all our people could be told the farmers have treated me well—so well they'll even let me become the wife of their prince."

Wandering Star looked at Morning Sun and smiled. "You've made a good choice."

"But I know you can't tell our people I'm alive," Rose Leaf continued. "Many Numbers said you'd also be required to tell them how you know that. Then they'd have to kill you."

"I can't tell the people," Wandering Star agreed. "But I'd like to let your mother know you're alive and well."

"Can you do that?" Many Numbers asked. "Can an exile speak with your people's queen?"

"I can tell somebody who might get word to her," Wandering Star replied.

"Secretly?" Spring Rain asked.

"Secretly," Wandering Star replied.

"Safely for you?" Rose Leaf asked.

Wandering Star shrugged his shoulders. "There's not a lot of safety among our people."

"Then don't tell anybody," Rose Leaf said. "Is my mother well?"

Wandering Star hesitated. "Do you wish to know the truth?"

"Yes."

"She refuses to be seen in public."

"Do you know why?"

"She went into seclusion the day you were abducted. She tells people her life ended when the farmers' prince and his comrade took you away. She couldn't have any more children."

The farmers' prince in the last war with the hill people was now the valley people's king, Tall Oak, and his comrade was Green Field. Hill warriors had captured them, but they'd escaped, taking the hill people's infant princess with them, seeking revenge for having their testicles removed upon the hill king's order.

"My mother still has my father," Rose Leaf said, "even if they can't have more children."

Her father, Lightning Spear, had lost his manhood the first day of the war. That was the reason why he'd decided to inflict the same wound on the captive enemy prince and his comrade.

Wandering Star scowled. "Your mother detests your father. They live in separate tents."

"You must detest him yourself," Rose Leaf said. "He sent you into exile."

Wandering Star took her hand. "You should know what your absence means to our people. They lost the war and the king's only child at the same time. If your father dies without a male heir from you, the kingdom will probably go to a man most of our people live in fear of."

Wandering Star explained that Lightning Spear was the king of all their people as well as the chieftain of their most numerous tribe. His closest relative, other than Rose Leaf, was arguably a distant cousin called Thunder Hunter, the chieftain of the second-most-powerful tribe. Wandering Star liberally used the words "cruel" and "bloodthirsty" to describe him.

Wandering Star turned to Morning Sun. "You're very fortunate," he said. "You get to choose the person who'll be your mate, and she gets to choose you."

The hill people had the same law the valley people had, requiring parents to choose their children's mates. The hill-people's king and tellers, though, enforced their law.

"My father would choose my mate for me?" Rose Leaf asked.

"He would," Wandering Star replied. "He'd force you to become the mate of some chieftain's son, whether you desired him or not. Maybe one of Thunder Hunter's two sons."

"Well, would I find them attractive?" Rose Leaf asked, not without giving the prince a naughty smile as she looked his finely muscled body up and down.

"Not the older son," Wandering Star replied. "He's called Dark Storm."

"What about the younger son?" Rose Leaf asked. "Is he pleasing to the eye?"

"That's War Cloud. Very pleasing to see, yes. Pleasing to live with? Not at all, I'd say. He's as brutal as his father—maybe worse. He begs his father to let him execute people."

The princess, Rose Leaf, no longer amused, took Morning Sun's hand.

"Then I'm glad I'm living with the farmers in their valley," she said, her dark brown eyes tearing. "And I can only thank the gods for sending Green Field and Tall Oak to rescue me."

*****

Shortly after Spring Rain and Blue Sky began their guard duty on the fifth day after Morning Sun and Rose Leaf went missing, Blue Sky saw something moving in the clump of bushes where he'd first spotted Wandering Star the previous autumn.

Blue Sky rose to his feet, yelling his hill friend's name.

Wandering Star hurried up the ravine to the guard post.

He'd returned earlier that morning but hadn't wanted to reveal himself to the guards who'd preceded Blue Sky and Spring Rain on duty.

"I was afraid they'd kill me," he said. "They'd have every reason to."

He appeared to Blue Sky as if he might be ill, too fevered to stay asleep for long.

"My people," he said, "captured Morning Sun and Rose Leaf."

Blue Sky's comrades had prayed to the gods they'd never hear those words spoken.

*****

Wandering Star explained how his people did it.

11

One warm afternoon the previous spring, Long Arm and his family were encamped below sunrise pass. Long Arm walked up to the pass to invite Wandering Star to join his family for their evening meal. They'd killed a deer that morning.

He was still at a distance when he saw Wandering Star bathing naked in the brook outside his tent with a beardless young man—a farmer. Wandering Star had shaven off his own beard, too.

Keeping himself unseen, Long Arm moved close enough to hear what they were saying. The farmer was attempting to learn the hill people's language by using it every time he spoke.

Long Arm, who could understand almost everything the farmer said, learned that he'd come down a hidden gully in the ravine from the valley people's encampment above it.

Long Arm also figured out that the farmers sent their apprentice tellers to that encampment. And the youthful farmer was an apprentice teller who was infatuated with his new hill-man friend.

Wandering Star had once been a teller himself.

But that was before Lightning Spear expelled him from the tellerhood and exiled him from his people for publicly expressing his increasingly favorable views of the farmers, who needn't, he was telling their people, be their enemies.

His exile, though, hadn't stopped some of the hill people, Long Arm's family included, from using his services as a hunting guide and gratefully sharing their kills with him.

Blue Sky, the youthful farmer who spoke as rebelliously as Wandering Star did, was also the warrior who'd refused to retreat from the farmers' guard post the previous autumn.

Long Arm privately told Lightning Spear what he'd observed.

The king asked Long Arm to spy on Wandering Star and his farmer friend.

Long Arm did his job well. The two people he was furtively observing never suspected anybody was just outside Wandering Star's tent listening to them.

Long Arm eventually began to understand what they were saying even when they were talking in the farmers' language. Now he could speak it as well as Blue Sky, Spring Rain, and Many Numbers, having Wandering Star for their instructor, could speak the hill people's tongue.

Long Arm overheard Wandering Star and his farmer friend conversing about a young woman called Rose Leaf, who'd just recently found out, thanks to Wandering Star, that she was the hill people's abducted princess. She and Wandering Star's friend had spent their childhood as sister and brother. In the course of his eavesdropping, Long Arm figured out where the farmers' prince and Rose Leaf had built a hut they shared during her full-moon visits to sunrise pass.

After Long Arm heard Blue Sky tell Wandering Star his people's king had ordered the guard post moved so their guards would have a view of the gully, he warned Lightning Spear they had little time left to take advantage of the situation and rescue the princess.

The king told Long Arm to do whatever he needed to do to bring her back to him unharmed. And he also wanted the farmers' prince, preferably alive.

Long Arm enlisted his younger brothers and a number of their cousins to take part in the raid. But first they needed to capture Wandering Star and deny him any opportunity to assist the farmers, who'd become so friendly with him they'd invited him to live in the valley with them.

Long Arm and his men were closing in on Wandering Star one evening when the farmer companion unexpectedly happened upon the scene and spotted Long Arm, who'd sneaked around Wandering Star in the shadows to prevent him from escaping upward in the ravine.

After the farmer left that night, and Wandering Star ventured forth from his tent to find out what was going on, Long Arm and his men captured him at spear point.

They found Rose Leaf and the prince where Long Arm had figured out they'd be. He'd deduced from what he'd overheard, but still not without some effort, which campfire was theirs.

Long Arm and his men tied leather straps in and over the mouths of all three of their captives, to keep them from calling out to the farmers' guards. They led them down the gully, out of the ravine, through the hills, and over a barren plain to Lightning Spear's encampment.

*****

"I'm sorry," Wandering Star said. "I'm sorry I didn't know what Long Arm was doing. I'm sorry I wasn't able to stop him and his men from taking Rose Leaf and Morning Sun."

"Have they been harmed?" Blue Sky asked.

"Not yet," Wandering Star replied.

"Not yet," Blue Sky repeated. "What will Lightning Spear do with them?"

"He says Rose Leaf will live with our people, whether she wants to or not. She's our princess, and she'll never live with your people again. But he won't let her be harmed. He hopes she lives a long and happy life. She's his only child. He says she'll enjoy all the privileges of a princess. Her first son who survives his childhood will become our next king."

"What will he do with Morning Sun?" Blue Sky asked.

Wandering Star, still in the guard post with Blue Sky and Spring Rain, looked away from them, toward the hills where his people lived.

"What will your king do with Morning Sun?" Blue Sky repeated, raising his voice.

Wandering Star turned to Blue Sky. "Lightning Spear says he'll order him killed."

"Why hasn't he had him killed already?" Spring Rain asked.

Wandering Star was taking Blue Sky's and Spring Rain's questions like well-aimed arrows. They could see on his face the pain he felt each time one of them hit. Spring Rain's query had apparently caused him so much discomfort he couldn't put words together for a reply.

"Why aren't you still a prisoner?" Blue Sky asked him, impatiently. "Did you escape? Why couldn't Morning Sun and Rose Leaf get away with you?"

"I didn't escape," Wandering Star said. "Lightning Spear ordered me to come back here to deliver a message to your people's king."

"A message?" Blue Sky asked. "What possible message does your king have for ours?"

"Lightning Spear is offering a deal," Wandering Star replied, his voice faltering.

"A deal?" Blue Sky asked.

"He'll trade your people Morning Sun for the valley."

"Where are the gods?" Spring Rain asked, a believer committing blasphemy.

"That's Lightning Spear's deal?" Blue Sky asked, his booming voice befitting someone of his brawn. "He'll order Morning Sun killed unless we give him our valley?"

"He assured me he'll do that," Wandering Star affirmed.

"That isn't a message," Blue Sky spat. "It's an ultimatum—an evil ultimatum."

"I pleaded with Lightning Spear to let Morning Sun go home," Wandering Star said. "I told him you farmers will never give up your valley. I told him if he kills your prince, he'll only enrage your people. I said he might regret doing that. I begged him to let Morning Sun go."

Blue Sky stared at Wandering Star. The two of them had chosen to see through the darkest-night lies their peoples told, and often believed—in which the other people was always the eternal enemy. Now the two rebels could see where their naive optimism had taken them.

"I tried to explain it to Lightning Spear," Wandering Star began again. "I told him the farmers' prince and the persons closest to him don't hate our people. I told him who your father is. I told him even the emasculated comrade doesn't hate him for what he did to him and Tall Oak. I told him Green Field only wishes none of them had suffered their injuries. I told him Green Field and his mate, Gentle Brook, were good parents for Rose Leaf and raised her well. I offered to lead Morning Sun out of there at night. Then the king could tell the people I'd helped the farmers' prince escape, and he wouldn't have to admit letting him go. I'd be a traitor. I'd have to live with your people from then on, but I told him your king has already agreed to that."

"What was his response?" Spring Rain asked.

Wandering Star shook his head. "He told me if I wanted to help the farmers, I'd tell them to go back to wherever it was they came from. If they did, their prince could go with them."

"You were right," Spring Rain said. "Our people will never give him our valley. Not even to get a prince back. This Lightning Spear must not understand who we are."

Blue Sky was staring at Wandering Star. "Get me over there to Lightning Spear's encampment," he said. "There must be woodlands for us to hide in when the sun is up. Show me where Lightning Spear's tent is. We'll figure out some way to get me in it at night. I'll kill him while he's sleeping. Then we'll find Rose Leaf and Morning Sun and bring them home."

"We can't do that," Wandering Star scoffed, shaking his head again. "Lightning Spear made Long Arm his chief warrior. He's got his huge family guarding Rose Leaf and Morning Sun. We couldn't get any where near them. Besides, killing Lightning Spear wouldn't do us any good. Until Rose Leaf gives birth to a son, the person most likely to become the next king is Thunder Hunter. Believe me, he'd be worse to deal with than Lightning Spear."

Knowing the hill people's king had Rose Leaf and Morning Sun, Blue Sky wondered why he should wish to live on to see what came next—why he wouldn't be better off dead.

"There's more to it than what the king wants," Wandering Star continued. "My people are no longer what they were. Now they have their princess back—and your prince for good measure. They think the gods have answered their prayers. The future, they say, is theirs. So is the valley you arrogant farmers have pretended you own, where you can live and practice your ungodly farming."

"Then I'll take Lightning Spear's ultimatum to Tall Oak," Blue Sky said. "I'll tell him and the people what's happened to Rose Leaf and Morning Sun. I'm responsible for it. I thumbed my nose at my people's laws. I went where I was forbidden to go. The people will rightly hate me."

"You won't go to Tall Oak without me," Wandering Star said. "I'll tell him what my people did. I'll deliver Lightning Spear's ultimatum. I'll also tell him none of this is your fault. You had no reason to guess Long Arm was spying on us."

"Neither of you," Spring Rain said, "should go to see Tall Oak. If you do, you'll get yourselves killed."

That was more than a possibility for both of them. Tall Oak could order Wandering Star killed simply because he was a hill person—who'd no doubt, despite his protestations, conspired with Long Arm and Lightning Spear in the abduction of Morning Sun and Rose Leaf.

Tall Oak could order Blue Sky put to death because he'd recklessly endangered the lives of the prince and the woman who was to become his mate. Blue Sky was talking while Long Arm was listening, figuring out where he and his men could find the prince and Rose Leaf. Even if Blue Sky didn't know anybody other than Wandering Star could hear him, the penalty for what he'd done, which was treason, was death.

"If Tall Oak wishes to have me executed, so be it," Blue Sky said. "If any harm comes to either Morning Sun or Rose Leaf, I'll just as soon be dead anyway."

Spring Rain extended his arm around Blue Sky's shoulders. "Don't say that," he begged.

Blue Sky and Spring Rain both knew that if life had taken a slightly different course, as the river in the valley sometimes did, they could've been lovers.

Blue Sky looked at Wandering Star. "But you don't need to die. You can turn around right now and go back to your people. Spring Rain and I won't stop you. You can live a long life. You can forget you ever had anything to do with me or my people."

"And let you die by yourself?" Wandering Star asked. "No, I'm going with you. I helped you endanger the life of your prince. If Tall Oak wants to kill both of us, we'll die together."

"I can't believe what you're saying," Spring Rain said. "Either of you. Let me tell Tall Oak what happened. Let me give him Lightning Spear's ultimatum. He can't blame me for it."

"They'll come and get us," Blue Sky said.

"They won't get you if you aren't here," Spring Rain countered.

"Where would we be?" Wandering Star asked.

"In the forest," Spring Rain replied, "hiding. I'll bring you food. Many Numbers will help me. We'll keep you alive. We'll think up some way to stay in touch with you secretly. So we can always find you, but nobody else will be able to."

Once in a while a valley dweller would attempt to escape a punishment, usually death, by hiding in the forest. In living memory, though, nobody had succeeded. All were soon recaptured or found dead, their bones picked clean by bears or wolves. In the winter fugitives either started a campfire and revealed their whereabouts—the only other fires on the valley side of the mountains were at the guards' encampments—or they wrapped themselves in as many hides as they could lay their hands on, but they still froze to death.

Blue Sky embraced Spring Rain. "I'm sure you and Many Numbers would do that. But I'd never let you. Sturdy Limb's people would follow you. They'd torture you to tell them what you know. Then after they executed Wandering Star and me, they'd use the same spears to kill you and Many Numbers. They'd keep each of us alive, but mortally wounded, as long as they could. You want four people executed instead of two? What's the advantage in that?"

Sturdy Limb, Tall Oak's brother, was the valley people's chief warrior. He'd relished the prospect of personally executing Blue Sky, Morning Sun, and their allies, including Many Numbers and Spring Rain, after what he'd hoped would be the failure of their recent rebellion.

Spring Rain's tears were trickling down his face like dew on the petal of a flower.

Blue Sky, who otherwise might've enjoyed kissing Spring Rain and tasting the moisture on his lips, gently shook his shoulders instead.

"I'm not hiding from anybody," Blue Sky loudly insisted. "Tall Oak is our king. The gods require him to execute people for their crimes. I can't blame him if he wants to punish the individuals responsible for the capture of Morning Sun and Rose Leaf. And I, without question, am one of them."

Chapter 2

Early that evening, at the higher of the two stopping places on the path between the town and sunrise pass, Blue Sky and Wandering Star came upon the king's party, who were preparing for their second night in the forest. Sturdy Limb was present with his deputies, a number of allies among the court people, and his three sons. Law Keeper, the first teller, his high tellers and their usual entourage were with them. As were Solemn Promise, Many Numbers, and Green Field.

After a deputy spotted Blue Sky and Wandering Star coming down the path, the news of their arrival quickly spread. The travelers stopped their work and chatter and stared at them.

Blue Sky and Wandering Star approached Tall Oak. Sturdy Limb was at the king's side.

High in a tree above them, a bird had begun singing an evening song.

"I'd rather live in hell forever," Blue Sky said, "than tell you what I have to tell you."

The king's party murmured

"Hill warriors," Blue Sky continued, "came up the gully in the ravine, captured Morning Sun and Rose Leaf, and took them to the hill people's king."

"No!" many in the crowd screamed back at him, as he knew they would. "No! No! No!"

He waited for them to finish.

"I take full responsibility for my part in it," he said. "The hill people's king had a man spying on Wandering Star and me. He listened outside Wandering Star's tent. We didn't know he was there. We freely spoke of anything we pleased. The spy learned our language. He figured out how to find the clearing where Morning Sun and Rose Leaf slept—and how to get there secretly. Morning Sun and Rose Leaf are Lightning Spear's prisoners. He hasn't harmed them yet. But I helped to place their lives in jeopardy. I deserve whatever punishment you see fit to give me for that. Whatever penalty you choose, I'll accept it."

Green Field and Many Numbers, standing together but apart from the crowd, winced.

The bird in the treetops sang on.

"You can put me to death now," Blue Sky said. "I only ask two things. First, that you spare Wandering Star. I was a guard. I was responsible for the safety of the prince and Rose Leaf. I was responsible for the safety of the kingdom. I failed in every way possible. I insisted on knowing the truth. I scoffed at our people's laws. Wandering Star had nothing to do with it. He's innocent."

The valley people believed gods often disguised themselves as birds when they paid a visit to the human world.

"Second," Blue Sky continued, "when the hill warriors came into our kingdom to abduct Morning Sun and Rose Leaf, they entered by way of the gully your chief warrior and first teller assured you didn't exist. And after I proved to you it did exist, they still felt they could ignore it."

Tall Oak, who could see where Blue Sky was taking him, closed his eyes.

"They are as responsible for the abduction of Morning Sun and Rose Leaf as I am," Blue Sky drove on. "If they'd moved the guard post, the abduction never would've happened."

"We've heard enough!" Sturdy Limb yelled.

"We've heard enough!" Law Keeper echoed.

Most of the deputies, court people, and tellers chose to demonstrate their support for their leaders with loud exclamations: "No more!" "Shut him up!" "Kill him!" "Yes, kill him! That'll shut him up for good!"

"When you order me killed for the abduction of Morning Sun and Rose Leaf," Blue Sky persisted, raising his voice above the uproar of the crowd, "I only hope you don't neglect to order your worthless chief warrior and first teller killed with the same bloody spear. The farmers despise them as much as I do and will gladly see them dead. They'll thank the gods you're their king."

Those remarks struck the deputies, court people, and tellers like a fist repeatedly jabbing them in their guts.

The world they'd lived in so comfortably was suddenly sliding away from them.

"You can let their lackeys off," Blue Sky offered. "They can always claim to have been stupid and lazy. And I wouldn't blame you for believing it. The evidence is overwhelming."

20

Out of the corner of his eye, Blue Sky saw Many Numbers and his father wincing again.

The bird had reached the end of its mournful evening song.

"Place your weapons on the ground!" Sturdy Limb screamed.

Blue Sky and Wandering Star looked at one another and did so.

"Morning's Sun's cousins," Sturdy Limb added, staring at his sons, "will collect the prisoners' weapons."

The three brothers also exchanged glances and did what their father told them to do.

Wandering Star turned to Tall Oak.

"May I speak?" he asked.

The king looked at him as if he were startled to hear his voice.

Sturdy Limb replied for his brother.

"No hill person," he snapped, "has anything to say to our king!"

"Wandering Star's a hill person," Blue Sky said to Tall Oak, "but you know his sympathies are with us. He doesn't wish to see any harm come to our people."

"He's the enemy!" Sturdy Limb shouted back. "He has nothing to say to our king!"

The deputies, court people, and tellers loudly agreed.

Sturdy Limb had carefully handed out positions to his allies, as Law Keeper had to his. The king and queen took little interest in that sort of thing. Blue Sky would've been the last to blame them for their indifference, but he also suspected it explained why the chief warrior and first teller often seemed to be more in command of the day-to-day affairs of the kingdom than Tall Oak was.

Ignoring the chief warrior, Blue Sky kept his eyes fixed on the king's. "It can't hurt you," he said, "to hear what Wandering Star, enemy or not, has to say. Your nephews took his weapons."

Tall Oak turned to Wandering Star. "You may speak."

"Lightning Spear asked me to pass on to you his offer," Wandering Star said. "He'll return Morning Sun to you alive and unharmed, but only if your people leave the valley."

The deputies, court people, and tellers gasped.

"Your people's king is the tool of the hell-gods!" Law Keeper snarled.

"If your people don't leave the valley," Wandering Star nevertheless continued, "Lightning Spear asked me to promise you he'll order his warriors to kill Morning Sun."

"Evil!" the tellers, deputies, and court people cried. "Evil! Evil!"

"What will Lightning Spear do with Rose Leaf?" Green Field asked.

"He knows Rose Leaf is his daughter," Blue Sky replied. "He believes he's brought her home. He won't let her come back to live with us. But he doesn't wish to see her harmed. To the contrary, he wants to see her thrive. That's not surprising since she's his only child and heir."

Tall Oak turned to Wandering Star. "Are you supposed to take my answer to your king?"

"Yes."

"Where is he now? I assume Morning Sun and Rose Leaf are with him."

"He's a two-day journey on the other side of sunrise pass. Where he always has his encampment this time of the year. Morning Sun and Rose Leaf are with him."

"What do you think?" Green Field asked Wandering Star, the hill man who'd become his son's lover. "What should Tall Oak say to your people's king?"

"I don't think Tall Oak should give an answer until Lightning Spear demands one," Wandering Star replied. "Up to that time, Morning Sun lives, and you haven't lost anything."

"What would you have us do in the meantime?" Green Field asked.

"We could offer them something less than the valley," Blue Sky interjected. "We could let them hunt in the forest on our side of the mountains."

Blue Sky glanced at the faces in the crowd and knew how badly he'd blundered.

"Never!" Sturdy Limb spat.

"Never!" the crowd responded.

"We'll never do that!" Sturdy Limb continued, his voice growing in volume. "Those damned people in the hills have our prince and your sister. You'd let them come into the kingdom so they could

22

abduct the king and queen, too. They could take our young people as well, rape them, and make them their slaves. What you're saying is absurd! Absurd!"

"Absurd!" the crowd repeated.

Perhaps the bird had flown away, taking its sad song with it. Perhaps, being an immortal in disguise, it simply wanted nothing more to do with humans and their endless quarrels.

"I say we kill them both," Sturdy Limb offered, after the shouting began to wane. "Right here, right now. Valley Defender will do it. He loves his cousin the prince. He'll do it for him."

Valley Defender was the oldest of Sturdy Limb's three sons. A year older than Morning Sun and Blue Sky, he'd done his encampment duty on sunrise pass the previous autumn, winter, spring, and summer.

Valley Defender looked at his father as if he couldn't believe what he'd heard. He hadn't previously performed the work of an executioner. In the valley people's stories, though, the gods favored young males who avenged the murder or betrayal of a relative, especially if the person murdered or betrayed was of royal blood.

Tall Oak raised his hand for silence and turned to Sturdy Limb.

"Have Morning Sun's cousins take the prisoners away from us," he said.

The crowd murmured its approval.

"Hold them at spear-point," Sturdy Limb loudly ordered his sons. "If they make even the slightest attempt to escape, don't hesitate. Kill them both. Instantly. You'll be heroes."

*****

Blue Sky assured the cousins—who used to run about in the courtyard with Morning Sun, Rose Leaf, and him when they were all still children—that Wandering Star and he, having voluntarily surrendered themselves to the king, had no wish to escape. The cousins soon took their father's command to hold their prisoners at spear-point to mean they could sit with them around the campfire they'd started, with their spears at their feet. The two younger cousins, not having come of age yet, weren't supposed to kill anybody, not even a prisoner attempting an escape.

23

Valley Defender admitted he'd wanted Rose Leaf for his mate. And he'd still want her if he could have her. Her turning out to be a hill person didn't matter to him.

Sturdy Limb had his people take food to the cousins for their evening meal. The deputies brought nothing, though, for Blue Sky and Wandering Star. Sturdy Limb had said it would be a waste of provisions to feed them since they were going to die in the morning anyway.

But the cousins weren't hungry. The two boys gave the prisoners their food without touching it. The prisoners, who hadn't eaten all day, eagerly and gratefully devoured it.

Valley Defender tried to eat his food but soon ran into the forest, where his brothers and the prisoners could hear him throwing up.

When he returned, he offered the prisoners the rest of his food.

Splitting it with Wandering Star, Blue Sky asked Valley Defender what was wrong.

"What's wrong?" Valley Defender gasped. "My father says I'm supposed to kill you."

"He's right about that," Blue Sky said. "Morning Sun doesn't have any brothers to avenge him. You're his closest cousin who's come of age."

"He wants me to kill you," Valley Defender repeated, emphasizing the last word.

"I'd prefer you do it," Blue Sky said. "You're big and strong like Morning Sun. You can do it quickly and get it over with. Use your best spearhead. If it needs sharpening, I can help you."

The cousins' mother had died giving birth to the youngest of them. Sturdy Limb had been too occupied with his many duties as the chief warrior to raise his sons. Rainbow Evening, the queen and their mother's sister, had cheerfully done so in his place.

Valley Defender had recently caused a stir. Tall Oak had ordered the execution of a young man who, having chosen not to work, lived off what he could beg from his relatives. He'd attempted to kill his father and mother with his blade for coming up empty-handed. Even so, the parents, their injuries still oozing blood, pleaded with the king to spare their son.

But Sturdy Limb's insistence that the kingdom would be better off not having such a person living in it had won the day.

Valley Defender, who'd come of age, could've witnessed the execution, but he conspicuously chose not to—and unmistakably angered his father.

"I'll ask Tall Oak," Blue Sky said, "if you can slit my throat. That'll make it easy for you."

Persons facing execution almost always asked the king to order their throats slit. That was, of course, a quicker and less painful way to die than a wrong-doer faced in the traditional execution, which consisted of the repeated thrusting of a spear into the offender's belly.

Unless the king specified otherwise, the executioner could make a death as painful and drawn out as he chose. But Tall Oak, like his father before him, had made it clear he ordinarily preferred throat-slitting. Only if the victim's family and neighbors insisted upon a traditional execution, in view of the egregious nature of the prisoner's crime, would Tall Oak order one.

Sturdy Limb had never bothered to conceal his disagreement with his brother on that point. He said any person who deserved death deserved a painful death as well, and never a quick one.

The chief warrior also argued that the adult males who came from all over the kingdom to witness an execution deserved to be entertained for an entire day—at the end of which they'd be blissfully intoxicated, expressing their heartfelt thanks to the chief warrior for performing his job as chief executioner with such aplomb.

Sturdy Limb had also been heard to say his brother wasn't responsible for the lamentable dearth of traditional executions. For that, he blamed Green Field and Gentle Brook, individuals who took no part in ruling the kingdom, who had no duty to impose order among the people, and who could therefore pretend that justice needn't be hard and cruel.

"You expect me to slit your throat?" Valley Defender asked, again stressing the word indicating the opened throat would be Blue Sky's.

Blue Sky supposed Tall Oak would probably give in to Sturdy Limb this time and order a traditional execution for him. He could at least beg for a throat-slitting for Wandering Star.

"You killed a man," Blue Sky said to Valley Defender, "in last summer's battle on sunrise pass. Your comrades said your spear went all the way through his body. They said after that you grabbed his spear and slit his throat with it. They said you were covered with his blood."

"You were the one?" Wandering Star asked, looking at Valley Defender, after hearing this story for the first time. "You did that? I thought I'd seen you before. I was in the bushes next to the gully. I watched you do it. You frightened the man's comrades. They ran. One of your comrades got the man who stumbled. But you won that battle all by yourself."

"Can't you do at least as much for me?" Blue Sky asked. "Thrust your spear in my belly if Tall Oak orders it. Then slit my throat. I'll lie on the ground and make it easy for you. Do the same thing for Wandering Star. Don't listen to the crowd. They'll be screaming about traitors and evil hill people. But you're the executioner. You get to decide. They can't blame you for wanting to get the business over with, up here in the mountains, as quickly and cleanly as possible."

"Last summer was different," Valley Defender insisted, shaking his head. "That was a battle. I killed a man I'd never met. Among men I'd never met. If we didn't kill some of them, and chase the rest of them away, they'd kill us. I had no choice. That man I killed wasn't you."

Valley Defender turned to Wandering Star.

"That man wasn't you, either," he said.

Their people, Blue Sky thought, would be fortunate if Valley Defender became their king someday—if the hill people's king actually carried out his threat to execute Morning Sun.

The youngest of the three cousins went to fetch some wood for the fire. He came back with the fuel and a question: "Will they make us watch?"

Tall Oak and his father had ruled that females and males not yet of age couldn't witness an execution. Every time, though, some older boys, employing one stratagem or other, with varying degrees of success, managed to surreptitiously view the proceeding.

Morning Sun's cousins had never been among those boys.

Morning Sun and Blue Sky were, though, for an execution shortly before they came of age. It was a traditional one, too. Sturdy Limb himself did the killing, as he invariably did in that kind of execution, which was always delayed by him until all the males of age from the most distant reaches of the kingdom could arrive to view the gruesome but satisfying death of another human.

The on-lookers also realized that if they chose to misbehave, they could be the unfortunate person being made an example of in some subsequent execution.

By then, Rose Leaf almost always insisted on doing whatever Morning Sun and Blue Sky did, but the day of the execution they wanted to view, she told them she had no desire to join them.

"You're lucky," Valley Defender said to his brothers. "I wish I weren't of age yet. I wish I hadn't killed a hill man. He was only hunting. I didn't know that. I wish I were still a boy."

Blue Sky's father would have to watch. And cradle his son in his arms while he died.

"Morning Sun's still alive," the middle cousin said. "So is Rose Leaf. Why does anybody have to be killed?"

A thoughtful brother of a king might well ask such a question. To be sure, someone might counter that the prince was already as good as dead since the kingdom had two choices: give him up to a youthful death at the hands of the hill people, or give up the promised valley. That might lead, though, to the difficult but perhaps not impossible task of creating more choices than those.

Tall Oak and Sturdy Limb left the three cousins and their two prisoners together in the forest without further instructions throughout the night.

Blue Sky told the cousins it would be pointless for them to stay awake guarding Wandering Star and himself. They could all go to sleep, assuming sleep was possible for the two of them facing execution in the morning.

Blue Sky and Wandering Star, exhausted by the events of the day, did in fact fall asleep.

But when Blue Sky, having drunk Valley Defender's wine, got up in the middle of the night to relieve himself, he heard the youngest cousin, lying between his brothers, sobbing.

*****

Before dawn, the chief warrior and several of his men, all with spears raised, marched up the path to the clearing where Blue Sky, Wandering Star, and the cousins had spent the night.

In a booming voice Sturdy Limb ordered his sons to "take the prisoners to the king."

"Will he order them killed?" the middle son asked.

His father, detecting apprehension in the boy's voice, gave him a hard look.

"Take the prisoners to Tall Oak," he repeated.

Drawing closer, he saw his sons' spears on the ground and scowled again.

"At spear-point!" he added, making certain his sons heard the disgust in his voice.

*****

Tall Oak looked at Blue Sky, the son of the man who'd saved his life in the last war.

Sturdy Limb, with his deputies next to and behind him in the order of their rank, and Law Keeper, with his high tellers similarly arrayed, stood on either side of the king.

Tall Oak knew rank was vitally important to the chief warrior and first teller he'd appointed to run the kingdom. He usually couldn't say, though, where specific persons ranked, or why. Tall Oak had little interest in the day-to-day administration of the kingdom. He'd let Sturdy Limb and Law Keeper do it for him.

And yet he often seemed to enjoy hearing Rainbow Evening, Green Field, and Gentle Brook—and later all three of their children—ridicule his chief warrior and first teller.

Blue Sky had tried to convince the king that often what his officials did wasn't for his benefit or the people's. Tall Oak took the view that since Sturdy Limb and Law Keeper were the only persons willing to run the kingdom for him, he had to tolerate their "occasional mistakes."

At the moment, Sturdy Limb, making no effort to conceal his contempt, refused to look at his brother, who was openly weeping.

28

The chief warrior could only wait, though, for the king to pull himself together.

There was nothing anybody could say or do. Perhaps that's what Tall Oak wanted.

Green Field and Many Numbers once again stood together but apart from the others.

When Tall Oak did speak, still staring at Blue Sky, his voice was admirably strong.

"Law Keeper and the other tellers present spent most of the night considering your case. The first teller has advised me they've arrived at a unanimous decision as to what I should do with you for endangering the lives of Morning Sun and Rose Leaf."

Shafts of sunlight broke through the evergreens above them like spears parting flesh.

"Law Keeper will explain their decision," Tall Oak said.

"You chose to disobey the gods," the first teller said, glowering at Blue Sky. "They've always warned us not to question the things we see in this perfect world they created for our people, and not to demand answers where they've decided we should have none. They tell us of the people who chose to eat from the tree of knowledge, tasting only the loss of their promised valley after they did so. They tell us of the young man who sought to soar in the sky with the eagles and achieved nothing more than a quick fall back to earth and a needless early death."

It was difficult for Blue Sky to believe the person speaking was the first teller of a people who imagined their obvious superiority to their enemy was based on their vast knowledge and their willingness to use it whenever and however they could.

The crowd nevertheless murmured their agreement with everything the first teller said.

"You chose to disobey," Law Keeper continued. "You've not only seen fit to question the things of this world but to challenge the gods themselves. Many persons have given evidence of the despicable remarks you've made. You know full well how often you've blasphemed. And you, along with every other person in the kingdom, know the penalty for doing so is death."

"Put him to death!" one of the more exuberant court people that morning cried.

Blue Sky's father and Many Numbers beside him simultaneously cringed.

"The rules of our people," the first teller said, "wisely prohibit traveling beyond the borders of the kingdom, which our mountain guard posts mark. You, though, arrogantly disobeyed that rule. And merely, I must say, to satisfy your abnormal curiosity—and your shameless lust for a hill man."

The first teller, his voice booming now, chose to stare at the object of Blue Sky's lust.

"Not just once," he bellowed. "But, as you told us yourself, 'many times.'"

The first teller's gaze drifted downward toward the hill man's loincloth.

"'Many times,'" he repeated. "You told us that yourself. I heard you say it. 'Many times.'"

One of the high tellers nearest Law Keeper wisely chose that moment to clear his throat.

"And in so doing," Law Keeper abruptly continued, "you placed the prince and his future mate in grave danger. Your transgressions directly led to their abduction by our eternal enemy."

"Put him to death!" several of the deputies and court people yelled. "Kill him!"

Solemn Promise, for some reason standing much closer to the chief warrior than Blue Sky had seen him before, was the most conspicuous of the younger court people, many of them Morning Sun's companions, refusing to lend their voices to the clamor.

Tall Oak, frowning, put his hand to his mouth and whispered in Law Keeper's ear.

Curiously, Blue Sky thought, none of the tellers were demanding he be killed. It wasn't because they were above sending up a cry for a prisoner's execution. They were often quick to add their voices to those of the court people. They knew the court people were stating Sturdy Limb's position, and therefore their own leader, Law Keeper, would soon be saying the same thing—"in the interest of the unity of the people," he liked to claim.

"Of course," he now whispered back to the king. "I'll get to the point."

Blue Sky, unlike most of the people present, could read his lips.

The first teller turned to Blue Sky again. "You've gone so far beyond reason that the other tellers and I have unanimously determined you've taken leave of your senses."

Sturdy Limb, looking at Law Keeper as if the first teller might've taken leave of his own, began pounding the earth with the butt end of his spear.

"What in hell does that mean?" the chief warrior demanded.

Cowering like a thief caught in the act, the first teller chose not to say.

"It means," the king chose to answer for him, "I can neither hold the prisoner responsible for what he's done nor punish him."

Blue Sky could hear Valley Defender behind him exhaling a sigh of relief.

"I accept the finding of the tellers," Tall Oak added.

Valley Defender patted Blue Sky's shoulder with the flat side of his spearhead.

His father saw what the oldest of his three sons was doing and glared at him.

"On the other hand," Tall Oak continued, speaking to Blue Sky, "having lost your mind, you can no longer exercise the privileges of a person of age in this kingdom. You can no longer perform guard duty. You can never fight in our people's army. You can never become a teller."

Tall Oak had obviously told Law Keeper what he expected the tellers to decide.

Sturdy Limb's patience with his brother was gone.

"You're making him another prisoner I have to feed and keep alive?" he asked.

"No," the king replied, still staring at Blue Sky. "I'm placing him in the care and control of his father and mother, as if he were still a child, for the rest of his life."

Wandering Star embraced Blue Sky. "You live," he said, whispering.

"Not unless you do, too," Blue Sky quickly whispered back.

Blue Sky spoke in the hill people's language, to make certain nobody near them could understand what they were saying.

31

"If Sturdy Limb tries to kill you," Blue Sky said, "I'll grab a spear and attack him. He and I'll both die with you. Some good might come from this."

"Wandering Star," Tall Oak said, his voice seeming to come from a distance, like a god's.

"You can grab a spear yourself," Blue Sky continued, whispering. "You can help me kill Sturdy Limb. You can kill as many of his men as you please. But don't touch Valley Defender, his brothers, or Solemn Promise. My people need them. They might inherit the kingdom."

"I won't help you do any of that," Wandering Star whispered back, using his people's words. "Your people need you, too. Keep yourself alive. Sturdy Limb isn't worth your life."

"Do you expect me to stand here and let him get away with killing you?"

"I'll warn your king you intend to kill his brother. I'll tell him you need to be restrained during my execution."

Blue Sky looked at Wandering Star. That wasn't an empty threat.

"Then I'll kill Sturdy Limb," Blue Sky whispered, "after you're dead."

"Wandering Star," Tall Oak said again.

The silence of the crowd was also making its presence known.

"That would be a better way to do it," Wandering Star agreed, his mouth to Blue Sky's ear. "I just ask you to be damned sure he's worth it, and you can get away with it."

"I promise you I'll do that," Blue Sky said, still embracing his hill-man companion. "Don't give them any reason to separate us. I'll be with you until the end."

Keeping one arm around Blue Sky, Wandering Star turned to the king.

"I'm asking you to do a favor for my people," Tall Oak said.

Sturdy Limb turned to his brother. "You're asking him to do us a favor?" he exploded. "You're asking for a favor from a hill person? Why can't you just tell him what he has to agree to do or we'll kill him? And we still only regret we didn't kill him the moment we first saw him?"

Sturdy Limb's own deputies and allies seemed shocked by their leader's outburst.

Tall Oak ignored his brother's remarks.

The king had kept his best friend's son out of danger, at a high cost in face to the king's brother, and the brother wanted something for it.

"I'm asking you," Tall Oak said to Wandering Star, "to return to your people's king. I'm asking you to tell him I don't have an answer for him yet. Please also tell him I presume in the meantime he'll wish to keep my son and Rose Leaf safe. Will you do that?"

"You live," Blue Sky whispered in Wandering Star's ear.

"We live," Wandering Star whispered back.

Wandering Star turned to the king again.

"I'll be glad to do that," he replied. "I don't want to see your people harmed. I don't want to see Morning Sun and Rose Leaf harmed."

Tall Oak turned to Many Numbers.

"Will you go to the apprentice tellers' encampment and retrieve Spring Rain?" he asked. "I can't overlook the part you and he have played in this unhappy business. Both of you will need to return to the town. You can remain tellers. The people often report to me how kind you are to them. A king is always glad to hear his people make comments like those. But, I'm very sorry, neither of you can serve in the army again."

"Warriors in my army," Sturdy Limb barked, "don't question authority."

Many Numbers and Spring Rain had helped the prince, Rose Leaf, and Blue Sky lead their rebellion the previous spring. And the farmers adored Spring Rain and Many Numbers as much as they did Morning Sun, Rose Leaf, and Blue Sky.

Blue Sky knew the punishment of Many Numbers and Spring Rain wasn't what Tall Oak was giving up to let Green Field's son live. It would be something far more important than removing from the army two misguided young tellers—who'd naively chosen to believe the love of the people was worth more than the favor of those placed in positions above them.

"I'll bring Spring Rain home," Many Numbers said to the king, ignoring the chief warrior.

Tall Oak approached Green Field.

"Please go to your village now," he said. "Take your son and keep him there with you and Gentle Brook. I'm sorry, my friend. I know you love him despite his endless provocations. I don't blame you. At his age we shared his faults—and look what happened to us. I'm truly sorry."

Sturdy Limb, viewing the two heroes of the last war embracing, rolled his eyes. He was still waiting for what came his way out of a deal so lopsided in favor of Green Field and his know-it-all son, who'd outrageously presumed his friendship with the prince could let him do and say anything he pleased. Not the least of which was his insolent remark, however true, that the farmers detested the chief warrior so intensely they'd gladly see him dead.

*****

Green Field and Blue Sky stayed ahead of Tall Oak's party all the way down the mountain.

"You can thank Many Numbers," Green Field told his son, shortly after they'd started out, "for saving your life."

During the previous evening's debate, Sturdy Limb had insisted, loudly and at length, the gods required Tall Oak to order Blue Sky killed.

Many Numbers, though, said a king could find him out of his mind, since he clearly hadn't intended to endanger Morning Sun and Rose Leaf. Blue Sky wasn't an evil person, Many Numbers argued. Like others who'd lost their minds, he'd simply misapprehended reality. Besides, killing Blue Sky wouldn't bring back the prince and Rose Leaf. Having them returned to the kingdom unharmed was what the king's advisors should be talking about, not the unnecessary execution of a person the farmers and their prince loved.

Sturdy Limb chose not to respond to Many Numbers' argument. He instead merely wished to draw to Tall Oak's attention the necessity of ordering the execution of all those persons who'd assisted the villain in his endangerment of the prince—whoever those persons might be.

Law Keeper cried out that he was prepared to name two such individuals.

34

Many Numbers' suggestion didn't come up again until, much later in the discussion, Tall Oak asked Law Keeper if a king could find that a person such as Blue Sky was out of his mind.

Sturdy Limb insisted the proposition was so absurd no king should need to ask the first teller whether it was possible. If a king could rule Green Field's son had lost his mind, why couldn't he do the same thing with every other person who came before him deserving execution? Why wouldn't people kill their neighbors whenever they chose, if they had no reason to fear punishment for doing it?

While his brother spoke, Tall Oak twice leaned over and whispered to Law Keeper. Whatever it was the king said, the first teller realized this time he couldn't choose to side with the chief warrior without opposing the king. He begged the latter for time to confer with the other tellers regarding the "highly unusual" question Tall Oak had "so astutely" asked him.

It took Law Keeper and the high tellers most of the night, but they finally agreed Tall Oak could find Blue Sky out of his mind. They further concluded he obviously was.

"It was a wise thing for Tall Oak to do," Blue Sky said. "I don't give him enough credit. I doubt if my execution would've done the kingdom or him any good. The people would soon forget the many youthful blunders I've committed. But they'd always remember the king who ordered the execution of the only child of the man who'd saved his life in the last war. Our people might've wished to pass that story down as a perfect example of ingratitude in high places."

Green Field and Blue Sky had stopped beside a brook to bathe and spend the night. The stream was a tributary of the creek that ran past their village, which their people referred to as the "home village" because it was once the home of the ancestors of the present royal family.

"Whatever Tall Oak's intentions were," Green Field said, "I'm just glad you're still alive. What you and Wandering Star did had consequences you couldn't foresee, but it wasn't wrong. Nobody can blame you for wanting to be with him. I don't. Your mother doesn't either. We know how easy it is to fall in love with a hill person. We did—many others did, too—with Rose Leaf."

The sun was poised just above the mountains on the other side of the valley.

"What will Tall Oak do," Blue Sky asked, "to get Morning Sun and Rose Leaf back?"

"I doubt if he knows yet what he should do," Green Field replied. "Solemn Promise told us Sturdy Limb insisted in private Tall Oak should raise the army and attack the hill people."

Blue Sky looked at his father. "That will get Morning Sun killed."

Green Field, frowning even more than he usually did, made no response to that.

When Green Field and Blue Sky were saying their goodbyes to Many Numbers and Wandering Star, they noticed Tall Oak and Sturdy Limb speaking with Solemn Promise, who soon left, heading up the path to sunrise pass without waiting for Many Numbers and Wandering Star to go with him. Solemn Promise was ordinarily far more polite than that.

"Spring Rain told me a story," Blue Sky said. "One of our kings sent an army over the mountains to punish the hill people. The story doesn't say, though, what the hill people did to earn their punishment. It does say, whatever the reason was, we killed every last one of them."

Green Field nodded his head. "That's how I remember the story."

"Then why are the hill people still out there?"

Chapter 3

Green Field and Blue Sky emerged from the forest early the next evening. One of East Land's grandchildren saw them coming down the path, and she soon rousted the whole village to meet them. They wanted to know, of course, what had happened to Morning Sun and Rose Leaf.

Green Field and Blue Sky were the first to arrive with the answer to that question. Since a number of the king's entourage no longer had legs muscular enough to propel them speedily up, or even down, the mountains, Tall Oak's party was at least a day behind.

"Please tell us they're safe and unharmed," East Land pleaded.

After surviving the last war with the hill people, in which East Land had acquired hero status, the grateful valley people called him by the name of his family's village, the village farthest to the east on the path from the valley people's town to sunrise path.

"I'm sorry," Green Field said to his former comrade in arms. "We have reason to believe they're still unharmed, but we can't tell you they're safe."

As they listened to Blue Sky and Green Field's story, the younger children clung to their parents.

After the story reached its conclusion—with a village of humans young and old staring hopelessly at one another—East Land's older son was the first to speak.

"The hill people can't take our prince and Rose Leaf," he said. "This means war."

"Your hill-man friend was like us," the older son's mate said to Blue Sky, as her youngest child, a little girl, tightly grasped her skirt. "He'd never harm Rose Leaf and Morning Sun."

East Land's family had met Wandering Star during the celebration after the rebellion.

The woman's mate, the father of her children, shook his head. "Their king says they'll kill our prince unless we give them our valley? He's asking for war."

"I only wish," East Land said, looking at Green Field, "I could fight those damned hill people again."

In the last war, he'd stayed with Tall Oak and Green Field to the end of their futile battle on sunrise pass and taken a number of wounds. Like so many others, he was fortunate he survived.

He could never fight in another war, though.

His two sons, on the other hand, could.

*****

Older children raced to neighboring villages to let their people know what had happened, as they did whenever there was news to be told—and retold by youthful messengers from the recipient villages. And soon, once again, every person in every village in the kingdom, as well as the town, would hear the news.

"Is it true?" the people from nearby villages, gathered in a group along the path, asked when Green Field and Blue Sky reached them.

Learning that the messenger children hadn't gotten the ultimate facts wrong, they insisted upon hearing the full story from Green Field and Blue Sky.

By the time Green Field and Blue Sky approached their own village, Gentle Brook was waiting on the path with their neighbors, who'd gone to her as soon as they'd heard the news.

She embraced Blue Sky, making no attempt to wipe away her tears.

"Sturdy Limb blames you?" she asked. "And you're the one who begged him and Tall Oak to move the guard post. For that, he thinks Tall Oak should let him kill you?"

She spoke loud enough to let the persons surrounding them hear and pass her words to the many others behind them.

"If Sturdy Limb had killed you," she continued, "he'd be facing his own death now. The farmers would gladly kill that man. And I'd do whatever it took to strike the first blow."

*****

Gentle Brook had asked their neighbor, Autumn Wine's younger grandson, to run to the town ahead of the other children to tell Fair Judge what had happened. That way, she could be the one to let

38

Rainbow Evening know. Gentle Brook rightly suspected none of the other court people wished to take on that task anyway.

Fair Judge was a female teller who'd become the queen's companion after Tall Oak lost his manhood in the last war with the hill people.

When Gentle Brook, Green Field, and Blue Sky arrived at the court, Fair Judge was still with the queen, sitting beside her in the chair Tall Oak usually occupied.

Fair Judge had acquired her name because the people, knowing it made Law Keeper angry, had insisted upon it.

"What do we do?" Rainbow Evening asked Green Field.

A noisy crowd had gathered in the courtyard below the king and queen's open windows.

"Not attack the hill people," Green Field replied.

"Is someone saying we should?" the queen asked.

"Yes," Gentle Brook replied. "Sturdy Limb is saying that."

Fair Judge glanced at the nearest window. "The people in the courtyard," she said, as if she were discussing the weather, "are clamoring for war."

Rainbow Evening frowned. "We'll lose Morning Sun and Rose Leaf."

Fair Judge put her arm around the queen's shoulders.

The din in the courtyard grew. It was possible all the court people and tellers who hadn't gone up to sunrise pass with Tall Oak were out there. And a large number of farmers from the nearby villages were with them, adding their voices to the uproar.

Rainbow Evening turned to Green Field. "You've got to stop him," she said.

Rainbow Evening's companions knew she wasn't talking about her brother-in-law, the chief warrior, but her husband himself, the king.

"You've got to tell him he can't do that," she pleaded.

"I promise you I'll let him know what I think," Green Field said. "But I don't hold out much hope he'll listen to me this time."

"We'll lose Rose Leaf and Morning Sun," Gentle Brook said, echoing her cousin.

By then, they could easily tell the loudest voices in the courtyard were all in favor of war.

"Tall Oak is our king," Green Field said. "We must obey him, no matter what he decides."

Blue Sky suspected his father meant that, for this question, unlike the rebellion over the king's refusal to allow the prince to marry the woman he loved, they might well have no other choice in the matter. This time, an appeal to the people could easily fail.

"No matter what," Gentle Brook said, "we have to let Tall Oak know we disagree."

"We'll do that," Green Field replied.

They listened to the voices in the courtyard, calling on the gods to accompany them in another war.

"We have to let the people know, too," Blue Sky said, "whether they agree with us or not."

Fair Judge turned to Green Field and Gentle Brook.

"Your son is right," she said. "Whether the people agree with us or not, we have to make our case. Then, whatever happens, the people will always know of our opposition. They'll also know we weren't afraid to face their disapproval when we voiced it."

*****

After Tall Oak and his party returned to the town, he assured the people he'd decide what to do "at the appropriate time," which presumably meant when Wandering Star returned from his meeting with Lightning Spear.

In the meantime, Sturdy Limb let it be known what he'd do: attack the hill people without remorse.

Law Keeper agreed. He said handing the hill people their rightful punishment was the only thing the valley people could do if they wished to regain the favor of their benefactors in heaven.

The valley people also learned that Green Field, Gentle Brook, Fair Judge, Many Numbers, Spring Rain, Blue Sky, and Rainbow Evening, the queen herself, believed going to war with the hill people would be most unwise. Many persons, including the prince, would surely be killed.

Sturdy Limb had a word for the seven vocal dissidents, even if they were persons the people—especially the farmers—favored. The enemy had abducted the prince and his chosen mate, and those "cowards" incredibly thought their people should let them get away with it.

*****

In any event, the wheat and barley harvests were at hand. Until Tall Oak made his decision, there was nothing anybody could do but go into the fields and work.

After Green Field, Blue Sky, and Gentle Brook finished their harvest, they planned to help neighbors who had sons in encampment, as they were expected to do. They'd also help neighbors who were too old or ill to bring in their crops on their own.

The first neighbor they called on, though, was Autumn Wine.

They were used to working with her grandsons. Accordingly, the sooner they got their work done, the sooner the five of them would be available to help others as an efficient team.

Soon after they began working together in Autumn Wine's fields, she confronted Blue Sky as he mowed her wheat.

"I hear you blame yourself for what's happened," she said.

Green Field, Gentle Brook, and the neighbors close by paused in their work, listening.

"I have no choice," Blue Sky said. "I broke a law, a good and reasonable law. I went past the guard post. If I hadn't broken the law, the prince and Rose Leaf would still be with us."

Hearing Blue Sky admit his wrongdoing, Autumn Wine grimaced.

"This must be hell for you," she said. "You spent your childhood with them."

"But we have every reason," Blue Sky countered, "to see them with us again soon."

Autumn Wine shook her head. "Not if the hill people took them."

She looked at Blue Sky as if he were in fact the child Tall Oak had decreed him to be.

"I saw what they did in the last war," she continued, her white hair as short as the old men wore theirs. "You were still in Gentle Brook's arms. You can't remember what those people did."

41

"No," Blue Sky agreed, "I can't. You know about that. I admit I don't."

"They came this way," she said. "I saw them with my own eyes. Between the forest and the town they burned every village. They killed all our livestock they could find."

She was raising her voice without intending to.

"We had to run away and hide in the forest," she said. "Otherwise they would've killed all of us. That's what those hill people would've done."

The neighbors were hanging on every word she spoke. Having lost most of her family in the last war, she had a few more for them. She put her hand on Blue Sky's shoulder.

"They'll kill Morning Sun," she said, shaking Blue Sky, again without seeming to have any wish to do what she was doing. "They'll kill the prince our people fell in love with. They'll make your sister a slave, bearing the children of a man she detests. That's what the hill people will do."

*****

Older children from a neighboring village came running the next morning with more news from the town. They vied to be the first to tell the story to those who hadn't already heard it.

Solemn Promise had returned from sunrise pass and spoken privately with Tall Oak and Sturdy Limb as soon as he reached the court.

After they'd finished their discussion, Sturdy Limb had appeared in the courtyard and announced that Tall Oak would address the people that afternoon.

*****

Spring Rain and Many Numbers, who'd spoken with Solemn Promise, met Blue Sky, Green Field, and Gentle Brook on their way to the courtyard.

Tall Oak had asked Wandering Star to deliver a message to Lightning Spear so that Solemn Promise could secretly follow him and find out where the hill people's king and army were camped.

42

Solemn Promise had successfully completed his mission.

"He's a brave man," Blue Sky said, feeling at least as much envy as he had when Solemn Promise told him he'd be sharing an encampment hut on sunrise pass with the prince.

Lightning Spear and his army were ensconced at the far end of an empty plain surrounded by low rocky hills. Solemn Promise was certain he could find the place again. Going there and coming back, he'd fastidiously memorized a series of landmarks, as well as the general directions it took to get from one to the next.

Many Numbers and Spring Rain both thought Solemn Promise was capable of doing that.

"Tall Oak doesn't care what the hill people's king has to say?" Blue Sky asked.

"Not at all," Many Numbers replied.

"He and Sturdy Limb have already decided what they'll do?" Gentle Brook asked.

"So we hear," Spring Rain replied, softly, taking her hand.

When the five of them got to the courtyard, all but a few of the tellers and court people chose to pretend they didn't notice them.

Even the farmers were keeping their distance from them.

Fair Judge, though, conspicuously joined their group, embracing each of them.

*****

Tall Oak, Rainbow Evening, Sturdy Limb, Law Keeper, Solemn Promise, and Morning Sun's cousins—followed by the high deputies and tellers, strictly according to their rank—filed into the courtyard, all of them looking as if they'd arrived for a funeral.

Only Rainbow Evening, Solemn Promise, and the cousins dared to exchange grim-faced glances with the persons who'd made known their opposition to another war with the hill people.

As Tall Oak and Rainbow Evening mounted the stairs to the dais, the crowd's murmurs fell to whispers. Sturdy Limb had ordered his people to place Morning Sun's chair where it would be if he were expected to attend court that afternoon.

Every person present remained standing in any event. The matter at hand was war.

"Our people will never give up the smallest parcel of this valley," Tall Oak began. "This valley the gods promised us we'll have forever. I'd never consent to our people giving up a speck of it, no matter what we'd get in return. I'd never ask our people to do so even for the lives of my only child, the prince you love, and the woman he wishes to be his mate. No matter how dearly his mother and I love them, I'd never do that. I'd always choose the valley over any individual in it."

Rainbow Evening and Gentle Brook made the mistake of looking at one another.

Their eyes filled with tears they were neither able nor willing to stop.

"On the other hand," Tall Oak continued, "if an enemy king were to abduct any person from our kingdom and place that individual in captivity, I'd answer him for that. I'd answer him for his intolerable cheek. And my answer would be the same whether the person he abducted was a prince or a person with no hopes whatsoever. My answer would also be the same whether the captive was the future mate of the highest prince or the bride-to-be of the most unfortunate man who ever lived."

The crowd murmured its approval.

Sturdy Limb, who was in his usual place next to the dais, but this time with Solemn Promise nearest him on his other side, smirked at Green Field, savoring his victory.

"This is my answer," Tall Oak resumed. "This is my answer to the promise of the hill people's king to kill my son and keep in captivity the woman he loves: I'm ordering every able-bodied male of age in the valley to immediately assemble between the town and the eastern forest. Here we'll muster the mightiest and most powerful army this kingdom has ever seen."

Almost all the men and older boys in the crowd loudly shouted their approval. Many of the adult males raised the spears they'd thought to bring with them.

And almost all the women and girls stood quietly, neither speaking nor gesturing.

"And I'll personally lead that army," Tall Oak declared. "I'll lead our army to the hill people's presumptuous king and his army."

The shouting in the courtyard grew louder.

"Let the gods themselves hear us!" one man cried.

"And when we've met the hill people's king," Tall Oak continued, "I'll give him my answer to his outrageous demand: I'll order him to release the youth and young woman he's taken from my kingdom—or he and all his warriors will die that day on the points of our spears!"

*****

After the king and queen came down from the dais, Rainbow Evening went to Gentle Brook.

They wordlessly embraced.

The crowd, observing them, fell silent.

Reaching them, Tall Oak stopped, waiting for Rainbow Evening.

He and Green Field exchanged nods, but neither spoke.

The two women clung to one other, weeping.

Sturdy Limb stood next to Tall Oak, scowling.

Rainbow Evening and Gentle Brook parted, wiping their eyes.

Valley Defender and his brothers joined their father and Tall Oak.

Rainbow Evening turned to Blue Sky and embraced him.

Valley Defender moved toward them.

Sturdy Limb raised his spear and held it across his eldest son's chest, stopping him.

Despite the spear, the chief warrior's younger sons skirted around their father and brother, and went to embrace their aunt Rainbow Evening and their cousin Gentle Brook.

Stepping forward, Green Field reached over Sturdy Limb's spear and placed his hands on Valley Defender's shoulders.

Valley Defender, the hero of the previous summer's skirmish on sunrise pass, wasn't ashamed to shed tears in public.

Sturdy Limb glared at him in disgust.

Valley Defender spoke nevertheless, breaking the silence.

"I don't want Rose Leaf and Morning Sun to be harmed in any way," he said.

"That's enough!" Sturdy Limb yelled at his oldest son. "Wars aren't for the cowardly!"

Blue Sky imagined grabbing Sturdy Limb's spear and sinking it deep in his guts, making certain the chief warrior would die, however long his death took.

Then Blue Sky realized Spring Rain had hold of one of his arms and Many Numbers the other, and his mother was whispering to them: "Don't let him go."

*****

"What good will it do?" Gentle Brook asked.

She, Green Field, and Blue Sky had accompanied Spring Rain and Many Numbers to their ivy-covered house near the bluff-top woods.

"Sturdy Limb thinks it will do some good," Many Numbers said. "He tells everybody killing a lot of hill warriors will teach their king and the rest of their people a damned good lesson."

"Teach the hill people a lesson?" Gentle Brook asked. "How will that help Morning Sun? How will it help Rose Leaf? Won't they both end up dead?"

Spring Rain extended his arm around her shoulders.

Many Numbers turned to Green Field. "What would you do?" he asked.

"I'm not the king," Green Field replied. "It's not my decision to make."

"Tell us anyway," Many Numbers insisted. "If you were the king, what would you do?"

For more than a few moments, Green Field stood silent in the late afternoon sun.

"I'd try to stall," he finally replied. "When Wandering Star returns, I'd ask him to go back to Lightning Spear again and tell him we need more time. What his king is asking us to do, I'd point out, is no small matter. For one thing, we honestly don't know where our ancestors came from."

"Lightning Spear is five days away from us," Many Numbers said. "That gives us ten days for Wandering Star to go back and forth. What would you do then? Ask for more time?"

"Why not?" Spring Rain asked. "It would keep Morning Sun alive. We could go on hoping he and Rose Leaf would return someday unharmed. I'd send Wandering Star back and forth as many times as we could and he would."

"But what would you ultimately do?" Many Numbers asked, still looking at Green Field, who seemed to be taken with Spring Rain's argument. "To get Rose Leaf and Morning Sun back? That's what we want more than anything else."

"More than anything else," Gentle Brook quickly agreed.

"I don't know," Green Field said. "I can't imagine right now what I'd ultimately do. I'd be hoping for something to happen."

"That won't bring them home," Many Numbers said, his remark as blunt as a fist to the face.

"We could offer to meet with Lightning Spear," Blue Sky interjected. "Maybe we'd find out what to do. How to please him, maybe, short of giving up the valley. Or how to get into his encampment and sneak Morning Sun and Rose Leaf out."

"Sneak them out?" Many Numbers asked.

"Tall Oak could send me over there with Wandering Star. He knows every hill and hollow between sunrise pass and Lightning Spear's encampment. He could get me in without being seen. Solemn Promise did it on his own. He could go with us. We could figure out some way for Rose Leaf and Morning Sun to escape. Lightning Spear has had other captives get away from him."

Gentle Brook looked at Blue Sky and shook her head.

"Those hill people will catch you and kill you," she objected. "We'll lose you and Solemn Promise as well as Rose Leaf and Morning Sun. What do we gain from that?"

"If they catch us, our people will lose two persons," Blue Sky said. "If they don't catch us, though, we'll prevent a war and a lot more deaths than our own, and we'll have Rose Leaf and Morning Sun back. I'm willing to risk my life for that."

This time Blue Sky had convinced the usually doubting Spring Rain.

"I'll go with you," he said. "Tellers are supposed to risk their lives. I'll ask Solemn Promise to put your proposal to Sturdy Limb and Tall Oak. Maybe they'll listen to him."

"And he can tell them I'll go in his place," Many Numbers said. "He can stay home this time. I understand the woman who's been seeing him on sunrise pass is with child."

47

Many Numbers would make this another of the valley people's stories in which men who went with men exposed themselves to danger in place of men who had children to raise.

"But it won't work," he continued. "Solemn Promise can put it to Sturdy Limb and Tall Oak, but they'll call our rescue plan half-baked and laugh it off. They won't want to distract the people's attention from the war they insist has to be fought. Sturdy Limb knows what he's doing. When Morning Sun's dead, he and his sons are next in line to the kingship."

Green Field stared at Many Numbers. "I've thought that thought myself," he admitted. "But I've hoped thinking it was unjustified. Am I a fool?"

Many Numbers stared back at Green Field. "Nobody would call the least foolish person in the kingdom a fool."

*****

The people didn't seem to have any misgivings about Tall Oak's decision. The day after his declaration of war on the hill people, able-bodied men began arriving in the villages between the town and East Land's village. They could see no reason why the hill people's king wouldn't give up Morning Sun and Rose Leaf as soon as he realized how many valley warriors his army would have to fight to keep them.

"He may be as evil as hell itself," one farmer said, "but that doesn't mean he won't want to stay alive. He gives us Morning Sun and Rose Leaf back, and we'll let him go on living."

Once again, the farmers between the town and the eastern forest put the farmers from elsewhere up in their houses and barns. As long as it didn't rain, the livestock could stay out to pasture at night, making room indoors for warriors. A large number of them slept in the houses and barns in the home village. Green Field, Gentle Brook, and Blue Sky fed them and gave them wine.

"If it takes my life to do this, so be it," one of their guests said. "That must be the way the gods want it. I'll always be remembered as a hero in the stories our people will tell. So be it."

Reports came from many parts of the valley that the women who lived together without children, as well as the women whose

48

children were old enough to fend for themselves, were harvesting crops for their neighbors deep into the night. Even very young children were insisting upon helping. They only let sleep itself stop them. They began working again the next day at dawn.

*****

A messenger came out from the town to speak privately with Green Field, Gentle Brook, and Blue Sky. The young man found them in a neighbor's barley field.

He told them Tall Oak and Sturdy Limb wished to express their deep gratitude to them for so generously assisting the army. The king had already thanked Many Numbers and Spring Rain for their contributions, one of which was teaching the hill people's language to Solemn Promise and Valley Defender, who were to deliver Tall Oak's counter-ultimatum to Lightning Spear.

In view of all those exertions, Tall Oak and Sturdy Limb added, the five of them, along with Fair Judge and the queen, needn't concern themselves with the planning for the coming war with the hill people.

The messenger, who had the same close-set eyes and slender frame that Spring Rain, Many Numbers, and Wandering Star had, was the son of farmers who lived a great distance from the town. Like Valley Defender, he'd finished his encampment year the previous autumn. He and his mate had one child, and a second was on its way. He'd arrived well ahead of his slower village comrades. He came, he said, to see what he could do to help the kingdom in its time of need.

After delivering the communication from the king and his chief warrior, he began helping the recipients of the message harvest their neighbors' barley, gently collecting the cut stalks in his arms in order not to spill their seeds on the ground.

As he worked, he kept looking at Green Field. Finally, he couldn't hold back any longer.

"Are you the Green Field," he asked, "who saved Tall Oak's life in the last war?"

Green Field, Gentle Brook, and Blue Sky straightened themselves up from their work.

"I served with Tall Oak in the last war," Green Field replied.

49

"He's the Green Field," Gentle Brook said, "who saved Tall Oak's life in the last war."

Having learned that, the visitor didn't have to ask if they were the family the hill people's princess, the woman the prince wanted for his mate, had lived with as daughter and sister.

Tall Oak and Sturdy Limb had chosen their messenger well. No court person, teller, or farmer living near the town would've kept such a communication confidential. And no matter how obliquely the king and his chief warrior worded their refusal to wait upon some fanciful rescue attempt Green Field's son and the orphan boys had dreamed up, in the ears of the court people and tellers the message would've been cause for endless speculation and rumor.

But the young man from a faraway village had no reason to think the message included anything more than kingly encouragement and gratitude. He told Green Field, Gentle Brook, and Blue Sky he assumed it had to be kept confidential or other less-deserving people would expect to receive similar dispensations from the king and his chief warrior, and waste their valuable time.

"You're welcome to stay in our village," Gentle Brook said to the messenger, taking his hand. "You can sleep in our house. We'll find a place for you."

*****

Wandering Star didn't show up within the time anticipated for his return to the valley.

The belief arose among the people that Lightning Spear, angered by the response Wandering Star had taken to him from Tall Oak, must've ordered him killed.

People began speaking of him, even in Blue Sky's presence, as if he were dead.

*****

Sturdy Limb ordered the guards down from all the encampments except those on sunrise pass, who would join the army when it reached them.

50

Sturdy Limb also removed Green Field from the army. And Tall Oak let him do it.

Without needing to mention any names, the chief warrior spoke of the matter in court.

"Almost all our able-bodied men will go off and fight a war our kingdom cannot refuse to fight—and cannot fail to win," he said. "Those few who question the wisdom of fighting the war will stay home, where they belong—with the old people, women, children, and cowards."

Autumn Wine's older grandson offered to go to court and demand an apology from Sturdy Limb for making those remarks.

Green Field persuaded him, though, it could never be worth the time it would take him away from the harvest and the preparations for the departure of the army.

*****

Spring Rain arrived in the village to say Rainbow Evening wouldn't come out of her room.

The next day being dark and rainy, the harvest came to a halt up and down the valley.

Gentle Brook walked to the town in the rain to see her cousin the queen.

Rainbow Evening had learned Sturdy Limb was insisting on taking his two younger sons with the army although they hadn't yet come of age. He said it would be wrong to deny them their fair share of the glory. After all, they were fourth and fifth in the line to the kingship.

Rainbow Evening, whose fondness for Morning Sun's cousins was well known, had pleaded with Tall Oak not to give in to his brother on the point. She'd threatened to retire to her room and never appear in public again if he did so. When Tall Oak did give in, she made good on her promise, abruptly leaving the court as soon as he rendered his decision.

Rainbow Evening admitted to Gentle Brook she'd laid down rules for Morning Sun he'd enjoyed ignoring. People had accused her, she said, of wanting him to be the perfect prince. And in a sense, she conceded, maybe she did. But she wasn't about to apologize for imagining that her son could come as close to being what the people needed in a king as anybody ever would.

Looking out at the courtyard through the nearest window, as from the interior of a cave their ancestors were said to have dwelt in, Rainbow Evening and Gentle Brook silently watched the rain, which their people's stories often referred to as the "tears of the gods."

"There was nothing we could do," Gentle Brook said, upon her return, "but cry ourselves."

*****

The time for the army's departure arrived.

At dawn that day Tall Oak, Sturdy Limb, Law Keeper, Solemn Promise, and the three patently reluctant cousins stood on a rise facing the army. The wall separating their people's peaceful farmland from the horrors of the outside world was immediately behind them.

Tall Oak first turned to the people who would remain in the valley. Among that group, those present who would've kept the army in the valley—Green Field, Gentle Brook, Blue Sky, Fair Judge, Many Numbers, Spring Rain, and Rainbow Evening—stood conspicuously alone.

"I leave you now," Tall Oak said, "to deliver my answer to the hill people's king."

In the army certain warriors within earshot of Tall Oak repeated his statement to their comrades immediately behind them, after which it echoed to the most distant ranks.

Tall Oak turned to the army. "You're my answer to the hill people's king. I'll take you to him and show him what you look like. He'll know in a glance how proud of you I am."

There was a long pause between each statement. The army stretched halfway to the town.

"I'll tell that king, so deeply in debt to the hell gods already, he has two choices, and only two," Tall Oak continued. "He can give us back the youth and the young woman he took from us, or he and his army can die."

Tall Oak turned again to the pastures where those who'd remain behind were standing.

"In my absence from our promised valley, our gift from the gods, one of you must rule in my place as regent," he said. "Therefore, until my return with this army in full victory, all the powers I have as your king will belong to my comrade who saved my life—Green Field."

It was obvious from the looks on the faces of Sturdy Limb, Law Keeper, and their closest allies that Tall Oak had intended to shock them as much as he did everybody else.

The army and the people remaining behind stared wordlessly at Green Field.

Tall Oak had put him in a position where he could no longer refuse to help run the kingdom. With all of Tall Oak's powers, he might even have to send someone to his death.

"No better choice!" East Land blurted out, cracking the silence like thunder.

The warriors leaving for battle, as well as the people staying home, immediately took up the cry: "No better choice!"

As the army moved into the forest, and the warriors passed Green Field, they gave him their people's traditional salute, raising their spears above their heads and waving them in synchrony with their comrades.

Chapter 4

In order to help Green Field rule the kingdom and assist with the harvest, Many Numbers and Spring Rain spent their days near the home village, their nights in Rose Leaf's room.

The third evening after the army left, Blue Sky's family and their guests were eating at their table, which they'd taken outside. Spring Rain, looking up, wondered if an animal had gotten out of its barn. He saw something in the twilight shadows at the other end of the orchard.

Blue Sky, on the other hand, saw a person facing them, but he couldn't tell who it was.

The person was standing motionless, as if fearing to come any closer.

"Who's there?" Blue Sky shouted, getting up from the table with his spear.

"Wandering Star," came the reply, far more hesitantly than Blue Sky would've expected.

Blue Sky dropped his spear and ran to him.

When he got close enough to see his hill friend's face, he could also see how wary he was.

Blue Sky nevertheless threw his arms around the man who'd become his lover.

"I'm so damned glad to see you," Blue Sky said, leading Wandering Star through the orchard to the table. "People said you must've been killed. I tried to ignore them, but it was getting more and more difficult to do."

Tentative no longer, Wandering Star sat down at the table and helped himself to the food and wine his hosts and their other guests set before him.

"When was the last time you ate?" Blue Sky asked, taking pleasure in his friend's pleasure.

Wandering Star finished chewing before attempting a reply.

"Yesterday morning," he replied. "I found some ripened grapes in your forest."

"Where have you been?" Many Numbers asked. "We expected you back several days ago."

Wandering Star wiped his mouth.

"Your comrades on sunrise pass shot arrows at me," he replied. "From the guard post."

"They did what?" Green Field asked.

"You didn't know that?" Wandering Star asked.

"Why would they do such a thing?" Gentle Brook asked. "They knew who you were."

"They were warning me," Wandering Star replied. "I was in range of their arrows, but they all hit the ground in front of me. They yelled at me. Noon Breeze did most of the talking. He told me I couldn't come back to the valley. I had to go away, or they'd have to kill me."

"Why did they do that?" Green Field asked. "I thought they considered you a friend."

"Noon Breeze said Sturdy Limb ordered them to kill me. He said they weren't supposed to be speaking with me. The chief warrior gave them orders to kill me as soon as I showed up."

Spring Rain's face darkened. "Noon Breeze and his comrades were supposed to kill you, but they didn't? They disobeyed Sturdy Limb's order?"

"I'm grateful to them for that," Wandering Star replied.

"The only guards there were the apprentice tellers," Many Numbers said. "Law Keeper ordered the supervising tellers back to the town. Noon Breeze must've put himself in charge."

"And saved one hill man's life," Spring Rain added.

"I'm especially grateful to him for that," Wandering Star repeated.

"How did you get here?" Blue Sky asked.

Gentle Brook brought their hill guest another bowl of food.

After she'd met Wandering Star at the conclusion of the spring rebellion, she'd told her son he'd chosen well. She'd even admitted she admired his body as well as his mind.

"I went to another of your encampments farther north," the guest replied, eating again. "I couldn't believe what I saw when I got there. It was abandoned. I walked right through it."

Blue Sky shook his head. "Sturdy Limb hadn't considered you might know more than one way to get into the valley. Hill people are too stupid to figure those things out."

"It took me a long time getting through your forest," Wandering Star continued. "I tried to be as careful as I could coming down the path from the encampment. I didn't want to run into any of your people. I thought they might not be as easy on me as Noon Breeze and his comrades had been. After I came out of the forest, I did most of my traveling at night."

Wandering Star had taken Tall Oak's message to Lightning Spear. He'd also seen both Morning Sun and Rose Leaf. His people hadn't harmed either of them. To the contrary, they were treating them quite well.

Lightning Spear, though, had told Wandering Star to assure Tall Oak he wouldn't hesitate to order Morning Sun killed if his people didn't abandon their encampments in the mountains and begin leaving the valley. He preferred they depart at the south end of the valley and follow the river downstream back to wherever it was they came from. He promised he'd release Morning Sun alive and well as soon as the last of their people left the valley.

"Did he say," Green Field asked, "how much time we have to leave the valley?"

"No," Wandering Star replied. "He said he'll order Morning Sun killed if he becomes convinced your people have no intent to leave the valley. In the meantime, he'll keep him alive. Your people's prince is valuable to him only as long as he's living. Dead, he's worth nothing."

Blue Sky nodded his head. "Tall Oak could've had you go back to him again with all sorts of excuses as to how long it was taking us to get ourselves ready to leave the valley?"

"Tall Oak could do that," Wandering Star replied. "He should do that."

Blue Sky realized his hill friend had misunderstood one aspect of his question.

"And Morning Sun and Rose Leaf," Gentle Brook asked, "would still be alive, unharmed?"

"They will," Wandering Star replied, as if his knowledge of the valley people's language had regressed.

"Tall Oak could've also," Blue Sky asked, testing just to make sure he was right, "offered Lightning Spear something less than the whole valley for Morning Sun?"

"He can," Wandering Star replied, "for whatever it's worth."

"Time, at least," Green Field said. "It would've been worth that."

"It will," Wandering Star said, as if he were fully agreeing with Green Field's remarks.

Many Numbers heard what Blue Sky and the others were hearing.

"It's too bad," he said, looking at Wandering Star, "we don't have any time left for what you're saying we should do."

"What do you mean?" Wandering Star asked, looking up from his food.

"Our army has gone to attack your people," Many Numbers replied. "Solemn Promise followed you and found out where Lightning Spear and his army are."

Wandering Star finished swallowing the food he'd been chewing and laid down his bowl and spoon. He looked at the other people around the table as if he didn't know who they were.

"That's right," Blue Sky said. "Our army has gone to teach your king a lesson."

"Don't tell me that," Wandering Star said, almost whispering.

"Sturdy Limb didn't want you coming back to the valley," Many Numbers said. "If you found out we were planning to attack your people, he said you'd go back to Lightning Spear and warn him. He said if you returned to the valley, he'd have to put you in one of his cages."

"But he didn't tell anybody he'd ordered you killed," Spring Rain added.

"Although it stands to reason he did," Many Numbers said.

"I told Tall Oak that Many Numbers and I would hold you prisoner in our house," Spring Rain added. "We'd make sure you didn't go back to your people. He told me he'd think about it."

Blue Sky's friends had apparently decided it best he not know about those negotiations.

"It's clear what Sturdy Limb and Tall Oak were doing," Blue Sky said. "They didn't want to hear anything Lightning Spear had to say. They were determined to make a show of force with our army. There wasn't anything anybody could've said to stop them."

Wandering Star was still staring at his hosts as if their words made no sense to him.

"Your army has gone to attack my people?" he asked.

Blue Sky laughed the laugh of a hardened cynic. "All the able-bodied men in the valley except the four at this table have gone to kill Lightning Spear and your people's warriors."

"Unless," Many Numbers said, "Lightning Spear lets Morning Sun and Rose Leaf go."

Wandering Star shook his head as if a blow to it had left him dazed.

"Did Lightning Spear really think he'd get any other response?" Blue Sky asked.

Wandering Star kept shaking his head. "It's what he wanted your people to do."

A bird was singing in the village orchard. Night was coming on. A god was speaking.

"How do you know," Green Field asked, "what Lightning Spear wants us to do?"

"I told him," Wandering Star replied, glancing at Blue Sky, to whom he hadn't previously made the fact known. "I told him that's what he should want your people to do."

The bird in the orchard sang on.

"Before I became a teller," Wandering Star said, "I went to Lightning Spear and told him how I thought he could start a war with your people and win it. I still believed my people should fight your people and take back the valley you stole from us. I still believed that."

"What did you tell him?" Green Field asked.

"I told him I believed you were a proud people. If he provoked you enough, you'd bring down all your might on him and our people."

"You were right," Many Numbers said. "That's what Tall Oak is doing."

"I thought," Wandering Star continued, "Lightning Spear should mount an attack on one of your encampments. Not sunrise pass, but the weakest of them we could find. Your people's guards would kill many of our warriors, or most of them, or maybe even all of them. But we'd also kill so many of yours our deed couldn't go unpunished. Your king would send an army to do it."

"That's what our king and chief warrior are doing now," Many Numbers repeated.

"Then your prince fell into Lightning Spear's hands," Wandering Star said.

"And that became the provocation," Spring Rain said.

Wandering Star looked at him. "A far greater provocation than any I'd imagined."

"What good does it do Lightning Spear?" Many Numbers asked. "If we've got an army coming to kill him and his warriors? He'll either give up or die."

"The provocation had a second purpose," Wandering Star replied. "That was to bring the warriors from our out-lying tribes in to fight under Lightning Spear."

"He can't just summon them," Green Field asked, "as our king does?"

"He can always summon them," Wandering Star said. "But unless their chieftains see some good reason to obey the summons, they'll only send back what my people refer to as 'lame excuses instead of healthy warriors.' That's what too many of them did in the last war. That's why your people won it. Despite your king's stupid order to retreat to your town."

Blue Sky, horrified, could see where Wandering Star's story was going.

"Are your out-lying tribes," he asked, "coming to fight under Lightning Spear now?"

"No chieftain is ignoring the summons this time," Wandering Star replied. "The gods have obviously chosen Lightning Spear to lead our people back into the valley. And they've clearly picked this moment for him to do it. Acting through Long Arm, they gave him his daughter back."

"Our army will still crush yours," Many Numbers said. "The few of your people's warriors who'll survive will curse the same gods they're heaping praise on now."

Wandering Star was shaking his head again.

Before he came of age, he said, he'd traveled all around the valley hunting and fishing. He'd pitched his tent as close to the valley people's encampments as he could. He'd realized the guards were replaced every autumn by generally younger-looking guards. He'd guessed the new guards were all the men who'd come of age during that year. He'd figured out how many encampments the valley people had. He'd made a rough count of the number of guards he saw in each of them. He'd compared his information with what he'd learned from his people who usually hunted near the encampments. He'd concluded his people's tellers had made a profound mistake.

"They always insisted," he said, "your people were far more numerous than ours."

"Aren't we?" Spring Rain asked.

Wandering Star looked at Spring Rain again. "And your tellers made the same mistake."

"We've always thought," Green Field said, "we were more numerous than your people. That's why we won the last war. We had many more warriors than your people did."

"It won't be like that this time," Wandering Star countered. "You think you're more numerous because all of you are concentrated in your valley. Farming lets you live like that."

Wandering Star had once tried to explain this to Blue Sky when they were drinking wine. And Blue Sky had laughed him off. What his hill friend was saying was too absurd to be true.

"My people are scattered over the hills," Wandering Star continued. "There aren't many of them near your encampments. Most of them have no reason to get close to the valley. But the lands Lightning Spear can claim as his, the lands where our people live, extend many days' travel in every direction beyond the boundaries of your little valley. I told Lightning Spear I was certain our people greatly outnumbered yours. He listened to me, but the high tellers said it was another of my many lies. Everybody knew I made things up just to oppose them. They insisted on having me punished for talking the way I did. They pleaded with Lightning Spear to at least warn me I'd be executed if I wouldn't stop. He eventually gave in to them on that. It was the easiest thing for him to do. Nobody agreed with me. I can't blame him. But he believes me now. Nobody imagined how many warriors would obey his summons. I'm sure your army is huge. But I'm just as certain Lightning Spear's warriors will vastly outnumber yours. My people say they can see more campfires on the plain than stars in the night sky."

The bird in the orchard was still singing.

"I saw Thunder Hunter arrive with his warriors," Wandering Star said. "Lightning Spear publicly promised him when the war is over, and our people are hunting and fishing in the valley again, Thunder Hunter's older son, Dark Storm, will become Rose Leaf's mate. Their descendants will rule the kingdom after Lightning Spear dies."

"Rose Leaf won't have him," Gentle Brook said. "She only wants Morning Sun."

"I'm sorry," Wandering Star said. "Among my people she won't have a choice."

"Solemn Promise didn't see a vast number of warriors," Spring Rain said.

"Solemn Promise wouldn't have seen them," Many Numbers said. "Wandering Star had to have been there for several days after Solemn Promise turned around and came home."

"Solemn Promise could've spared himself the risk of getting killed," Wandering Star said. "I could've told Tall Oak and Sturdy Limb where Lightning Spear and his warriors are. Lightning Spear wants them to know where he is."

"Why?" Green Field asked. "Why does he want our warriors to know where to find him?"

"So they'll be sure to walk into his trap," Wandering Star replied.

"Which is what?" Many Numbers asked.

"To reach Lightning Spear and his warriors, your army will have to cross my people's plain," Wandering Star replied. "Tall Oak and Sturdy Limb won't know it, but most of Lightning Spear's warriors will be hiding in the surrounding hills. After your people's army enters the plain, my people's warriors will have them trapped—trapped and greatly outnumbered."

The moon was rising over sunrise pass.

"Your warriors will soon run out of food and water," Wandering Star continued. "They can't fight a long battle. In late summer Lightning Spear's warriors won't run out of anything, not with their own people at their backs."

The bird in the orchard had reached the end of its song.

Blue Sky rose to his feet. "I'm leaving now. Somebody's got to warn Tall Oak."

Wandering Star and the others at the table stood up as well.

"I'm going with you," Wandering Star said.

"You're damned right you're going with me," Blue Sky said. "You're going to show me how to get there."

"You can't get there in time," Many Numbers said. "Our army has to be stopping at sunrise pass tonight. Solemn Promise said it'll take them two more days to reach the plain."

"He was right about that," Wandering Star agreed.

"They'll attack the next morning," Many Numbers said. "You can't get there by then."

"I don't want to hear that," Blue Sky said. "We won't be stopping at night to sleep. We'll take just enough food and water to get there alive. We won't need bows and arrows or shields. We can find food in the forest this time of the year. We'll run as much of the way as we can."

His father and mother looked at one another, making the same mistake Gentle Brook and Rainbow Evening had made in the courtyard.

"I brought this war on," Blue Sky said. "I have to do whatever I can to stop it."

"You're not the king," Gentle Brook said. "You didn't order the army to leave the valley to attack the hill people."

"I put the king and chief warrior in a position where they thought they had to attack the hill people," Blue Sky said. "I'd say that makes me responsible for what they've done."

"You can't possibly get there in time," Many Numbers insisted.

"But we can't possibly not attempt to get there in time," Wandering Star countered. "The two of us brought this on. What choice do we have? We've got to try to stop it."

Green Field looked at his son. "You don't think you need my permission to do this?"

"No," Blue Sky replied, embracing him. "You've got to prepare the people in case we fail."

Gentle Brook embraced her son, too, weeping.

Green Field stared at Wandering Star. "If Tall Oak and Sturdy Limb had let you come back," he said, "I take it you would've told them about the trap they were walking into."

"I tried to tell the apprentice tellers," Wandering Star said. "They convinced me they'd have to kill me if I said another word. They had their arrows aimed at me. They promised they wouldn't fall short the next time they fired them. I was well within their range. I didn't want to test them. They'd made me feel I was their friend. I didn't want them to have to kill me."

"And you would've been dead," Blue Sky added. "And not much help to anybody then."

*****

Blue Sky and Wandering Star ran and walked through that night, ran and walked through the next day, stopping only to relieve themselves, fetch water from the nearest brook, and find grapes and berries to eat as they walked. When darkness came again, they walked on, struggling to stay awake.

It was afternoon of the second day when they passed the abandoned apprentice tellers' encampment and began their descent into the hill people's land. It was bleaker and more desolate than Blue Sky had imagined from what he'd seen of it from sunrise pass. Bizarre rock formations dotted the landscape as if the gods who'd created them had been drinking far too much wine.

Blue Sky and Wandering Star had to reach the plain by the next morning. What took an army two summer days to accomplish, they'd have to do in one evening and one night.

And that night, even as they walked on, dreams came.

After pausing to relieve themselves, they sat side by side on a log, leaning against one another. Hill people were chasing Blue Sky through the forest again. But now it wasn't just him they were chasing. They were chasing all his people. He turned and saw Autumn Wine. She'd fallen. And soon found out what a fatal thrust of a hill warrior's spear in her belly felt like.

She screamed, but Blue Sky was the one doing the screaming.

"We fell asleep," he heard Wandering Star saying, shaking him. "We fell asleep."

They were lying entwined on the ground next to the log.

They jumped to their feet and hurried on, into the darkness.

The hill people came back, though, again chasing Blue Sky's people with spears raised for the thrusting, slashing, and throat-slitting it would take to kill them all.

Blue Sky turned to see how close they were. He was on their land now. He fell.

Wandering Star lay down next to him and embraced him.

He was sobbing like a child. So was Blue Sky. And neither of them could stop.

It took from them what little strength they had left. They fell asleep.

When the hill people came back again, as Blue Sky knew they would, he woke.

Wandering Star, waking, stood up and pulled Blue Sky to his feet.

"We've got to hurry now," he said.

*****

Toward dawn of the next day, Wandering Star was peering into the distance.

When they reached the crest of a rise, he suddenly stopped.

"We've failed," he said. "We've failed."

"What makes you think we've failed?" Blue Sky asked, not bothering to hide his anger.

He followed Wandering Star's gaze and saw a cloud of dust.

"Tall Oak's army," Wandering Star explained. "By the time we reach them, they'll all be in the trap."

Although they feared they'd exhausted hope as much as they had themselves, Blue Sky and Wandering Star ran on.

*****

A flat featureless plain, gravelly like the bottom of the lake in the upper valley, lay before them. The sun was rising behind the hills on the other side of it.

Tall Oak's army was moving forward from the southern end of the plain.

Solemn Promise had ably as well as bravely done what he'd been asked to do.

Wandering Star pointed his spear toward the northern end of the plain, where hill warriors were massed.

"Lightning Spear's with them," he said. "But that's only a fraction of his army."

He motioned with his spear at the hills on either side of the plain.

"That's where most of his warriors are," Wandering Star said. "And all of them believe right now the gods are on their side. The gods brought their abducted princess home. The gods even brought them the farmers' prince. At long last the gods have answered their pleas."

"A lot of my people's warriors will die today," Blue Sky said, staring at Tall Oak's army marching so confidently across the plain. "That must be what the gods really want."

"I'm leaving you here," Wandering Star said.

Blue Sky turned to him. "Where are you going?"

"To beg Lightning Spear not to kill your people."

"You're not leaving me here," Blue Sky said. "I'm going with you."

"Lightning Spear will order his warriors to kill you. You can turn around here and go home. You can find the way. Go help your father and your people. They need you. You can't do anything here."

"My people's warriors are facing a disastrous defeat. I can't possibly leave and go home. I brought it on. You brought it on. What difference will it make if your people's warriors kill me? My people are dying this day. Let me die with them."

Wandering Star embraced him.

"At least you'll be with me when I die," Blue Sky said.

*****

They stayed atop the ridge on the western side of the plain, forcing themselves to keep running. Ahead of them, Tall Oak's rear guard had already entered the plain.

Wandering Star waved his spear at a pocket in the hills below them.

"See?" he asked.

66

A group of Lightning Spear's warriors were moving in the opposite direction of Tall Oak's army, from which they were keeping themselves hidden in the hills.

"They're closing ranks behind Tall Oak's army," Wandering Star said. "With the warriors coming from over there."

He waved his spear in the direction of the hills on the other side of the plain.

"Tall Oak doesn't know it yet," he continued, "but Lightning Spear has already got his army surrounded. Tall Oak and Sturdy Limb don't have any way out of the trap they're in."

The hill warriors stared up at Wandering Star and Blue Sky on the ridge. So did all the warriors they passed. Blue Sky was surprised they made no attempt to accost two beardless men.

He couldn't hear what they were saying, but he could read their lips: "Wandering Star's back." They'd know, Blue Sky realized, the king had twice sent him to see the farmers' king.

"They must know I'm a farmer," Blue Sky said. "Why don't they try to stop me?"

Blue Sky and Wandering Star were talking in the valley people's language.

"They know who you are," Wandering Star said. "Think about it. You're with me."

"Why does that matter?"

As they ran, Wandering Star turned and gave his farmer friend an irritated glance.

"Think about it," he said. "I predicted this could happen. They all know that. I'm the person who told the king how to bring it about. I'm in Lightning Spear's favor now."

"How do they know who I am?" Blue Sky asked.

Wandering Star gave his farmer friend a look showing how little patience he had left.

"I told you to think about it," he said. "You're a farmer with me. You've got to be the farmer I go with. They've all heard and reheard the story countless times by now. You're the farmer who mistakenly believed he was the brother of our princess. They all know that."

Blue Sky had never thought about it that way, but Wandering Star was obviously right. All the hill people would know what had happened. It was undoubtedly one of the most delightful stories they'd ever heard. Wandering Star hadn't just predicted this day would happen, he'd also gotten a farmer to go with him, a farmer who, when he wasn't giving in to his desire for a hill man, was letting Long Arm know where to find their people's princess and his own people's prince. Which proved to the hill people at last, after all their suffering, the gods in fact favored them, not the farmers.

Blue Sky imagined they must've viewed him as some kind of fool the gods had sent to do their work. When the hill people came to his part in the story—the part where a young farmer fell in love with a hill man and betrayed his people to satisfy his lust—they must've laughed at his folly.

"They also know," Wandering Star added, "you're a farmer who wishes to befriend and understand them. If that makes you feel any better. Long Arm didn't leave that out of his story. I promise you they won't attempt to kill you as long as you're with me. Lightning Spear will have to order you killed."

"I assume he'll do that."

"I can't see why not," Wandering Star said. "My people believe every farmer should be killed. There's no exception for a deluded farmer who wishes to be our friend."

"Not even for a seduced farmer who wished to be your people's friend?"

Wandering Star grabbed Blue Sky's arm, stopping him.

"We can't separate now," he said. "It's too late for that. If the warriors see you by yourself, they'll kill you. They'll have to. We've got two choices. We go back far enough for you to get home by yourself. Or we go ahead and take our chances with Lightning Spear."

"I told you before. I'm not going back. I'm staying with you."

Blue Sky glanced at Tall Oak's army. Noon Breeze and the apprentice tellers were in it. Early Harvest and his cousins were in it. Solemn Promise and Morning Sun's other town companions were in it. Autumn Wine's older grandson and the other able-bodied males from the home village were in it. Valley Defender and his brothers were in it. The messenger was in it.

"We've only got one choice this damned day," he said. "We go to see your king."

*****

Tall Oak's farmers, tellers, and court people, all of them transformed, as night becoming day, into warriors and an army, boldly marched across their enemy's worthless plain. They were still unaware of the extreme danger they were in. The closer they approached the hill warriors assembled at the northern end of the plain, the more they must've imagined how overwhelming their victory would be—and how Lightning Spear had to see it as well. Blue Sky had insisted the hill people could be reasoned with. Maybe there would be no fighting that day.

That Lightning Spear and his warriors stood their ground and made no attempt to escape could've been taken as a hopeful sign that he had no intention to fight but would hand over Morning Sun and Rose Leaf as soon as he learned that was all he had to do to ensure he and his warriors would live to see another day.

Wandering Star and Blue Sky had outpaced Tall Oak's warriors. There was nothing remaining between them and Lightning Spear's visible army but empty plain.

Lightning Spear decided the farmers had come across the plain as far as they needed to.

He gave the command, which was loudly repeated by his men so that no warrior hiding in the surrounding hills could fail to hear it: "Rise! Make yourselves known!"

At the bottom of the hills below Blue Sky and Wandering Star, Lighting Spear's warriors were rising to their feet, filing around the hillocks they'd been hiding behind, making themselves known to the enemy. Their comrades were doing the same thing up and down both sides of the plain—as they were doing behind Tall Oak's army, having closed ranks there.

Blue Sky could see the warriors on the near flank of Tall Oak's army taking notice, slowing their pace considerably, falling silent. From the flanks to the innermost warriors the news must've spread like a late-summer field fire leaping in a strong south wind.

Tall Oak's army, as huge as it was, came to a stop, its roar fading to a whisper in the early-morning breeze.

The valley people's warriors stared at the hills confused, no doubt wondering how they'd gotten themselves on a dusty plain surrounded by an army far more numerous than any of them could've imagined it would be.

What they saw was worse than anything they'd seen in their most terrifying dreams.

*****

"This is our chance," Wandering Star said, laying down his spear.

Lightning Spear's warriors were streaming out from the hills onto the plain.

"They'll walk to Tall Oak's army," Wandering Star said, "to save their strength for the battle. But we've got to run."

Blue Sky lay his spear on the ground next to Wandering Star's, and they ran.

They ran past Lightning Spear's warriors. They ran across the plain and into the open between the armies.

Tall Oak's warriors, immobile now, stunned by the vastly superior numbers of their adversary, had surely already given up any hope for a quick victory that day and the start of a triumphal return home the next. They must've begun considering the probability—even the inevitability—of a calamitous defeat for their beloved kingdom, and their own slaughter in it.

The warriors with Lightning Spear at the northern end of the plain were under orders to stand their ground. Lightning Spear was biding his time as his warriors on the flanks and at the rear of Tall Oak's army marched steadily toward their foe.

With evident curiosity the hill warriors in the first ranks looked out at Wandering Star and Blue Sky running across their front. Like their comrades who'd been hiding in the hills, though, they made no attempt to keep them from reaching the king.

Blue Sky could hear some of them shouting in their language to those in the rear.

"It's Wandering Star," they yelled. "With his thief companion. Both unarmed."

As Wandering Star and Blue Sky drew closer, they slowed to a walk.

"Lightning Spear," Wandering Star said, again speaking the valley people's language, "is the one sitting in the chair. Only the king can sit in a chair before a battle."

Lightning Spear was staring at them.

The first warrior on his right was the king's new chief warrior, Long Arm.

Wandering Star told Blue Sky who the others were.

The first warrior on Lightning Spear's left was the powerful chieftain, Thunder Hunter. Standing beside Thunder Hunter was his elder son, Dark Storm, to whom the king had promised Rose Leaf after the hill people won back their valley. And the next warrior in that direction was War Cloud, Thunder Hunter's younger son.

On Long Arm's side of the king stood the first teller, Heaven's Voice, and his high tellers, according to their rank. On the side of Thunder Hunter and his sons stood the chieftains of the lesser tribes, which were all the tribes other than the king's and Thunder Hunter's.

One of the warriors in the first rank behind War Cloud caught Blue Sky's eye. Wandering Star said he was a cousin of Dark Storm and War Cloud's. He was also a teller. They called him True Hunter.

Nobody had yet tried to keep Wandering Star and Blue Sky from approaching the king.

"Wandering Star!" Lightning Spear suddenly shouted. "Did you come to see my warriors destroy the farmers? Just as you told me they would?"

As was the custom for the valley people's army, certain hill warriors close enough to hear the king repeated the question to their immediate rear, and succeeding ranks made it echo around the plain.

"No," Wandering Star answered, loudly. "I don't wish to see anybody die today."

Lightning Spear, fearless now on the morning of a victory he'd never imagined himself achieving, laughed as he let his warriors repeat the brash exile's reply.

"Then be certain not to look," he said, "in the direction of the farmers' warriors."

The king pointed with his spear at Tall Oak's army behind Wandering Star and Blue Sky.

"Because if you do," he added, "you'll see every one of them die this day."

71

Lightning Spear's warriors responded to those remarks with their own laughter, and it, too, made its way around the plain.

Solemn Promise, Valley Defender, and the apprentice tellers must've been interpreting. The valley warriors were shouting back to their rear and out to their flanks reasonably accurate versions of the conversation between the enemy king and the hill man seeking to save them.

"They're already your prisoners," Wandering Star said. "You don't need to kill them."

Lightning Spear paused to let the warriors in both armies consider those remarks, too.

"Why would I wish to hold them as prisoners?" he asked. "They're the people who stole our valley from us. Why shouldn't I wish to kill them all?"

"Including their old men," Thunder Hunter added, "their women, and their children."

"You can trade their army for their forest," Wandering Star replied. "The stories from the last war are true. They use only a small part of the valley near the river for farming. There's no game there. Most of the valley is forest. That's where the game is. They only take wood from it."

Lightning Spear stared at Wandering Star, even after the echoes died.

"You can take fish from the river," Blue Sky said, speaking the hill people's language. "It's filled with fish. So is the lake in the upper valley. Your people can fish there, too."

The warriors near Lightning Spear looked at one another, even as they repeated the farmer thief's statements to their comrades behind them. Only Long Arm and the few who'd come in contact with the prisoner, Morning Sun, had previously heard a farmer speak their language.

"All we need is the farmland," Blue Sky added. "It's of no use to your people."

Fair Judge had wondered if the forest would grow down to the edge of the river if their people didn't farm that land. And wouldn't the wild animals come with it? Many of the weeds the farmers pulled from their fields were in fact newly sprouted trees that grew in the forest.

Lightning Spear smiled, almost graciously, while Wandering Star and Blue Sky set forth their proposals for the terms of the surrender of the valley people's army.

Thunder Hunter and his two indignant sons, though, exchanged angry glances.

Blue Sky knew what he was saying sounded insane, but that was no reason for him to stop.

"Your people and my people can live in the valley together," he said. "We don't need to kill one another anymore."

After the echoes faded that time, they gave way to a low rumble as Lightning Spear's warriors on the flanks of Tall Oak's army trooped across the plain, closing in on their enemy.

"The whole valley belongs to my people," Lightning Spear said.

His warriors repeated that remark with loud and prolonged cheering.

"And," he said, "the day we take it back from the thieves who stole it from us has arrived."

The cheering grew louder.

"That might be," Blue Sky said. "But many of your warriors won't be alive tomorrow to celebrate their victory. They'll never hunt in the valley. What good will it be to them?"

Even those words went out to the hill warriors farthest from the king.

"They'll go to their graves," Lightning Spear replied, "knowing they died in the most glorious battle their people have ever fought."

That statement appeared to need no celebration to confirm its truth.

"They'll go to their graves," Lightning Spear added, his voice rising, "knowing they defeated your people at last, as the gods always intended we would. Knowing the valley is ours again and will continue to be forever. Knowing the difference for our people will always be the battle in which they fought as heroes."

Concentric arcs of those words spreading outward among the hill warriors warned Blue Sky that they might not fear the possibility of death in the coming battle, even a bloody, agonizing, day-long death at the end of an enemy spear. Not if their gods' fulfillment of their promise of the return of the valley to their people and the extermination of its usurpers was at hand.

"Now get out of here," Lightning Spear said to Wandering Star, rising from his chair.

As an exile, Wandering Star wasn't allowed to fight in his people's army.

"The thieves die today," Lightning Spear continued. "The gods command it. I'm only their servant. Leave the battlefield. Since you don't have a beard anymore, my warriors might mistake you for one of the thieves and kill you along with them."

His army greatly enjoyed that remark.

Thunder Hunter was glaring at Blue Sky.

"Either of my sons," he said to the king, "will be honored to kill this thief for you—this impudent thief who dares to speak to you without being asked. Which of them do you wish to carry out his execution?"

War Cloud, who was uncommonly pleasing to see, stepped forward, laughing.

"I'll gladly kill him," he said, pointing his spear at Blue Sky's bare midriff. "And since we've got a battle to fight, I'll make it quick. Too bad, though, we won't have time to watch him suffer."

Long Arm glanced at Thunder Hunter and War Cloud with what appeared to be contempt. Blue Sky assumed he thought Lightning Spear hardly needed to depend upon a son of mighty Thunder Hunter to put to death a man bearing no weapon—a man who had to have been the most pathetic character, farmer or not, who'd ever made an appearance in their people's stories.

Wandering Star threw his arms around Blue Sky.

"I beg you," he said to Lightning Spear. "Please don't kill him. His king has prohibited him from joining the fight against our people. Nor does he wish to fight our people, or do us any harm."

Neither Lightning Spear nor anybody else made any attempt to keep those remarks from going out to their warriors.

"I beg you," Wandering Star repeated, making no attempt to hide his tears from his king and his people's warriors. "I beg you not to kill him. I love him."

If Wandering Star hadn't had his arms around him, declaring his love for him and imploring he be spared, Blue Sky might've preferred suffering death at the swift and certain hand of War Cloud to witnessing the remainder of that day. But he also knew that, as long as Wandering Star was in the world with him, he did wish to live, no matter what else he might have to live through.

Lightning Spear looked at Blue Sky. "My daughter speaks favorably of you. She tells me you and she were raised as brother and sister. I'm certain killing you would greatly sadden her."

"Maybe she needs to be told," Thunder Hunter loudly interjected, "no farmer deserves to live—not even one who was stupid enough to think he was her brother."

War Cloud guffawed at his father's remark.

"I'm ready to kill this farmer," he reminded Lightning Spear, the tip of his weapon almost touching Blue Sky's belly.

"His guts on the ground," Thunder Hunter spat, "will inspire our warriors."

Wandering Star glared at his people's second-most-powerful chieftain. "Our warriors don't need to see this man's guts spilled for inspiration. He comes to us as a friend, unarmed."

Both peoples told a story in which the gods praised a king for protecting an unarmed enemy messenger. But they both also had reasons for insisting the story couldn't apply to them.

Lightning Spear turned to Thunder Hunter and said something only they could hear.

If Blue Sky read his lips accurately, he was arguing that Wandering Star's farmer friend might prove useful to them later on.

And this deluded man, the hill king laughed, would surely never pose a threat to them.

Thunder Hunter appeared unconvinced, even agitated.

Blue Sky could feel the tip of War Cloud's spear-head against his abdomen.

Thunder Hunter was saying something only he and the king could hear.

Blue Sky believed he was arguing no farmer could ever be of any conceivable use to their people.

War Cloud, smirking, slowly drew the tip of his spear-head across Blue Sky's belly.

Wandering Star looked down at the cut War Cloud had made.

Blue Sky thought it appropriate the first blood drawn in the war would be his.

"Don't move," Wandering Star whispered to him, in the valley people's language, taking hold of the shaft of War Cloud's spear and pushing the head of it away from Blue Sky.

War Cloud, laughing again, pushed back, creating a stand-off in which only Wandering Star's continued resistance kept him from slicing another and perhaps deeper cut.

War Cloud was undoubtedly hoping Blue Sky would make a defensive move similar to Wandering Star's, giving him an excuse to kill the intruding farmer without waiting for the king to make up his mind.

He must've felt he wasn't free, though, to kill Wandering Star, a man the king had just publicly thanked for dreaming up a ploy to take the valley back from the farmers—and maybe wipe them off the face of the earth for good.

Lightning Spear stared at the blood running from Blue Sky's wound onto his loincloth.

So did Thunder Hunter, Long Arm, and all the other warriors who were close enough to see it. They knew what Lightning Spear had done to Blue Sky's father in the last war.

Wandering Star had told Blue Sky most of them—even Long Arm, who was a youth, and Dark Storm and War Cloud, who were still children then, as Wandering Star was—were present that day and saw it.

There were so many hill warriors marching across the plain the pounding of their feet had become a low unrelenting rumble like thunder preceding a storm.

Lightning Spear suddenly roused himself.

"We have a battle to fight," he declared.

"Do you wish," War Cloud asked the king, raising his voice, "for me to kill this thief?"

Lightning Spear looked at Wandering Star, who was still blocking War Cloud's spear from Blue Sky's body.

When the king turned to Blue Sky again, it's possible he smiled at him, ever so slightly.

Then he pulled himself together once more and gave his order: "Let him go."

Chapter 5

The hill warriors laughed as Wandering Star and Blue Sky ran past them again, no doubt amused by their failure to persuade Lightning Spear to stop the battle. It was a result the interlopers had every reason to foresee. The only surprise was the farmer thief's continued existence.

By the time Wandering Star and Blue Sky reached the top of the hill where they'd laid down their spears that cloudless morning, the armies were about to clash.

Blue Sky thought how pleasant it would've been in the valley that moment—driving the livestock to pasture, preparing for a full day in the fields harvesting, having no knowledge of a harsh foreign plain where nothing grew.

Blue Sky even dared think how pleasant it would've been if Sturdy Limb and Tall Oak hadn't decided to lead all but four of their able-bodied males of age out of the safety of the valley to punish the hill people. And to confront the now-obvious truth: in the fertile valley his people loved they hadn't bothered themselves to learn who their enemies outside their valley were, not even how tragically numerous they were.

The unfortunate hill people were always lesser beings who deserved nothing more than instant death. They merited no further attention.

It's possible every valley warrior on the plain had already begun looking back with regret to the time when he could still imagine the encampment guards were all his people needed to keep the savage hill people out of their valley. If the number of hill warriors they confronted that day had come pouring over the mountains during the last war, the valley people would no longer exist.

*****

Both sides chose to remain behind their shields and not use their bows. The shooting of arrows could only delay the close fighting with spears that would decide the outcome of the battle.

Tall Oak and Sturdy Limb, having limited supplies of food and water, had no desire to extend the battle over several days. And

Lightning Spear and Thunder Hunter wanted a quick victory on the plain followed by a swift and massive invasion of the valley and the slaughter of its suddenly defenseless old men, women, children, and cowards.

At that moment the hill people had two questions. How had the farmers gotten away with their subterfuge for so long? Why had Wandering Star been the only one to see the truth?

And the valley warriors on the plain also had questions as few. Why had they left the protection of their valley? How could the abduction of any two people—even if they were a beloved prince and the equally beloved woman he'd chosen as a mate—justify it?

Once the sides got close enough to eliminate any possibility of using bows and arrows, all the warriors dropped their shields, freeing up both hands for the thrusting of spears.

The valley people's warriors went into their traditional defensive mode. The warriors in the outer ranks, who were the current guards and those who'd served as guards in the most recent years—and therefore the youngest and ablest of them all—stood shoulder to shoulder. This time, though, they were in a line of comrades they'd never imagined themselves being a part of: a closed circle with no beginning, no end, and no way out.

It wasn't going to be the battle Tall Oak and Sturdy Limb had brought their army to the plain to fight—in the highly improbable event Lightning Spear would choose to force a fight.

The valley warriors presumed they were more powerful both in numbers and in fighting ability. Therefore, when Valley Defender and Solemn Promise delivered Tall Oak's ultimatum, they'd make it clear the valley people's army had one purpose: to capture and kill Lightning Spear if he refused to give up Morning Sun and Rose Leaf. That would require the hill people's army to encircle their king in order to defend him.

As they did so, the valley warriors would surround the hill warriors and methodically kill them, picking them off one at a time until there were no longer enough of them left to prevent the capture, torture, and prolonged execution of their king.

Valley Defender and Solemn Promise would promise Lightning Spear that, even as the battle raged, he could stop it by ordering the release of Morning Sun and Rose Leaf, in effect trading them for his own life. He wouldn't know that after he'd fulfilled his part of the bargain, Sturdy Limb, Law Speaker, and their allies would insist that the valley warriors should nevertheless kill him and any hill warriors who were still alive.

It would be the promised punishment given and lesson taught. The valley people had agreed on one matter with the seven persons who'd opposed attacking the hill people: their warriors couldn't kill old men, women, or children. So they'd need to show those survivors, especially the boys, why they and their descendants must never provoke the farmers again.

Standing on the ridge with Wandering Star, Blue Sky assumed his people's warriors had passed along, comrade to comrade, new instructions from Tall Oak and Sturdy Limb during the interval between the rising of Lightning Spear's hidden warriors and the dropping of shields.

Blue Sky imagined his people's warriors taking some comfort in the knowledge that they'd be in the sort of defensive battle they'd spent almost all their training time with their comrades learning to fight.

He could even imagine Tall Oak and Sturdy Limb might calculate that, despite being so badly outnumbered, they could eventually wear the hill warriors down and win the battle. Maybe they'd included a statement to that effect in their instructions to their warriors.

Whatever the reason, when the fighting began, the outer ranks of the valley people's army held their ground.

"Defense is what your people do best," Wandering Star said. "You live in a valley, surrounded on every side by your enemy. Defense is all you really know."

The first hill warriors to make contact with the encircled valley warriors seemed uncertain as to what they were supposed to do. They randomly stepped forward, thrusting their spears in the general direction of their adversaries, who easily parried them well short of the point where they could cause any harm. Then the hill warriors would jump back a step or two as if they expected their opponents to break out of their line and come after them.

The valley warriors, though, weren't accepting the invitation to do that. They were displaying their discipline, maintaining their line, never letting a gap open between them and their nearest comrades, forcing their opponents to fight one-on-one, nullifying the benefit of the hill army's far greater numbers. That would always give an advantage, even on a level field, to warriors fighting defensively, especially if they were far better trained than their opponents.

Wandering Star had once pointed out—and Many Numbers had readily agreed he had to be right—farmers had more time than hunters to practice fighting. Hill people mostly trained for war with humans by hunting and killing animals.

The valley people trained with other humans as mock opponents in games as entertaining for their endless boasts and jibes as they were necessary for the safety of the kingdom. While the men and boys couldn't actually kill or harm one another, they could see what would probably result in serious injury or death—perhaps their own if they weren't careful enough, if they let their minds stray.

The initial screams in the battle on the plain came from Lightning Spear's side.

In the fighting nearest Wandering Star and Blue Sky, a hill warrior whose opponent had batted his spear out of his hands stepped back from the front line to get a spare. Whenever that happened to a valley warrior, a comrade behind him would immediately either hand him a replacement spear or take his place in the line.

No comrade, though, came forward to take the hill warrior's place. That left his valley opponent free to thrust his spear into the belly of his nearest comrade's adversary in the hill people's line—no doubt the missing man's brother, companion, or cousin.

That hill warrior fell, screaming, his entrails spilling out of his body onto the plain.

The hill women, children, and old men gathered on the hillside below Blue Sky and Wandering Star drowned out the wounded hill warrior's screams with their own like thunder overwhelming the whimper of a human.

Both of the valley people's warriors who now found themselves without opponents were free to thrust their spears into the bellies of the opponents of the comrades on either side of them. That left three hill warriors mortally wounded—all of them no doubt screaming, though Blue Sky couldn't hear them above the cries of their comrades and the hill noncombatants ringing the plain.

Hill warriors rushed to take the places of the three fatally wounded men as a fourth, momentarily distracted, took a thrust in his gut.

The hill warriors fought on. Being careful, though, not to trip on their fallen comrades, they kept glancing down, taking their eyes off their opponents.

The valley warriors, from their sandals to their loincloths looking as if they'd gone wading in vats of red wine, quickly impaled two more of them.

The hill warriors, stunned, withdrew.

The valley warriors did what they'd learned in their training to do. They stood fast in their line, refusing to pursue their opponents. Above the screams of the fallen and the din of the battle around them, Blue Sky could hear them shouting back to his place the occasional comrade tempted by the enemy's confusion to break from the line and score himself a quick heroic kill.

Blue Sky could see that what was happening nearby was happening all over the battlefield.

The front-line warriors of Lightning Spear's army were retreating, carrying their wounded comrades with them, and the next line was moving forward to attack. The valley people's front, though, wasn't moving forward or backward, but was staying where it was supposed to be, with the correct amount of space between each warrior and his comrades on either side of him.

Blue Sky could see as well that the two armies had different visions of what their front was supposed to be and do. In Tall Oak's army the front line's goal was to remain unbroken, with the warriors freely replacing one another in it as need be, to deliver a mortal wound to a fallen enemy warrior here, to replace a wounded, exhausted, or poorly performing comrade there.

In Lightning Spear's army, on the other hand, the front was succeeding waves of warriors throwing themselves against the enemy, aiming for penetration and the disarray it would bring.

The hill people's wounded and dying warriors needed attention. Around the plain, men too old to fight were leading boys still too young to die to the battlefield.

They had leather pouches filled with water slung over their shoulders. Some of them carried stretchers consisting of two saplings and hides.

The old men and boys were the only non-warriors among the hill people allowed to have contact with the army. Wandering Star said Lightning Spear and Thunder Hunter were worried that cowardly warriors would avoid fighting by hiding among the people—with the help of their mates, mothers, and sisters—if the people in general were allowed to go near them.

The front-line warriors on both sides clashed again.

Women and children on the hillside below Wandering Star and Blue Sky wailed. But no matter how loud they cried, they could no longer drown out the screams of the wounded and dying.

One of the hill warriors broke away from his comrades as if he were crazed, running ahead of them straight at opponents dripping with his comrades' blood. One of the valley warriors quickly thrust his spear into the attacker's gut, but not before the hill warrior had landed his spear in another valley opponent's belly.

Two valley warriors behind the wounded man grabbed his spear and pulled him out of the line. Another quickly took his place and impaled a second hill warrior insensibly charging ahead of his comrades—and throwing his life away with nothing to show for it.

Behind the valley people's line, the two comrades, one under each of the injured warrior's arms, dragged him away from the front and gently laid him down.

He'd either somehow get up on his feet and fight again, or he'd remain on the ground in the agony of a slow death, listening to the curses and screams of the battle, tasting the dust of the plain mixed with other men's blood, hoping death would come before his comrades ran out of water, wasting it on a compassionate attempt to slake his horrendous thirst.

All around the battlefield Blue Sky and Wandering Star could see the attack of the second wave of hill warriors was as costly to them as the first. When the hill warriors pulled back again, they were lugging away far more dead and wounded comrades than their valley opponents had need to.

A third wave ended with the same lopsided outcome.

The lesson was evident: the disciplined defense of Tall Oak's army required far fewer warriors than did the front-to-front, wave-after-wave offense of the hill people.

Even if the hill people were ultimately victorious that day, a great many of their warriors could expect to die—never to see the abundant valley they paid for with their lives.

Worse still, the anticipated victory might somehow slip away.

*****

Wandering Star took Blue Sky to a nearby hollow and asked him to help pick the unripened seed pods of a weed the valley people sometimes saw growing in clearings in their forest. Here it was particularly abundant.

Wandering Star and Blue Sky bundled the pods in their shirts, having no need to wear them that late-summer day, and left their spears in the hollow, having no need for them either.

A number of the hill people had brought with them pots for boiling water, assuming they'd prepare meals while their army slaughtered the thieves. In view of the hell-godly tenacity of the farmers, though, few hill people seemed interested in cooking, whether to celebrate an unfolding victory or simply to alleviate the usual midday hunger.

Wandering Star borrowed several pots from people he knew. He and Blue Sky filled them with water from a nearby brook, set them on stones and started fires under them. They threw in the pods and brought the mixture to a boil.

As the exile and his farmer companion worked, the old men and boys who'd gone out to the army were bringing wounded and dead warriors back with them, one to a stretcher for the wounded, two for the dead.

Another group of older men—many of whom, Wandering Star said, had fought in the last war with the farmers—were starting out with more boys for a trek across the plain. They'd been digging graves, but the boys couldn't take their eyes off the battle. A few of them loudly wondered why the gods would let thieves kill their fathers, brothers, cousins, and friends in a battle the hill people had every reason to win.

Another wave of hill warriors attacked the valley warriors' front line. When the assault came to its bloody end, a frightful number of newly killed and wounded hill warriors lay on the ground.

Tall Oak's warriors were doing what they'd interminably practiced with their comrades during their boyhood, their year in the encampments, and all the years thereafter as long as their comrades considered them able to fight.

And except for those who'd fought in the last war, as Green Field had, or in the occasional skirmish in the mountains, as Valley Defender had, they'd only seen practice.

But there on a dusty, barren plain, surrounded by a monstrous army they'd had no warning of, they were thrusting and slashing with their spears, taking and re-taking their places in the front line, pressing water to the lips of the wounded, bearing off the dead—all as if they performed those gruesome tasks every day.

A woman on the hillside below Wandering Star and Blue Sky screamed. The children with her wailed. Other women and children took up her cry.

The old men and boys returning from the battlefield had gotten close enough for the people on the hillsides to identify the wounded and dead they were carrying with them.

The women and children who saw their own among the first to fall that day ran out from the surrounding hillsides and onto the plain to retrieve their mates, fathers, sons, and brothers.

More than a few of the women who remained behind on the hillsides, knowing there was no good reason why they wouldn't be the next to scream and hear their children sob—some of them having already sighted uncles, nephews, and cousins among the wounded and dead—were openly damning the gods for so suddenly withdrawing their favor.

When Wandering Star got to the wounded warriors, with his farmer companion assisting him as a well-behaved child would, he offered them a drink of the pod tea he'd brewed.

In some cases he pleaded with them to take it. He insisted, no matter how bitter it tasted, it would ease their pain. The men, most of whom knew they'd die anyway, were in no position to turn down a person making that kind of promise.

If the liquid dribbled down their chins, as it sometimes did, Wandering Star told the men's wives, companions, children, and mothers they should wipe it up with their fingers and put it back into the wounded men's mouths, and never let it go to waste.

When Wandering Star was still an apprentice teller, he was traveling from encampment to encampment with the two older tellers he'd been assigned to assist but had displeased by refusing to go with them. They heard an old woman was on her deathbed asking to see the tellers.

When they arrived, the woman appeared to be jabbering incomprehensibly. The tellers paid her no attention and busied themselves consuming the food the woman's encampment companions provided, as they were expected to do whenever tellers came for a visit.

Wandering Star, though, chose to listen to what the woman said.

He determined she was asking for the unripened seed pods of a plant that grew nearby. He asked her why she'd want anything so useless as she lay dying. Nobody ate them. He eventually figured out she'd been brewing a tea with them and drinking it to ease her pain. But she'd run out of the pods and could no longer fetch them herself.

He went where she told him to go and gathered the pods. After she started drinking the tea he made for her, she did in fact babble incomprehensibly—when she wasn't sleeping. In her few lucid moments, she thanked him for making her pain much more tolerable.

Wandering Star understood the pod tea was her family's secret. And it had to be a secret. The tellers had long ago insisted their people couldn't consume the fruits of that particular plant because there was no story in which the hill-people's gods had approved eating them, just as there was no story that approved farming. The pod plants were therefore in the same category as snakes and rats. Humans simply didn't and couldn't eat them.

Despite the prohibition, Wandering Star told Blue Sky, his people did roast and eat snakes and rats if they were hungry enough and couldn't find anything else—but they wouldn't dare let the tellers know they'd done it.

The hill people's first teller, Heaven's Voice, and his high tellers used Wandering Star's advocacy of drinking the pod tea to dull pain as one of their many reasons to expel him from the tellerhood. It was proof of his obstinate refusal to submit to the wisdom of his elders.

On the plain, though, the effectiveness of the tea soon became apparent. The exile and his companion went from one wounded man to the next, ladling out the tea into cups and letting the persons with the man know where they could find the pots it was brewing in.

*****

An uproar arose among the hill people. The most recent wave of attacking hill warriors had fractured. Groups of warriors here and there in the encircling front line refused to join the assault.

The valley warriors took immediate advantage. Their front line, undulating like a snake, pulled back in advance of the attacking hill warriors while moving forward on either side of them, closing around and pinching off the hill warriors who'd only done what they'd been told to do.

The valley warriors methodically impaled their bellies and slashed their throats.

When that wave came to its end, the valley warriors had suffered no new casualties of their own—and had also left few of the attacking hill warriors unscathed.

The women and children wailed.

A number of the hill warriors from the rearmost ranks of Lightning Spear's army ran toward the front line. The same thing was happening all over the plain.

"Thunder Hunter's men," Wandering Star explained.

So far, he added, most of the attacking warriors had come from the tribes of Lightning Spear and the lesser chieftains, and those warriors were stepping aside now as if in deference to superiors.

"Shameful," Wandering Star muttered.

Reaching the front, Thunder Hunter's warriors singled out the warriors who'd refused to join the last attack. Other warriors in the first ranks were identifying them.

"The informers are Thunder Hunter's warriors, too," Wandering Star said. "Some of them fight in the front ranks. That's how they find out who the cowards are."

As the valley warriors on the other side of the front stood silent and watched, Thunder Hunter's warriors lined up the warriors who'd disobeyed the order to attack and began counting, wresting the spears away from certain of the disobedient warriors and pulling them out of the line.

"One of every ten," Wandering Star said.

Thunder Hunter's warriors took turns impaling the unlucky tenth of the disobedient men.

Whatever the valley people's warriors might've thought, whatever the gods in heaven might've wished, the noncombatants on the fringes of the plain and in the hillsides screamed.

Thunder Hunter's warriors were killing men who spoke their language and worshiped their gods. And the warriors from the other tribes were making no attempt to stop them.

"Disgusting," Wandering Star spat.

Leaving the unlucky tenth to bleed, writhe, and die where they fell, Thunder Hunter's enforcers quickly marched back through the ranks and resumed their positions in the rear.

The women were now loudly questioning not only the commitment of the gods but also the character of Thunder Hunter's justice—and even, Blue Sky sometimes heard, the wisdom of Lightning Spear himself in letting Thunder Hunter's men take over the battle.

Blue Sky turned to Wandering Star. "I didn't think your people could get away with that."

"They can't," Wandering Star said, staring at the plain.

Three hill warriors came running from the rear of the army toward the hill people nearest Wandering Star and Blue Sky. Other three-warrior detachments—each with one warrior in the lead and another on either side of and behind him, as if they were spearheads—were racing toward the hillsides.

As the warriors approached, the people fell silent.

"Thunder Hunter's?" Blue Sky asked.

"His," Wandering Star replied, whispering. "Don't give them any excuse to kill you."

When the three enforcers reached the women, old men, and children weeping over the dead and tending the wounded, they brought themselves to a halt.

"It's come to the army's attention," the lead warrior announced, shouting so all the people nearby could hear him above the screams from the battlefield, "some of you are cursing our gods, our chieftains, and our king."

He and his two comrades strode among the dead and wounded and their families but stopped when they came to Wandering Star. They took a good, long, smirking look at his farmer companion's belly wound, knowing how he'd acquired it.

Apparently satisfied by their view of that, they continued on their way.

"The king's army wishes to remind you," the lead warrior said, shouting again, "the penalty for cursing gods, chieftains, and the king is death."

The people remained silent. All they could hear was the clamor from the battlefield as the two armies clashed once again.

A woman who'd been on her knees tending a fallen warrior, wiping away the blood and dust caked on his youthful face so his family and friends could kiss him goodbye, got herself up on her feet and turned to the lead warrior.

"This is my son," she said, pointing toward the young man lying on the ground.

The crowd murmured.

A younger woman who'd also been wiping the man's face stood up and put her arms around the older woman's shoulders.

"This is his mate," the older woman continued. "The mother of his two children."

The younger woman wept.

The older woman pointed at her son again.

"He's dead!" she screamed.

Thunder Hunter's lead warrior clenched his spear with both hands and aimed it at her.

"How many more of our sons is it going to take," the woman asked, "to win this war?"

"Shut your mouth," the lead warrior barked at her. "You're talking treason."

The woman persisted. "What good will a damned valley do us if our sons are dead?"

"The valley is ours," the lead warrior replied. "The gods want us to have it. This is our chance to get it back. It doesn't matter how many sons it takes. It doesn't matter if it takes them all."

"Takes them all?" the old woman demanded. "All? All our sons?"

"Not one more word," the lead warrior said, both hands on his spear, "or I'll kill you."

"All?" the woman repeated. "All our sons?"

The lead warrior thrust his spear into the old woman's belly, forcing her with his momentum out of the arms of her son's mate, toppling her over and pinning her to the ground.

The crowd screamed.

The lead warrior placed one foot on the old woman's ribcage and slowly withdrew his spear.

The crowd screamed again.

Standing over the old woman, the lead warrior swiped his spear-point as if it were a blade, slitting her throat—mercifully slitting her throat. She'd need no pod tea.

The crowd screamed a third time.

The son's mate fell to her knees, cradling the older-woman's head in her arms despite the spray of blood from her wound.

A boy, perhaps nine or ten years old, came charging out of the crowd toward Thunder Hunter's warriors.

"You killed my grandmother," he cried.

The lead warrior was still clenching his spear with both of his hands, even as the older woman's blood dripped from it.

Thunder Hunter's warrior nearest the boy turned to the lead warrior and shook his head.

A hill woman Wandering Star knew turned to Blue Sky, whispering, telling him the dead warrior was a younger brother of the boy's father, who was still fighting the farmers.

"You killed my grandmother," the boy cried again.

The nearest of Thunder Hunter's warriors let his spear drop to the ground, threw his arms around the boy, and wrestled him to the ground as if the warrior were a farmer and the boy a sheep in need of shearing.

He put his hand over the boy's mouth and lay on top of him.

The lead warrior, surveying the crowd, which had fallen silent again, its resentment obvious, stood motionless.

His legs were the red of the lower limbs of valley men when they butchered their animals. The dead woman, her son's mate, and a circle of plain around them wore the same red.

Wandering Star approached the warrior who'd subdued the boy.

"I know this boy," he said, getting down on his knees. "I'll take him."

The warrior relaxed his grip on the boy.

"I'll make certain," Wandering Star continued, quickly replacing the warrior's hand on the boy's mouth with his own, "he doesn't say another word."

The warrior who'd subdued the boy got to his feet.

Wandering Star looked up and saw Thunder Hunter's lead warrior, his spear still wet with the older woman's blood, standing over him and the boy.

The woman who'd whispered to Blue Sky approached the lead warrior.

"All of us pray the battle goes well," she said. "All of us are loyal to our king and our chieftains. All of us have faith in the gods."

Whether the lead warrior believed she'd spoken sincerely or not, he accepted her remarks with a slight nod of his head, perhaps as an excuse not to kill the boy and further enrage the crowd.

"Make damned certain," he said to Wandering Star, "I don't hear another word from him."

After Thunder Hunter's warriors left, Wandering Star removed his hand from the boy's mouth and returned him to his family.

The woman who'd assured the warriors of the people's allegiance and piety turned to Blue Sky again.

"They didn't dare touch Wandering Star," she said.

Chapter 6

The two armies continued the slaughter. Neither side's leaders could choose to stop it.

Lightning Spear and Thunder Hunter could only send wave after wave of their warriors against the surrounded farmers' front line. The king and the second most powerful chieftain could see their losses would always exceed their enemy's. They could also believe, though, they'd still have an army when the last farmer warrior lay dying. It might well be only a fraction of the size of the hill army when the battle began, but it would be an army, and the enemy would have none. The valley would be the hill people's for the taking.

Not attacking wasn't an option. Lightning Spear couldn't merely hold the enemy in the trap he'd sprung, waiting for the farmer warriors to die of hunger and thirst. Who could possibly say how long that would take? Would the promise of regaining the valley keep the hill warriors on the plain? They'd already displayed their capacity for indiscipline. The dark would come, and they'd sneak off, more of them during each succeeding night. Thunder Hunter's warriors, themselves greatly outnumbered by Lightning Spear's other warriors, might not be able to hold them in place.

Lightning Spear and Thunder Hunter could only imagine that if their army had to lose most of its warriors anyway, their loss as heroes who died fighting in a final war with the farmers would be far more fitting than their loss as deserters who ran back to their families. Death could bring with it a great victory. Desertion could yield another humiliating defeat.

Tall Oak and Sturdy Limb, having walked their army into Lightning Spear's trap, had chosen the only option they thought they had, which was to stand and fight. Early on in the battle, it was possible for them to imagine that standing and fighting the hill people's army, no matter how large it was, could still leave the valley people victorious.

By midday, though, the sun having reached its zenith unperturbed by clouds, Blue Sky and Wandering Star, viewing the battle from a hillside, could see Tall Oak and Sturdy Limb's warriors had given ground. Their army was shrinking.

No matter how bravely the valley warriors fought, the hill warriors, with their still superior numbers despite their losses, were pushing the farmers' front line back, and reducing, ever so gradually, the circle it traced on the plain.

It was impossible, though, to be on the plain or in the surrounding hills that day and not be vividly aware of the continued disparity in the losses of the armies, Tall Oak's few and Lightning Spear's many, even as the probability of Tall Oak's defeat and Lightning Spear's victory rose.

The hill people's old men, women, and children were digging a long grave in the sand and gravel all around the plain. They'd already laid in it, shoulder to shoulder, the first warriors who'd fallen that morning, covered them up, and placed stones on top of them, one stone for the first, two for the second, and continuing until they reached ten stones before starting again with one.

The hill people hoped they might later remember where a dead warrior slept, even if the only leads they had to go on were his number and the location of the comrades he was buried next to. For both the hill and valley peoples, the most unpardonable sin was forgetting a hero's death.

Anywhere Blue Sky and Wandering Star looked between the rearmost ranks of Lightning Spear's army and the hills, they could see old men and boys dragging dead and injured warriors back to their people.

And when the old men and boys returned to the battlefield, they took Wandering Star's pod tea with them. The hill warriors were giving it to their comrades to drink as soon as they fell.

Blue Sky wished he could've flown over the battleground to his people's dying warriors, grasping containers of pod tea with his feet like a bird—or a god in disguise.

The hill people were going about their grave-digging in silence. Even when families first gained sight of their dead or dying kin now, there was little screaming or wailing, usually only a quiet weeping acceptance of a loss already imagined. Glancing at the battleground on the plain from time to time, they simply shook their heads and resumed their work.

Having no old men, women, or children with them to dig graves, the valley warriors were heaping their dead on a pile of bodies at the center of their circle.

Blue Sky couldn't help but wonder who was lying there already. Solemn Promise and Morning Sun's other town companions? Valley Defender and his brothers? The men from his village he'd grown up with? Noon Breeze and the apprentice tellers? Early Harvest and his cousins? Tall Oak, Sturdy Limb, and Law Keeper themselves?

Still, though, the valley warriors maintained their line, blow after blow, relentlessly wounding or killing two or three hill warriors for every one of their own who fell wounded or killed.

And on and on they fought, long after they must've realized they could neither win the battle nor personally survive it.

No mere human on either side of the line separating the armies had anticipated such a day.

And once it arrived, no arrangement of words could possibly describe its horror.

*****

"This isn't the way it was supposed to be," Wandering Star grumbled.

He and Blue Sky had had little rest or food for several days by then, and yet they could neither eat nor sleep. They could only stare at the battlefield when they weren't picking pods, brewing tea, or fetching water for the wounded.

"How was it supposed to be?" Blue Sky asked, his tone exposing his lack of hope.

"Your warriors weren't supposed to be this brave," Wandering Star replied. "They were supposed to see how outnumbered they were and run."

Tall Oak and Sturdy Limb might've attempted a break-out, sending all their warriors in one direction, no doubt the direction from which they'd come. They might've hoped their army could smash through the encircling ranks of hill warriors, and enough of their survivors could outrun the hill warriors back to the valley and mount a defense there.

In doing so, Tall Oak and Sturdy Limb would've instantly given up the greatest advantage their army possessed: its order and discipline. Without which, the chances of a successful break-out came down to numbers alone. In an undisciplined fight, it wouldn't take many hill warriors to slow the valley people's army sufficiently to allow the other hill warriors to catch up and join the fray. Three or four hill warriors would be ganging up on each valley warrior. The hill warriors would quickly win such a battle with no substantial losses of their own.

In the valley people's training for warfare, they practiced running away, always posing as hill warriors when they did. It was easy for them to see a warrior gave up his best defense, the use of his spear, when he turned his back on his opponent. The warrior could only hope he was faster and had more stamina than his adversary. If he had two or more enemy warriors chasing him, he'd have to hope he could run faster and farther than each of them.

"Too brave," Wandering Star repeated, his eyes fixed on the battle.

The pile of dead bodies at the center of the valley people's army was scarlet, as was a broad band of ground on either side of the front.

"Your people's warriors stand and fight on," Wandering Star continued, as if in awe, "knowing they'll all die today."

"They stand and fight on, knowing they'll all die senselessly today."

If this is what the gods saw when they saw war, Blue Sky wondered, what could they be thinking when they ordered humans—humans they supposedly loved—to wage it for them?

"Along with a lot of your people's warriors," Blue Sky added.

"That's Tall Oak's goal now," Wandering Star said. "Bringing about as much senseless death on this plain as his warriors can manage."

"What good will that do him?" Blue Sky scoffed.

"It won't do him any good during his life."

"My mother was right. He's out of his mind."

"But he's your people's king," Wandering Star insisted. "Choosing to stand and fight today might do him a great deal of good in your people's stories."

94

"How can he ever be anything," Blue Sky scoffed, "but the most miserable king to make an appearance in my people's stories?"

Wandering Star glared at Blue Sky. "How many times do I have to beg you to think about what you say before you say it? With every hill warrior Tall Oak's army kills, he increases the chances his people, your people, the people he left at home in the valley, can ultimately survive."

"Survive?" Blue Sky asked. "My people? After this?"

"Survive," Wandering Star replied. "Your people's warriors know that, too. That's why they'll continue to fight until the last man among them is dead."

"That pile of bodies will be immense."

"And the stones above the graves for my people's warriors will be countless."

They stared at the battle. The number of humans already killed that day was countless.

"Both sides blundered," Wandering Star remarked. "Yours, by walking into this trap. Mine, by setting it."

"Maybe both sides," Blue Sky said, spitting out the words as if they were meat gone rotten, "are simply getting what they deserve— for hating one another for so many years."

Wandering Star looked at Blue Sky. "If that sin deserves this kind of punishment, the gods must deem it the most vile of them all."

"Maybe it is."

Blue Sky and Wandering Star couldn't eat, couldn't sleep, couldn't move. All they could do was stare at their peoples' warriors senselessly, needlessly killing one another.

But the killing didn't seem to bother the gods. Both peoples believed a cloudless sky was the way the gods revealed how pleased they were with the humans they favored.

And there wasn't a cloud in the sky that day.

*****

"People told me where I'd find you," Blue Sky heard a woman saying.

She was speaking the hill people's language.

"Picking your pods," she continued, "brewing your tea."

95

She was coming down from the rim of the hollow toward Wandering Star and Blue Sky.

"The injured warriors," she said, "are thankful you're making it for them."

Wandering Star stared at her.

"Those dying are doing it quietly," she added. "Their families are grateful to you for that."

She and Wandering Star embraced.

"Some people are thinking," she whispered but not so softly Blue Sky couldn't hear her, "you'd be a much wiser king than the one we have."

"They shouldn't say that," Wandering Star said. "Neither should you, in public."

The woman separated herself from him and turned to Blue Sky.

"So this is your farmer friend," she said. "People told me he's pleasing to see, even if he doesn't have a beard."

She peered at Blue Sky's wound.

"I heard War Cloud did that," she said. "Does it hurt?"

"I haven't thought about it," Blue Sky replied in her language. "People are dying."

"You could've gotten killed yourself," she said. "Running out in front of the army with Wandering Star, begging Lightning Spear to stop his damned war. Everybody thought that was going to end up with you dead."

Blue Sky couldn't tell whether she was criticizing or praising him.

"And it didn't do any damned good," Wandering Star said.

"I don't agree," the woman countered, pointing a finger in the direction of the battleground. "You let the people know there was an alternative to that."

At least in the hollows where Wandering Star and Blue Sky did their pod picking, the dreadful cacophony of the battle was muffled.

The woman turned to Blue Sky again, this time embracing him as well.

"Wandering Star told me you could understand our language and speak it," she said. "People call me Dancing Song. I'm his mother."

*****

When they reached the top of the hill, they met some children who'd come looking for them. Wandering Star and Blue Sky gave them pods to make tea for their brothers, fathers, uncles, and cousins Blue Sky's people's warriors had done their best to kill.

Vultures hovered above the battleground.

After the children left with the pods, Dancing Song turned to Wandering Star. "Many people are wondering if your father could somehow get himself killed in this battle."

Wandering Star shook his head. "They should be careful saying what they wonder."

Blue Sky looked at Wandering Star, who had his eyes fixed on the battlefield.

"You told me your father was dead," Blue Sky chose to say.

"Is he dead?" Dancing Song asked, glancing at the battlefield herself. "The people I've spoken with seem to think he's still alive. Out there, somewhere."

Blue Sky turned to Dancing Song. "Wandering Star told me his father was killed in your people's last war with my people."

"I know that's what he told you," Dancing Song said. "I found that out from Rose Leaf."

Wandering Star, refusing to take his eyes off the battlefield, chose not to respond.

"The man who was killed in the last war was my husband," Dancing Song continued. "But he wasn't Wandering Star's father."

Wandering Star turned to Blue Sky.

"I lied to you," he said. "I'm sorry, but I thought it was justified, under the circumstances."

Blue Sky stared at him. "Who is your father?"

Wandering Star was looking at the battlefield again.

"If my mother wishes to tell you who he is, she's free to do so," he replied. "I have no recollection of the act that brought me into this world."

Dancing Song looked at Blue Sky. "Wandering Star's ashamed of his mother," she said. "Did he ever tell you I'm a whore?"

Blue Sky was so unprepared for Dancing Song's question, he couldn't quickly reply.

97

Wandering Star turned to him. "I truly never thought it mattered. I'm not ashamed of my mother. She knows that. My father's the person I'm ashamed of."

Wandering Star had tears in his eyes.

"Do you wish to tell me," Blue Sky asked Dancing Song, "who his father is?"

"If you wish to know," she said, taking Blue Sky's hand as if the two of them were lovers, "I'll certainly tell you. Everybody should know the truth. That's what I believe."

Blue Sky's response was that of a demanding lover: "I wish to know the truth."

"Wandering Star's father," Dancing Song said, "is Lightning Spear."

*****

The boys too young to fight but old enough to work like men were bringing more of the mortally wounded and dead hill warriors back to their families. The women and younger children went out to meet them weeping.

The old men looked up from their work to see who they were and, without speaking a word, resumed digging grave space for them.

Wandering Star looked as if his farmer companion were seeing him naked for the first time.

"My father," Wandering Star said, "ordered his warriors to mutilate your father and your prince. Why would I want you to know that man was my father?"

The woman who'd pledged the loyalty of the people to their chieftains, king, and gods to spare a boy's life had told Blue Sky that Thunder Hunter's warriors couldn't touch Wandering Star. Blue Sky hadn't fully understood the point of her remark. Now he did.

"Your people must know you're his son," Blue Sky said.

"Of course they know," Dancing Song affirmed. "But they can't speak freely about it."

"Why can't they do that?" Blue Sky asked.

"They'd incur Lightning Spear's wrath," she replied. "He denies he's Wandering Star's father. Even though no other man in the kingdom would've dared go with me when he was putting Wandering Star in my body. The people know that."

"I still don't understand," Blue Sky said. "I thought Lightning Spear has a mate, she's the queen, her name is Thistle Dew, she's Rose Leaf's mother, and Rose Leaf is Lightning Spear's only child. I'm sorry. I don't understand. Something's wrong with my mind. I need sleep."

Dancing Song looked Blue Sky up and down as if she were deciding whether he might be a suitable lover. He'd seen his own mother look at Morning Sun, Early Harvest, Spring Rain, and Wandering Star that way.

"I'll tell you how it happened," Dancing Song offered.

When Lightning Spear was still a prince, his father arranged for him to become the mate of the daughter of the third most powerful chieftain in the kingdom. Only the king himself and Thunder Hunter's father ranked above him. His daughter was Thistle Dew.

The night of their wedding ceremony, though, she openly told Lightning Spear she wouldn't take any pleasure in their going together, and for her it would always be an onerous duty and burden. Persons who knew her said she'd hoped her mate would be a cousin she'd grown up with who'd hoped for the same thing.

Thistle Dew fulfilled her duties anyway. After several children of hers and Lightning Spear's had died in her body or soon after they were born, she gave birth to the child who thrived and eventually became known as Rose Leaf.

"I remember Rose Leaf as an infant," Dancing Song said. "Thistle Dew obviously loved her, even if the child didn't have the right father."

"How do you know," Blue Sky asked, "what Thistle Dew said to Lightning Spear on their wedding night?"

"They both told me," Dancing Song replied, pausing to let that revelation sink in. "The old king died shortly after the wedding ceremony, and Lightning Spear became king. One of the first things he did was to give my husband tribute for the privilege of going with me whenever he wished."

"I didn't think your people were allowed to do that," Blue Sky said.

"They're not," she said.

"They're not allowed to do that," Wandering Star chose to add, "in all cases except one."

"The exception being the king's case?" Blue Sky asked, unable to conceal his disgust with such a rule.

Screams from the battlefield, as the armies clashed again, were Blue Sky's answer.

Lightning Spear had made a deal with Heaven's Voice. The king would appoint him first teller. And Heaven's Voice would decide, after due deliberation with the high tellers he'd placed in their positions, that the king, but only the king, was allowed to trade his tribute to go with a woman who wasn't his mate.

The hill and valley peoples both told a story of a king who'd done that. Since he lived only a few years after reaching his manhood, the usual conclusion was that the gods had punished him for what he'd done. Heaven's Voice, on the other hand, made a novel argument: the gods had done that king a favor by letting him die young and escape old age, exactly as he'd wished.

But both peoples also knew some men paid other women and men to go with them—and usually got away with it with no loss except whatever it was they'd paid for something that could so easily disappoint. Neither Tall Oak nor his father punished persons for committing that crime. They'd even gone so far as to laugh and remark that the wrong-doers in the transaction, having been exposed in open court, had already been punished enough.

Lightning Spear, though, had ordered the execution of more than a few male culprits—but only when he'd wanted, for another reason, to see them dead. And his reason in some cases, both Wandering Star and Dancing Song affirmed, was merely to enjoy seeing the person put to death.

As for Dancing Song's husband, he considered himself "blessed by the gods" that the king wanted his mate so much he was willing to give up a part of his tribute for her.

"What would your people say about that?" Wandering Star asked Blue Sky.

Wishing not to seem superior, Blue Sky chose not to answer the question.

The valley people would allow their king to pay for a woman or man, especially if they knew his mate didn't wish to go with him, for whatever reason, good or bad. But they'd never let their king order a person punished for doing nothing more than what the king himself had done.

"I'm sorry," Blue Sky said to Dancing Song. "Going with Lightning Spear must've been difficult for you."

"But in fact," she said, "that part of it wasn't difficult."

Wandering Star was staring at the battle ground, pretending he wasn't listening.

"I never understood," Dancing Song continued, "why Thistle Dew objected to him so much. I confess I thought the youthful Lightning Spear was a good-looking man. I enjoyed going with him. His son turned out to be that kind of man, too. I've heard even the farmers like him."

She looked at Wandering Star as if she might've been willing to go with him herself.

"And see what we got," she added. "Our son passes out pod tea to the wounded warriors. He walks freely among the people with a farmer companion, both of them beardless. Who else has done that? Before this day dawned, nobody had imagined a story with those things in it."

"That son," Wandering Star said, "also brought on a senseless war with the farmers."

After Lightning Spear received his wound in the last war, Dancing Song told Blue Sky, he no longer wanted anything more to do with her. He sent her back to her mate's family. But by then her mate was dead, the king's tribute was gone, and they had no use for her or her child.

"Nor did my own family," she said. "Not after they'd watched me taking obvious pleasure in being the king's whore. They thought I'd shamed them. Maybe I had. I was young and foolish. I didn't understand the ways of the world."

Blue Sky took her hand.

She put her other hand on top of his. She had more to tell him.

"Wandering Star and I got by on our own," she said. "People had no reason to be surprised he grew up to think so differently from everybody else in the kingdom."

Blue Sky could see why Lightning Spear had chosen to give tribute for Dancing Song. Men who went with women must've enjoyed thrusting themselves into slender and yet fully feminine bodies like hers, his own mother's, and Rose Leaf's.

"Expulsion from the tellerhood," she continued, "even exile, didn't make a difference to Wandering Star. He went among the people as he pleased. They never had any quarrel with him. And he was still the king's son. That's why the warriors made no attempt this morning to keep him and you from seeing Lightning Spear and saying whatever you wished to say. Wandering Star is more remarkable than his father ever was. The people wish he were their prince."

Late afternoon had come. Only the vultures flying above the battlefield scarred the still cloudless sky. More of them had arrived for the eventual feast: dead valley warriors.

*****

"Long Arm was spying on Lightning Spear's son," Blue Sky said.

"That's right," Dancing Song agreed. "If some other man had been seen going with a farmer in the mountains, Lightning Spear would've simply ordered both of them killed. But he wanted to know what his son was doing. He was out to satisfy his own curiosity. He wasn't expecting Long Arm to bring him any information about our princess—or your prince."

"I used my position as the king's son," Wandering Star said. "No other hill man could've taken a chance on being seen bathing naked in a brook with a farmer. And look what it brought us."

Somehow still on their feet, Wandering Star and Blue Sky stared at the plain.

The valley army had appreciably shrunk. The warriors still fighting, who had no choice now but to leave their wounded comrades where they fell—which usually meant letting the hill warriors quickly finish them off with a spear thrust to the throat—were, head to toe, like the plain all around them, crimson.

Blue Sky turned to Wandering Star. "Your people must think the gods used you and me to achieve their purpose."

"Many of them say that," Wandering Star replied. "Many of the tellers say that."

"The purpose of the gods being what?" Dancing Song asked, looking at the battlefield. "This? The gods condoned spying on two people in a tent for this?"

Wandering Star looked at his mother. "Thunder Hunter's warriors killed an old woman for openly talking like that," he said.

Dancing Song nodded. "The people told me about it as I was coming this way. They also told me they think their next king should be the present king's son."

"That's the one thing they shouldn't speak of," Wandering Star said. "Nor should you."

Dancing Song, though, wasn't finished. "They heard what you said to Lightning Spear this morning. Many of them think your view of the matter was a lot wiser than his."

A hill woman and her three children were clinging to her mate and their father, even as one of the grave-diggers was prying his body away from them, insisting like the chief hell god himself, the god of death, the time had come to bury and be done with the man they'd loved.

"You wouldn't have allowed this to happen," Dancing Song said.

"Did the people say anything about Thunder Hunter?" Wandering Star asked.

"Some of them think Thunder Hunter's warriors would've attempted to kill Lightning Spear if he'd agreed with you and stopped this battle before it began."

"And once Lightning Spear was dead," Wandering Star added, "Thunder Hunter would've proclaimed himself king."

"Yes," Dancing Song agreed. "He would've done that."

"Maybe he's already done that," Wandering Star said, "if, as you and the people you spoke with hope, a farmer—or one of our people—has already killed Lightning Spear."

"Maybe," Dancing Song came back, "Lightning Spear shouldn't have made his deal with Thunder Hunter. Maybe that's the worst thing he ever did. Maybe he sold his people into slavery to Thunder Hunter and his warriors, all for a damned valley."

"Maybe," Wandering Star said, "everything you and the people are saying is true. Maybe it's also true they should still hope Lightning Spear, monster from hell that he is, survives this war. Maybe they should also hope his one legitimate child—who's called Rose Leaf, not Wandering Star—gives birth to at least one son, who'll then become their next king. Maybe that will settle the matter, and our people won't be fighting to see if Thunder Hunter or Dark Storm or somebody else, maybe even a bastard, is their next king."

"Two days ago I went to the king's encampment," Dancing Song said. "Thistle Dew took me to see Rose Leaf."

"Is she well?" Blue Sky asked.

"From her appearance," Dancing Song replied, "you'd have to assume nothing is wrong with her at all. But she misses your people. She told me she misses you and your parents. She also told me she loves your people's prince."

"He's still alive and well?" Blue Sky asked.

"Yes," Dancing Song replied. "I saw him, too. I can see why Rose Leaf is in love with him. But Lightning Spear says his warriors will kill him at the victory celebration at the end of this war, when our people have the valley again. The execution will be Lightning Spear's gift to the people."

Wandering Star shook his head. "The execution will be his gift to Thunder Hunter."

Blue Sky looked at the battlefield. The vultures were landing on the pile of dead valley warriors at the center of what remained of Tall Oak's army.

"Rose Leaf told me she'll never go with Dark Storm," Dancing Song continued.

"No," Blue Sky agreed, "she won't do that."

Wandering Star once again looked at Blue Sky as a parent would a child.

"Lightning Spear has promised her to Dark Storm," he said.

"Warriors will hold her down," Dancing Song said, "one of them with his hand over her mouth to stop her from screaming—and alarming the people."

Wandering Star was still looking at Blue Sky.

"They'll do that to your sister," he said. "To my sister. To our sister."

"They'd never do that," Dancing Song said to him, "if you were the king."

"I beg you not to say that," Wandering Star said, taking his mother's hand. "Think about it all you want. But I beg you, don't ever say that again when other people can hear you."

He pointed toward the grave diggers at the bottom of the hill.

"Do you see," he asked, "how many of Lightning Spear's warriors the boys are bringing back here for burial?"

Then he waved his hand in the direction of the battlefield.

"Look closely there," he said. "You can also see how many of the surviving warriors will be Thunder Hunter's."

Dancing Song took her time gazing at the battlefield.

"I see what you see," she said when she chose to speak again.

"Be sure to warn the people," Wandering Star said. "If those warriors hear them talking about making your bastard son their king, those same warriors will kill them. They'll kill you, too. And they'll surely find some excuse to kill me."

Dancing Song nodded her head.

"They'll do that," she agreed.

"And I don't know," Wandering Star continued, "what good we can do if we're dead."

Dancing Song stared at the battle field.

"I'll warn them," she said. "I see what you see."

The vultures were feeding on the pile of bodies at the center of Tall Oak's army. None of the valley warriors still fighting were making an effort to chase them away, even as they had to know the same birds would soon be picking at their own flesh.

And yet more scavenging birds—gods from hell in disguise perhaps—were flying in.

Blue Sky turned to Wandering Star. "It would've been better if you'd killed me."

"Killed you?" Wandering Star asked.

"That night last spring in the gully. According to my people's laws, I wasn't where I was supposed to be. And according to your people's laws, you were supposed to kill me. You should've held on to your spear. You should've used it. This never would've happened."

"That's nonsense," Wandering Star said. "I never could've brought myself to do such a thing. Anyway, I had a better chance than that one to keep this war from happening."

"What are you talking about?" Blue Sky asked.

"I didn't like the taste of your people's wine," Wandering Star replied. "I was five years old. I spit it out. I didn't get drunk like the adults and older children. I saw the princess crawling on the ground near the fire. My mother had told me she was my sister. I went to protect her, to make sure she didn't get burned. Then I saw she was crawling toward the two prisoners, the farmers my father's warriors had emasculated that day. One of them was covered with blood. He'd somehow freed himself and slit the throats of the three warriors guarding them. I was afraid he'd slit my throat, too. I cowardly hid behind a tree. I saw him cut the other prisoner's bindings. I saw the two farmers who were supposed to be killed the next day pick up our princess and run off with her."

Dancing Song looked at Blue Sky with tears in her eyes.

"He calls himself 'cowardly,'" she said, "and he was only five years old."

Wandering Star paid no attention to his mother.

"I should've come out from the shadows and made myself known," he said. "I should've clung to the princess. I should've forced the two farmers to pry her away from me. But I wasn't brave enough to do that. I found out later the two farmers weren't evil men. They probably would've left without her. But I wasn't brave enough to do what I should've done."

Dancing Song looked at Blue Sky again. "A five-year-old child 'wasn't brave enough.'"

Blue Sky turned to Wandering Star. "You hold yourself responsible for what's happened today—because of something you failed to do as a mere child?"

Wandering Star looked at the battleground for a long time before he attempted a response.

"No, I don't," he conceded. "My people and yours would've found some other way to make it happen. Maybe not this day. Maybe not here. But someday, somewhere—no matter what you and I did—it would've happened. And the tellers would've insisted it was the will of the gods."

On the hilltops packs of wolves had gathered, paying no attention to the living humans nearby. They ogled the battlefield instead and drooled, no doubt smelling, as the still-living humans could, the odor of death wafting across the plain on the warm evening breeze.

Suddenly, as if on a command only the wolves could hear, they moved down the hillside, darted between the hill people caring for their wounded and digging graves for their dead, and sprinted across the plain toward the dead and unburied farmers.

Once again, none of the warriors still standing on either side attempted to keep them away.

Under the circumstances, the wolves and vultures were as inevitable as death itself.

"But it doesn't matter what the tellers put in the mouths of the gods," Wandering Star remarked. "They'll never come up with any combination of words to justify this."

They'd first have to explain why the sky was cloudless all day that late summer day.

Chapter 7

The battle on the plain continued into the evening.

"It won't be over by dark," Wandering Star said.

Dancing Song was on her way to Lightning Spear's encampment.

She'd promised Blue Sky she'd tell Rose Leaf and Morning Sun he was still alive, he'd do everything he could to bring them home, and no matter what happened he'd always love them.

The moon would rise that night well after sunset.

The fighting had almost reached a stalemate. The hill warriors were still throwing themselves at the surviving valley warriors, but ineffectually, wounding few of their opponents. No doubt they were exhausted after fighting all day, but so were the farmers.

"Nobody wants to die now," Wandering Star said. "Not this close to the victory celebration. And your people are fighting harder than ever. They think they have a chance."

"A chance for what?" Blue Sky asked, scornfully. "A chance to be the last one to die?"

"A chance to be a survivor," Wandering Star replied. "A chance to survive this battle and go home. A chance to be a wounded but living hero. Like your father."

*****

Ignoring their own exhaustion, Wandering Star and Blue Sky hurried along the crest of the hills toward the southern end of the plain.

When they'd approached the plain before dawn that day, they'd come upon a woods where the valley warriors had tethered to trees the oxen that had pulled their supply carts over the mountains.

Entering the woods, Blue Sky and Wandering Star were relieved to learn the hill warriors who'd closed the encirclement behind Tall Oak's army hadn't come upon the oxen.

The animals were in fact well-rested and well-fed. Their handlers had left them ample water to drink and hay to eat. They'd need to be ready, the farmers had assumed, for the army's triumphal return to the valley.

Blue Sky and Wandering Star hitched the oxen to the carts, arranged them in a line, tied the reins of each team after the first to the back of the preceding cart, and led them toward the plain.

When full darkness came, they could tell from the shouting what was happening.

All at once—meaning it was done on a signal the valley warriors who were still fighting had been waiting for—they gave up their defensive stance, turned their backs on their opponents, and ran.

"Somebody figured it out," Wandering Star said. "The dark would give them a chance to escape alive."

The valley warriors were running in their direction.

The sounds of the battle were coming so close the oxen stopped, starlight in their wide-open eyes, and refused to go further.

Soon, though, the leaders of the hill warriors were ordering them to stop fighting.

"You were right," Blue Sky said.

The hill warriors, grateful perhaps, obeyed their leaders. The clamor of the battle ceased.

Wandering Star had explained it to Blue Sky: Lightning Spear and Thunder Hunter wouldn't let the hill warriors chase the valley warriors very far in the dark. They were too afraid their warriors would run off after that day's hellish fighting. Lightning Spear and Thunder Hunter would need to keep them together for the push into the valley.

"They think they can afford to let a few farmers get away," Wandering Star said.

*****

The hill warriors, shouting their praises to the gods for their great victory that day, and for their survival in the fighting that won it, were moving toward the northern end of the plain.

"The battle's over," Wandering Star said. "They're on their way to the king's encampment and his victory feast. I doubt he'll invite very many families of the dead warriors."

Blue Sky and Wandering Star led the oxen and carts forward, nearing the plain.

110

A man was standing at the edge of the plain straight ahead of them.

"We've got the oxen and carts," Blue Sky shouted to him in the valley people's language.

The man came toward them. He was tall and held his spear in his left hand.

Blue Sky ran to Early Harvest and embraced him.

He'd taken a deep spear thrust in the side of his belly, but none of his guts had spilled out.

"Others are back there," he said. "They've all been injured. Some of them can't walk."

"We'll get them," Blue Sky promised.

He and Wandering Star helped Early Harvest into a cart, where he could lie down on sheepskins and hay. Blue Sky convinced him to drink some pod tea.

Answering Wandering Star's questions, Early Harvest acknowledged he'd given the order to run when it got dark.

"You saved some lives," Wandering Star said. "Some very important lives."

*****

With no hill warriors around to stop them, Blue Sky and Wandering Star drove the oxen onto the plain, picking up survivors, most of them in groups helping one another, some of them sitting on the ground.

Noon Breeze was still walking. He'd taken two spear thrusts, one in his shoulder and the other in his thigh. Like all the others, he was covered with blood and wracked with pain.

He broke down in tears, though, when Blue Sky helped him into a cart.

The valley warriors had watched that morning as Wandering Star and Blue Sky made their futile effort to convince Lightning Spear to stop the battle. But the survivors soon discovered the original purpose of their would-be saviors was to warn Tall Oak and Sturdy Limb they were taking their army into a trap.

Noon Breeze looked at Wandering Star and grimaced.

111

"That's what you were trying to tell us at sunrise pass?" he asked.

"That's what he would've told you," Blue Sky said.

Noon Breeze reached out with his hand and touched Wandering Star on his lips.

"We should've listened to you," he said.

He took the cup of pod tea Wandering Star had poured for him.

"Sturdy Limb ordered us to kill you on sight," he said. "We weren't supposed to speak with you at all. You had nothing to say, his people told us, we needed to hear."

Noon Breeze made another face when he found out how bitter the tea was.

"And that's why all our comrades died?" he asked.

*****

After the moon rose, it was easier to find the survivors who'd been left behind on the plain. Toward morning, Blue Sky and Wandering Star weren't finding any more.

They'd loaded over three times ten times ten wounded warriors into carts that night. But that was still only a small fraction of the original army that had gone to the plain to teach the hill people and their king a good lesson.

Among the last of the wounded they found was Valley Defender. It was difficult to see how he'd survived. He'd suffered at least ten spear thrusts, two of them piercing his rib cage.

Somehow he was able to eat a few grapes and drink water and Wandering Star's tea.

"You must've been with Tall Oak and your father," Blue Sky said.

Valley Defender looked at Blue Sky, almost imperceptibly nodding his head.

Blue Sky had heard some of the non-fatally wounded hill warriors claim, after drinking the tea, they were with the gods in heaven.

"Are any of them still alive?" Blue Sky asked.

Valley Defender slowly shook his head.

112

"None of them?" Blue Sky asked, knowing—and fearing—where this conversation would take his people's kingdom.

Valley Defender kept shaking his head.

"All of them are dead? Tall Oak? Your father?'

Valley Defender nodded.

"Solemn Promise?"

He nodded again.

Blue Sky forced himself to continue.

"Your brothers?"

Blue Sky and Valley Defender looked at one another, two grown men weeping.

*****

Three of the wounded men died that first night in the hill people's woods. Blue Sky and Wandering Star dug graves for them. Despite his and Wandering Star's need for sleep, Blue Sky couldn't bear the thought of the men having survived the battle only to be left in the open and fed upon by scavengers.

They started out at dawn. The survivors knew they had to get back to the valley as soon as they could and warn the people that Lightning Spear's army was coming.

Wandering Star, on the other hand, surmised that his people's army wouldn't show up in the valley until the next full moon. They had too many dead and wounded of their own. If Lightning Spear and Thunder Hunter sent their warriors to pursue their enemy into the valley immediately, many of the families they'd leave behind would starve to death.

"You have these wounded men and their dead comrades to thank for the delay," Wandering Star said. "You should be just as grateful to Tall Oak and Sturdy Limb. Their only alternative was to kill as many of my people's warriors as they could."

"That's what they told us," Early Harvest said.

"They knew they were dying for the people at home?" Blue Sky asked.

"Of course they did," Noon Breeze replied.

They'd stopped beside a brook. Despite their wounds, Early Harvest and Noon Breeze were helping Blue Sky and Wandering Star fetch water for the others, most of them feverish and sweating. Whenever they woke up, they asked for water, drinking it until it made them vomit.

Blue Sky, Wandering Star, Early Harvest, and Noon Breeze were able to help most of the men sit down in the brook, which had retained its summer warmth, and wash the dried blood and grime off their bodies.

"We knew," Early Harvest agreed. "We had to make it as costly for the hill people as we could. Solemn Promise came around telling us that. He said it was the only hope we had."

"Killing," Blue Sky heard himself say, "is the only thing that made sense for either side."

"That's what war is," Wandering Star said.

*****

Although Wandering Star didn't think any of his people's warriors would be close by, he carefully led the survivors from one wooded area to the next. He knew whenever they got near a worthwhile berry patch or grapevine. He and Blue Sky would stop the caravan, quickly gather the berries and grapes and pass them out to the men in the carts.

The least severely wounded, attempting to follow the example of Early Harvest and Noon Breeze, would try to help. Blue Sky had to politely suggest to some of them they might want to stay in their carts and rest. It was good to see they wished to help, he'd remark, but they were only in the way, and probably postponing their recovery from their wounds as well.

After sleeping in the hill people's woods a second night, they began the climb to sunrise pass the next day. A surprising number of men insisted upon getting out of the carts and walking, making it easier for the oxen.

It was almost sunset by the time they reached the abandoned encampments of the apprentice tellers and the court people's sons. The survivors of the battle on the plain fell asleep that night no longer fearing they'd never see their promised valley again.

*****

Wandering Star didn't break it to Blue Sky gently.

They were sitting on the bank of the brook outside Wandering Star's tent, which was where he'd been forced to leave it the night Long Arm and his men had captured him.

"We part here," he said, "in the morning. You have to go ahead with your people. I have to go back to mine."

At that point, Blue Sky didn't want to go anywhere without Wandering Star.

Even if he hadn't fallen in love with him, he was certain his hill friend had a far better understanding of things than he did. Better than Many Numbers, Spring Rain, Fair Judge, and his parents, too. Wandering Star knew both his people and the valley people, but none of the valley people, not even the most curious and most willing to listen to unfamiliar stories, knew the hill people.

"I wish you'd come with us," Blue Sky said. "Nobody will object to your living with us now. The person who ordered the guards to kill you is dead himself."

Wandering Star shook his head.

"Your mother could live with us, too," Blue Sky said. "You should go get her."

Wandering Star was blunt.

"She'd miss her men friends," he said.

"Her men friends?"

"The men who bring her game and hides."

"And they go with her?" Blue Sky ventured to ask.

"And they go with her. They were fighting in the battle. She was worried about them. She didn't know who among them was alive and who dead or dying."

"Does Lightning Spear know about them?"

"He knows. But nobody dares speak of them in his presence."

"Not even you?"

"Only if he and I are alone, speaking privately."

"You speak with him alone?"

"He enjoys speaking with me alone."

It was late. The moon was rising. They'd fed all the wounded men and given each of them a jug of the bitter beverage they'd made by steeping Wandering Star's pods in water.

"Lightning Spear is my father," Wandering Star said. "I'm the only son he'll ever know."

"My people can't blame you for what your father has done. You never caused us any harm. You tried to warn us. You begged your father not to start the battle on the plain. You led these wounded men back to the valley."

Wandering Star placed his arm around Blue Sky's shoulders.

"I'm sure," he said, "your people won't blame me for what Tall Oak, Sturdy Limb, Thunder Hunter, and my father got them into. I'm certain I could live with your people. But can't you see? I'll be able to do your people more good if I'm with my own people now."

"I don't know how you can do that. Lightning Spear and Thunder Hunter don't care how many people they kill. But I do know I don't want to go through the rest of my life without you."

This time Wandering Star was brutal.

"You need to forget about yourself for a while," he said. "My people can wipe your people off the face of the earth. You need to think more about that."

Moonlight danced in his eyes no less than it did in the brook.

"A number of times I've been alone with my father," Wandering Star said. "He says everybody else just tells him what they think he wants to hear. He likes making fun of those people. He prefers it when I argue with him. He always thinks he wins the argument, though. He says if I were the king I'd be forced to accept his views. They come with the kingship, he says. But he still likes to hear mine, no matter how impractical he thinks they are."

Wandering Star looked at Blue Sky and laughed.

"Every time I was with him," he continued, "I easily could've killed him."

They were high in the mountains in late summer, and night had come.

Blue Sky was shivering.

"Of course, I wouldn't," Wandering Star added. "Not yet. Killing him would just hand over the kingdom to Thunder Hunter. Something's got to be done with him and his sons first."

"Something like killing them?"

Wandering Star pulled Blue Sky closer to him.

116

"My mother was right," he said. "Most of our people hate Thunder Hunter. More so now, I'm sure, after what his warriors did on the battlefield. I won't be the only person wishing to see him dead. And his sons, too."

He ran his finger gently over the scab of the wound War Cloud had inflicted on Blue Sky.

"I've got to go back," Wandering Star said. "I've got to see what I can do."

"You'll get yourself killed is what you'll do."

Wandering Star looked at Blue Sky and laughed again.

"And so will you," he said. "Lightning Spear and Thunder Hunter and their warriors will come to kill as many of your people as they can, and chase the rest of you out of the valley. In the hills, you'll starve. Why do you think you're so special you'll survive that?"

Blue Sky wiped his face with his sleeve.

"I probably won't," he said, "but I'm going to put up a damned good fight anyway."

Wandering Star took Blue Sky into his arms.

"That's what I want to hear," he said. "You can get your men home by yourself now. Lightning Spear's army is only a fraction of what it was. You and your people have to figure out some way to stop them. Defense is what your people do best. Don't forget that."

"I won't," Blue Sky promised.

He chose that moment, though, to think about himself.

He pressed his lips, wet as they were, against his hill companion's.

*****

In the morning Wandering Star folded up his tent with all his possessions in it, embraced and said goodbye to Blue Sky and each of the valley survivors he'd safely brought home, and went back to his people.

*****

During the afternoon of the first day of the journey down the mountain, thunderstorms blew up twice. Both times when the sky darkened, Blue Sky suggested they drive the oxen and carts into the forest and stop until the storm passed. He offered to find the survivors bushes to huddle under to keep dry. Both times they insisted they go forward despite the wind and rain. Both times the least severely wounded men had to get out of the carts and walk in order to keep the oxen from sliding in the mud, falling down, and possibly breaking a leg.

The survivors were of one mind. They had to get back to the valley as soon as they could.

The walking wounded trudged forward, refusing to halt until they reached the usual stopping place at the end of the first day down, and then only to rest the oxen.

Several times during the night the coughing of the survivors woke Blue Sky. Fearing the worst from their exposure to the rain and the chilly evening, he got up each time and made sure they had some of Wandering Star's pod tea to drink and dry hides to sleep on and under.

When morning came, though, with the sun rising in another cloudless sky, they were all still alive. They were all insisting, too, they were ready to start out again.

*****

During the steepest parts of their descent, many of the survivors got out of the carts, as they had before, to lessen the burden on the oxen. Blue Sky begged the most severely wounded among them to stop and rest as often and as long as they wished.

They scowled at him.

"If I die," one said, "it won't matter much."

"And if I live," another said, "I won't be any good for anything anyway."

"The people," a third said, "should know what happened."

"As soon as possible, they should know," a fourth said. "Your father should know."

A fifth, Autumn Wine's older grandson, offered his opinion as well, slurring his words as he did so, the pod tea drooling from both corners of his mouth: "It's all downhill from here."

118

Saving the lives of those men had become an obsession for Blue Sky. Despite their wounds, they'd escaped Lightning Spear and Thunder Hunter's slaughter on the plain. They'd all witnessed the wolves and vultures feasting on wounded comrades not yet dead.

Having come so far with those who'd suffered that horror, Blue Sky couldn't tolerate seeing another of them die.

*****

The third day going down the mountain, the survivors refused to stop at all, not even for a midday meal. They sent word to Blue Sky at the head of the line that their next resting place was on the other side of the wall, among their people.

The mountain path was no longer so steep there was any necessity for them not to ride in the carts. Early Harvest and Noon Breeze nevertheless insisted on walking with Blue Sky next to Valley Defender's cart. The survivors had insisted, even before they started out in the hill people's woods, it had to be the lead cart all the way home.

And, they specified, only the king and queen's two oxen could pull it.

In the middle of that afternoon, Blue Sky reached an agreement with Early Harvest and Noon Breeze, who'd continue leading Valley Defender's cart. Blue Sky would run by himself the rest of the way through the forest to the wall.

Two of East Land's grandsons were the first to spot him climbing over the wall. They were coming out of the village on the path, on their way to the pasture to drive their cattle, sheep, and goats back to their barns before the evening meal.

"Blue Sky!" the grandsons began shouting. "Blue Sky!"

He knew East Land's family would be the first to find out what happened.

All seven grandchildren, their two mothers and their paternal grandparents came running up the path to meet him. They'd heard—all the valley people had heard—that Blue Sky and Wandering Star had gone to warn Tall Oak and Sturdy Limb about Lightning Spear's trap.

They'd also heard that Many Numbers had pessimistically calculated that Blue Sky and Wandering Star didn't have enough time to deliver the warning.

And they'd learned that Wandering Star had even more gloomily compared the sizes of the armies that would clash on the hill people's plain.

Green Field had said the people left behind could only proceed with the harvest, forcing themselves to work longer and harder than usual to make up for the men who were gone.

"Where's Tall Oak?" East Land asked. "Where's Sturdy Limb?"

"They're dead," Blue Sky replied. "Almost all of our men who went to fight the hill people are dead. Every man who survived the battle is injured. They're on the path coming down the mountain. Many of them are in carts. The last of them should be here before the moon rises."

East Land's family stood huddled together staring beyond Blue Sky at the forest.

The littlest child among East Land's grandchildren, a girl, looked up at Blue Sky. She might've been too young yet to know what the word "dead" meant.

"Is my father coming home?" she asked.

Blue Sky closed his eyes. He and Wandering Star had buried the girl's father in the hill people's woods.

Blue Sky had imagined the questions—but not, no matter how hard he'd tried, his answers.

"Is my uncle coming home?" she persisted.

When Blue Sky was unable to respond to either question, the girl's mother and aunt, who were sisters who'd become the mates of brothers, fell into one another's arms, as did East Land and the girl's grandmother.

But the little girl refused to take her eyes off Blue Sky.

"Why are you crying?" she asked.

"I'm sorry," he said, taking her hand, facing her and the other six children who'd lost their fathers, the two women who'd lost their mates, and the mother and father who'd lost both of their sons. "I'm sorry."

*****

East Land's relatives, seeing that Blue Sky had returned, were arriving from their village, spilling out from the path into their immaculately harvested fields.

Blue Sky's appalling story swept through the crowd.

Several of the older boys ran to alert neighboring villages.

All the people in all the villages from the eastern forest to the town would soon learn the enormity of the defeat the kingdom had suffered in the battle on the plain. By dawn of the day after the next day, the news would reach the upper valley.

Blue Sky could tell when people coming up the path first heard the hill people had destroyed their army, and only a few survivors were coming home.

"No!" they cried. "No! No!"

They surrounded Blue Sky demanding to know—he could hardly blame them—whether their mate, son, or father had come home with the survivors.

And since Blue Sky knew, there was no way out of it for him. He had to answer the question no matter how many times it was asked, no matter how many times the answer was a shaking-of-the-head, trembling-of-the-lip "no."

The crowd grew larger and, although they meant Blue Sky no harm, unruly.

"No?" they asked. "You're telling me my son's dead? You're telling me he isn't coming home? You're telling me the hill people killed him?"

Blue Sky caught a glimpse of Early Harvest and Noon Breeze leading the king and queen's oxen down the mountain path in the late afternoon sun. They would soon reach the wall.

"Ask me your questions," Blue Sky said. "I'll answer them all. But promise me you'll leave these other men alone. They're all wounded. They could just as well be dead right now themselves. They came off the battlefield bleeding. I saw their wounds myself. I saw their blood. I saw their suffering. Please let them get their rest. Please don't ask them any questions about the battle. If it takes me a lifetime, I'll answer every question you ask me. I promise you I'll do it."

Voices in the crowd were repeating his pleas and promises to those out of earshot.

"And the only answer I'll give you," he said, "is the only answer that counts: the truth."

He motioned toward Early Harvest and Noon Breeze. Older children had removed the wall gate for them.

"Please let them take Valley Defender to my father and mother's house," Blue Sky said. "Those of you who can, please make sure the other wounded have everything they need."

East Land's niece and the woman she lived with came forward, took the reins of the oxen pulling the second cart, and led them toward their village.

"These two men will stay with us," the niece said.

The crowd, quiet now, made way for them and their cart, and for Early Harvest, Noon Breeze, Valley Defender, and their cart.

The people took Blue Sky up on his offer, swiftly admonishing anybody who dared asked a wounded man coming down the path if he'd seen their son, mate, father, brother, or friend.

But they spared Blue Sky, as he knew they would, none of their sorrow and anguish.

East Land's grandchildren brought him a bench from their house to sit on.

His father, Spring Rain, Autumn Wine, and other neighbors—all of them women, old men, and older children—came by with oxen and carts filled with food, water, and dry hides for the wounded men. They knew what Blue Sky was doing. When they saw him, they merely nodded their heads and went on their way into the forest.

Early Harvest had already told Autumn Wine her grandson had survived.

Many Numbers was further down the path toward the town. He'd remained behind to keep track of where the wounded men were spending the night. As their families arrived, he'd know where their mate, son, father, brother, or cousin was.

Gentle Brook, Blue Sky learned, was at their house with Valley Defender.

Into the evening and night, the people asked Blue Sky to retell the story of the battle.

He'd talked with every survivor. They'd accounted for all their comrades, who were either coming home with them or lying dead on the other side of the mountains.

Blue Sky could and did tell the people who came to him through the night their mate, son, father, brother, or cousin had stood, fought, and died, all so the people they'd left at home would have a better chance of surviving. But that didn't make the truth less unbearable to tell or hear.

Some of the people to whom the truth was most hard whispered the word "no" as if to the waning evening breeze. Some of them cried it out to their family and friends surrounding them. Some screamed it back in Blue Sky's face. Perhaps they were hoping, as he was, the gods could hear them—assuming, of course, the gods cared what happened to mere humans.

*****

After the day Blue Sky and his people's wounded warriors came home, whenever he heard the word "no" spoken sharply—or even when it was uttered in an ordinary tone of voice but with some disbelief—his mind became, for no apparent reason, fearful and dark. And whenever he heard that word cried out in a dream, as he often did, he'd wake, in tears, trembling.

*****

Farmers living nearby and the town people found places for all the wounded men to stay and recuperate, as well as for the persons who'd traveled a distance to learn what had happened to a man they loved—most often only to hear Blue Sky tell them he was dead.

Green Field, Spring Rain, and a group of older boys, some of them bearing torches, passed by with a team of oxen pulling an empty cart, on their way to the forest. When they came back, the cart was filled with pods. They went from village to village giving them to the people with instructions on how to brew a tea for the wounded men they were caring for.

It was dawn before the people waiting to speak with Blue Sky dwindled to one, a lone slender woman coming toward him on the main path from the town, shielding her eyes with her hand against the first sunlight of the day behind him.

Long before he could see her distinctly, he realized from the way she carried herself who she was: his mother.

He ran to her and embraced her.

"In all this sadness," she said, "at least you've come back alive. I'm one of the few mothers in this valley who has good reason to thank the gods."

If Lightning Spear had let War Cloud kill him, Blue Sky was certain his mother and father would've grieved inconsolably for the rest of their lives.

"I heard," she said, "Rose Leaf and Morning Sun haven't been harmed."

In the early morning light, Blue Sky's and Gentle Brook's shadows were greatly lengthened across East Land's pasture like the rooftop spears the tellers measured the seasons by in the courtyard.

Early Harvest had told Gentle Brook that Blue Sky had met Wandering Star's mother, and she'd recently seen both Rose Leaf and Morning Sun.

"We put Early Harvest and Noon Breeze in Rose Leaf's room," Gentle Brook said. "We put Valley Defender in your room. Rainbow Evening sat with him all night."

"I must see Rainbow Evening," Blue Sky said. "I'll promise her I'll do everything I can to get Morning Sun back alive. I don't want her giving up on him."

"She's taking it very hard," Gentle Brook continued. "She's lost Tall Oak. Morning Sun is gone. And she loved her nephews as if they were her own sons."

Blue Sky wondered if his lack of sleep was affecting his thoughts. It seemed to him there was something wrong with what his mother had said: "She loved her nephews."

"Rainbow Evening was with Valley Defender," his mother said, "when he died."

Their shadows became one again. Blue Sky, a grown man, clung to his mother as a frightened child would, weeping.

Chapter 8

"Valley Defender was still making sense," Many Numbers said, "despite that pod tea. I went through all the names with him, one by one."

"You're absolutely certain?" Green Field asked.

"Every person between Morning Sun and you in the line left with the army."

The "line" Many Numbers referred to was the valley people's line of succession to their kingship. Green Field and Blue Sky were distant cousins of Tall Oak and Morning Sun.

"Valley Defender was the only one who returned," Many Numbers added. "The last time he saw each of them, including his brothers, they were being laid on what he called 'the pile.'"

That was the crimson pile of dead valley warriors on the hill people's plain.

"He helped lay most of them there himself," Many Numbers noted.

Green Field, Many Numbers, Spring Rain, and Blue Sky were digging a grave for Valley Defender in the cemetery on the bluff overlooking the river. They were going to bury him next to his mother. The graves of his and Morning Sun's aunt, uncle, and grandparents, the old king and queen, were nearby. It was also where his brothers and father and Tall Oak should've been buried.

"You have no choice in the matter now," Many Numbers remarked, softly. "You'll remain the regent for the kingdom until Morning Sun returns."

"And Law Keeper?" Green Field asked. "Did anybody see him dead?"

"Noon Breeze helped lay him on the pile," Blue Sky replied.

"He was brave," Many Numbers said of the man he'd previously claimed to despise for attempting to force himself on Spring Rain. "At his age, he could've stayed home. Most of the high tellers could've done that, too. But they didn't have children and grandchildren begging them not to go. Their friends were all going, so they went along. They must've kept up with the younger men, too. And now they're all dead."

"All the tellers in the battle died," Spring Rain added. "All the apprentice tellers, too, except Noon Breeze."

"They killed a lot of hill warriors," Blue Sky said, chopping into the earth with his spade despite his lack of sleep. "That's what they were supposed to do, and they did it. We owe them more than we can ever repay."

Green Field looked at Many Numbers and Spring Rain.

"Which of you do I appoint first teller?" he asked.

"Neither of us," Many Numbers replied. "Even if we were otherwise qualified for the position, we're too young to be the first teller. You have to appoint an older teller."

Green Field scowled and lowered his voice. "One of those old men who stayed home?"

Some of the old men were nearby preparing the ceremony for Valley Defender.

"They know how old they are," Many Numbers said. "Otherwise, they would've gone with the army. None of them wants to be the first teller. Especially not now."

"But several older tellers are well-qualified," Spring Rain offered. "They know the stories and can tell you what they mean. They're also good at resolving disputes among the people."

"They're all women, too," Many Numbers added.

Many Numbers and Spring Rain had met with many of their people's remaining tellers during the night. They were dividing among themselves the dead tellers' duties.

"Has the first teller in our kingdom ever been a woman?" Green Field asked.

Many Numbers shook his head. "There's no story where the first teller was a woman."

"There's also no story," Spring Rain interjected, "where any god or goddess tells us a woman can't be the first teller."

"That's right," Many Numbers agreed. "Long ago, our people believed a woman couldn't even be a teller. But the gods never said that, either."

"What will the people say?" Green Field asked. "Are they going to accept a woman as their first teller?"

Blue Sky couldn't help himself.

"Right now," he said, "the vast majority of the people of age in this kingdom are women. Most of the men are lying on a battlefield far away. I saw them there myself. And I can assure you, we won't hear any of them raising their voices in dissent."

Green Field looked at his son and shook his head. Blue Sky had spoken so loudly the people arriving for Valley Defender's funeral were staring at him.

"The people will probably say something like this," Spring Rain more quietly responded to Green Field's question. "They'll probably say their kingdom has a regent who's not only wise but also brave. They might even say that's just what their kingdom needs right now."

"I wish I could believe I'm wise and brave," Green Field said, as he resumed digging. "In any event, I'll follow your advice. Please ask your fellow tellers to agree upon one person, and I'll appoint her."

Many Numbers nodded. "They'll thank you for the opportunity to do that."

"Many of them will also thank you for being wise and brave," Spring Rain said.

*****

Green Field turned to Blue Sky again. "How much time do we have before Lightning Spear's army arrives?"

"Just time enough," Blue Sky answered.

"To fall back to the town?"

"No."

"No?" Many Numbers asked.

"The hill people still have far too many warriors," Blue Sky replied. "If we fall back to the town, they'll slaughter us all. They'll chop at us the way they did the army—even if every old man, woman, and child among us joins the fight."

"What are we supposed to do then?" his father asked.

"We fall back to the upper valley."

"You'd give up the town?" Spring Rain asked.

"You'd give up the lower valley?" Green Field asked. "You'd expect all the farmers in the lower valley to give up their land?"

127

"We have no choice," Blue Sky replied. "We no longer have an army. Lightning Spear and Thunder Hunter still have a horde of warriors, and they don't care how many of them die. They'll surround the town and kill every one of us, no matter how long it takes them to do it. We can't stay in the lower valley. We can never defend it."

"You'd abandon the lower valley?" his father asked again. "You'd abandon most of our farmland? Shouldn't we just die in battle instead, if that's what the gods want?"

"I don't know what the gods want," Blue Sky replied. "I don't think anybody else does, either. Yes, I'd ask the lower-valley people to abandon their farmland. But only for now, and not forever. If we all die, we'll lose both the lower valley and the upper valley forever. If we survive, though, who knows what the future will bring?"

"If we're that out-numbered," Spring Rain asked, "how can we defend the upper valley?"

Blue Sky's family paid a visit to the upper valley once. Morning Sun went with them.

On their way they stayed with the families of warriors Green Field had fought alongside in the last war with the hill people. All their hosts invited relatives and neighboring families in for a feast. The children, of course, were eager to see the prince. Green Field and Gentle Brook always sat at the head table with the host farmer and his mate, who would often insist that the prince, Rose Leaf, and Blue Sky sit there, too.

Full Harvest, who was their host in the upper valley, invited a great number of guests to his festivities. The drinking, music-making, singing, and dancing continued late into the night.

Blue Sky's family and the prince came home on the river, floating on a raft the upper-valley people had given Green Field for his courage in the war. He guided the raft with a long pole.

Where the river was slow and gentle, he let Morning Sun and Blue Sky take turns with the pole. Rose Leaf, holding onto Gentle Brook during those interludes, tried to make them believe she was afraid the raft, with a mere boy guiding it, would get away from them, and they'd all drown.

After they safely returned, Morning Sun, Rose Leaf, and Blue Sky had many interesting stories to tell Valley Defender and his brothers. Most of them emphasized the height, steepness, and grandeur of the mountains surrounding the upper valley. The cousins were as sorry as the travelers were that their father Sturdy Limb hadn't let them go with them.

Blue Sky looked up from his digging and nudged Spring Rain.

"Here are two people who can answer your question," he said.

Early Harvest and Noon Breeze were approaching them.

They'd brought Valley Defender up to the town. He was in the same cart he'd lain in for the journey home from the plain. The king and queen's oxen were still pulling it, too. They were waiting for the procession to the cemetery to begin, munching on courtyard grass as they did so.

"The hill people will have to attack us through the upper gorge or over the upper-valley mountains," Early Harvest said. "The gorge is narrow. The mountains are steep."

Their summits were so high no trees, not even evergreens, would grow near them.

"I think they might be right," Many Numbers said to Green Field. "Two summers ago Spring Rain and I went up there to see the mountains and the lake. The upper valley has to be more defensible than this bluff."

"They won't come over the mountains," Noon Breeze said. "Any of our people can go up to the encampments and keep watch, just in case. The guards will only need to run down to the valley and warn us if they see anything we should know about."

"Who stops the hill people from coming through the gorge?" Spring Rain asked. "Since the only able-bodied men in the kingdom are the four people digging this grave?"

"The four of us and the men coming of age," Blue Sky replied. "Wandering Star was certain Lightning Spear's army won't set out before the next full moon."

The next full moon would rise several days after the end-of-summer ceremony.

"Some men coming of age wanted to go with the army," Many Numbers said, "after they heard Valley Defender's brothers were going. Tall Oak turned them down and sent them home."

"We can thank Tall Oak for that," Blue Sky said.

"After the ceremony they can fight all they want," Spring Rain said.

During the night Blue Sky had spoken with a number of men coming of age. He asked them to consider falling back to the upper valley. He tried to describe for them what their outnumbered brothers and cousins had done on the hill people's plain. He said if they fought that well in the upper gorge, their people might survive.

In one of their people's stories—the hill people told the same story—the brutally logical god of war insisted boys couldn't be warriors because the people always needed a reserve to continue the fighting in the event they suffered a devastating loss in a battle.

Green Field couldn't conceal his skepticism. "How are we going to convince the people to abandon the lower valley?" he asked Blue Sky. "Just because we say Lightning Spear's army is so huge? What if the people don't trust our judgment? We tried to tell them not to run off and fight the hill people. You saw what happened. They didn't waste any of their time listening to us."

"No, they didn't," Early Harvest agreed. "Neither did I. And I'm sure they all regret it now just as much as I do."

"I wouldn't expect the people to trust my judgment," Blue Sky said. "I've made too many mistakes for that. But I do believe they'll trust the judgment of the wounded men who fought in that battle on the hill people's plain and came back over the mountains to tell about it. They saw how many warriors Lightning Spear had standing when the battle was over. They all agree we should fall back to the upper valley. They say it's our only chance."

"The people are listening to them, too," Early Harvest said.

"The wounded men are already speaking with the people?" Green Field asked.

"Already," Blue Sky replied. "I promised them I'd try to convince you."

"They're talking with the people about giving up the lower valley?"

"Giving it up for now," Blue Sky replied, "but not forever. Maybe for a generation, but not forever. If we can save ourselves in the upper valley, everything we do after that will be aimed at returning to the lower valley as soon as we can."

"That's right," Early Harvest said. "We'll give up the lower valley—but not forever."

130

*****

A large crowd—court people, survivors of the battle on the plain, farmers, and their families—had gathered in the cemetery for Valley Defender's funeral.

The tellers—all of them women and old men but for Many Numbers and Spring Rain—led the funeral procession out from the town, singing. Behind them, Green Field and Blue Sky, now first and second in line to the vacant kingship behind Morning Sun, held the reins of the king and queen's oxen pulling the cart, which was filled with straw and furs so that Valley Defender was high enough for the spectators to see him.

Rainbow Evening, whose tears that day seemed inexhaustible, followed the cart walking between Gentle Brook and Fair Judge.

The royal cemetery had also served as the pasture for the king and queen's oxen.

Reaching their destination, surrounded by the survivors, most of them sitting on the ground, Green Field and Blue Sky lifted Valley Defender off the cart and placed him in his grave.

Many Numbers, singing as the god of war, and Spring Rain, as the goddess of love, stood next to the grave and sang their song, the chorus once again lamenting the inordinate demands of both the god and goddess, the former demanding death, the latter imposing grief.

The tellers continued singing as Green Field and Blue Sky shoveled the loose earth back into the grave, covering Valley Defender, giving him the rest he deserved.

When they finished, Green Field asked the people to begin driving their livestock and hauling their crops north to the upper valley that afternoon.

The people stared at their regent in silence, resigned to the outrageous necessity of ceding to the hill people most of their farmland as well as their town.

The survivors of the battle on the plain had done what they'd agreed among themselves most needed doing: they honestly told the people what had happened on the plain. The people, hearing the stories and retelling them to one another, and seeing for themselves how few of their warriors came home, could vividly imagine what might happen next in the valley.

"Those of our people still alive today must do what these men did," Green Field said, looking at the survivors, some of them noticeably feeling the effect of Wandering Star's pod tea. "We can each of us best serve our kingdom—and one another—by staying alive ourselves."

*****

Raising clouds of late-summer dust, the livestock rumbled across recently harvested fields toward the upper valley. Children walked behind and on either side of the herds, keeping them together. It was something they could do to help. Almost all the calves, lambs, and kids born that spring were grown enough to keep up with the older animals.

On the pathways going north, the mothers, grandmothers, and aunts of the children led oxen pulling carts, most of them still filled with that summer's harvest, the regent having warned of a retreat to the town. The children and animals too young to walk rode in the remaining carts.

The women often wept openly for the mates, sons, fathers, and brothers who hadn't come home from the battle on the plain. Often, too, they reminded one another the men died to save the lives of the people they'd left behind in the valley. It was the only way their loss made sense.

Many Numbers, Spring Rain, and Blue Sky went wherever they were needed to repair broken-down carts. Green Field had told them nobody, no matter how deficient their day-to-day maintenance work had been, was to have their livestock or crops left behind. The usual repair work required two of the three, together with whoever else was available, to lift up one side of a cart, the load still in it, while the third fixed a bad wheel as fast as he could.

Along the river old men led horses pulling chains of rafts tied together with vine and leather ropes and loaded with farming implements and household goods. Two horses, one on either side of the river, pulled each chain. Green Field had ordered that only boys coming of age that year or the next would ride the rafts, wielding poles to keep them a safe distance from the banks.

Early in the afternoon of the second day of the journey north, two of the boys, cousins guiding a raft chain, both of them at the end of their last summer before coming of age—and both of them reputedly desirous of the same young woman who'd come of age herself in the spring—exchanged hostile remarks.

Both of them had also lost older brothers in the battle on the plain. Blue Sky had explained that to them the night he returned with the survivors. They had demanded details. They wanted to know everything Blue Sky had heard about how their brothers had died.

Their remarks on the rafts escalated to the point where they commenced using their poles not just for guiding the rafts but also for dousing one another with surprising but well-deserved splashes of water.

Fortunately, at that time of the year the river below the upper gorge was at its slowest. In some places it was almost as serene as the lake when the breeze died. It wasn't taking a great effort on the part of the boys to keep the rafts in the middle of the stream.

The day was warm for so late in the summer, the clouds were few, and on the rafts there was no shade. Up and down the river, other boys soon chose to do as the rival cousins had done. They splashed their own cousins, brothers, and neighbors as often as they could, whether they held any grudges against them or not.

Almost all of them had brothers or fathers, or both—and almost all the old men guiding the horses had sons or grandsons, or both—lying now on the hill people's plain with no more life or beauty in them than autumn leaves rotting in the slush of late-winter. In view of that overwhelming horror perhaps, not even the crankiest of the old men with the boys objected to the splashing.

Green Field the regent, leading his own stallion and possessing all the powers of a king, glanced at the boys now and then, no doubt remembered his own losses from the last war with the hill people, and chose to say nothing.

One elderly gentleman mumbled within Blue Sky's hearing, "As long as the horses don't mind, I'll be damned if I'll say anything. Your father's in charge of the kingdom now. Sturdy Limb got himself killed. I'm with your father."

*****

133

It was taking a long time for all the lower-valley livestock, oxen, carts, and people to pass through the narrow passageway in the upper gorge. Green Field had asked the people to have the patience caution required. He didn't want anybody slipping into the river.

Even that late in the summer, the current in the gorge was swift, swirling, and dangerous. The upper-valley people said nobody was ever known to have fallen into it and survived.

Passage through the gorge was just as difficult for the horses and rafts. Because foot passage on the western side of the river was impossible—that bank rose straight up to the sky from the water the way both banks did at the lower gorge—the horses could only pull the rafts from the eastern side. Guiding the rafts therefore required considerably more thought and care than it did downstream.

Green Field decided the raft chains should be divided so that no pair of horses would be pulling more than two rafts at a time through the gorge. He'd also stipulated that only the boys who'd be coming of age that year, one on each raft, could do the poling.

The splashing of water accordingly diminished as much as attention to the river from which it came increased.

Green Field had asked them why they'd wish to take a chance on falling into the river and drowning, as a result of their own foolishness, when their father or brother or brothers had just died fighting in a war, and their family and all their people desperately needed them to stay alive.

Green Field, Blue Sky, Many Numbers, Spring Rain, and Early Harvest's younger cousin, Good Harvest, were at the narrowest point in the gorge. It was also where the passageway began its steepest south-to-north incline. Whenever a team of oxen came through the crowd, Green Field and his men helped them, pushing on their cart to keep the line moving up the slope.

Early Harvest and Noon Breeze were with them, but they weren't helping push the carts only because Green Field had asked them not to and sternly warned the people not to let them.

The seven of them argued at length that day how their few warriors were going to keep the hill people's army out of the upper valley. They agreed they were at the place where they'd need to stop, fight, and kill the hill warriors. But they couldn't agree on much else.

Many Numbers, not surprisingly, was quick to point out the flaws in the proposals the rest of them were bold enough to advance.

"We'll never kill enough of them," Many Numbers said to Blue Sky, as if it were his fault. "Not against an army the size of the one you and the survivors describe. They'll just keep coming at us the way you say they did on that plain. We'll kill a lot of them but never enough. They'll wear us down. We'll get tired. They'll kill us all, one by one."

Blue Sky shook his head. "On that plain we didn't have the advantage of higher ground."

"All they need to do is get in a few lucky thrusts," Many Numbers came back. "You said you saw that yourself on the plain. The survivors did, too. Most of the time the hill warriors missed, they said, but they still got the job done. They'll just keep coming at us."

Now Early Harvest was shaking his head. "I don't think we have any other choice."

Spring Rain looked at Many Numbers and nodded in agreement.

"That's what it comes down to," he said. "What else can we do?"

Noon Breeze agreed. "It's fight them here or give up."

"We won't give up," Green Field said. "We'll fight them here."

Early Harvest and Noon Breeze had insisted on coming with them to the upper valley, despite Green Field's order to all the wounded men to remain wherever they were and let themselves heal.

Early Harvest and Noon Breeze had also insisted on making themselves useful, sometimes tending the oxen for the women or the horses for the old men, sometimes herding livestock with the children, sometimes even poling the rafts and exchanging splashes of water with the boys to whom they'd become heroes.

They weren't the hard-to-believe heroes the boys had heard about in the strange stories the tellers told from long ago. These heroes existed in the here-and-now like the valley, river, mountains, and seasons.

If a warrior somehow survived the battle on the plain, he had to be a hero. No god needed to come down from heaven to tell the people that.

Blue Sky turned and looked all the way to the top of the cliff on the east side of the river, the cliff they'd be fighting under.

"Can't we get up there from the upper-valley side of it?" he asked.

Noon Breeze, Early Harvest, and Good Harvest looked where he was pointing.

"We can," Noon Breeze said. "I've been up there. You look down and you're right above the people passing through here."

"All the upper-valley people have been up there," Good Harvest said.

"But you can't get up there from the lower-valley side," Blue Sky said.

"No, you can't," Good Harvest agreed.

That side was as steep as the side facing the river, almost straight up and down.

"That's what the children told us," Blue Sky said to his father, "when we came back through the gorge. They wanted to take the prince, Rose Leaf, and me up there to show us how scary it was. They wanted us to see how far we could see from up there. But we were in a hurry. We were on our way home. You put your foot down and said we didn't have time for it. Remember how angry we got? Even the prince got mad that day. You told us we were all too damned spoiled."

The orphans, Spring Rain and Many Numbers, looked at one another and laughed.

"We were in a hurry," Green Field murmured. "I remember. It was getting close to harvest time. You and Rose Leaf and the prince didn't want to be reminded of that. You and Rose Leaf couldn't get enough of being the best friends of the prince. Especially among strangers."

All of the men with Green Field except his son snickered at that.

Blue Sky was still looking at the top of the cliff, as if he hadn't heard a word his father said.

"We can get up there," he asked, "but they can't?"

"That's right," Noon Breeze replied.

Many Numbers pointed toward the lower-valley end of the passageway.

"They'll be crowded together all along there," he said.

136

His finger was aimed at a cart coming up the passageway with one of the lighter loads of the day, a mélange of children, calves, lambs, and kids still too young to walk. All of them appeared to be sleeping soundly despite the life-and-death crisis their people found themselves in.

Despite the lightness of its load, Green Field and his men gave the cart a damned good push. The fathers of the children were lying on the hill people's plain.

Reaching the top of the steep incline, Green Field turned and shifted his gaze from the passageway where the hill warriors would be gathered to the cliff-top above.

"Are we agreed then?" he asked. "We'll fight them here?"

*****

The lower-valley people emptied the carts and rafts into the new barns and storage pits the upper-valley people were constructing and digging. When they were done, some of the older people and children from the lower valley stayed in the upper valley.

The rest of them, along with some of the upper-valley men and boys, went back to the lower valley with the empty carts and rafts. They took turns leading the oxen and horses on the pathways. They all, of course, preferred riding on the rafts, floating downstream on the current with no need to exhaust the horses. And in the afternoons when it got hot, the more splashing the better.

In addition to the older girls the same ages as the boys poling the rafts, there were younger children who'd insisted on returning to the lower valley to help reload the carts and rafts. They were often on the rafts engaging in water fights with their older brothers and sisters, occasionally dousing the adults by accident, like archers hitting comrades instead of the enemy.

Their victims now and then included the regent and his mate, who took the spray laughing every time. They were known for spoiling children.

And when the children weren't on the rafts, they were doing what they'd seen Early Harvest's young cousins doing in the upper valley: they were riding the horses.

*****

After Tall Oak's grandfather had ordered Green Field's recently married father and mother out of the town, they were in need of oxen. All the farmers who had them for trade were asking more than they were able to part with.

Then they learned from a neighbor coming back from the town that one of the river traders had some work animals the valley people hadn't previously seen. A trader from another land had brought these strange beasts to the river people's town. The river people had no interest in making any kind of a deal for them.

The river trader who'd brought them to the valley people's kingdom had only taken them because he valued his relationship with the foreign trader, who got nothing more than a few lambs for them. He'd at least rid himself of the bother of taking the unwanted animals home.

The foreign trader had assured the river trader the animals were of more value than oxen for farm work. They were stronger, harder-working, and less ornery.

Their greater size and strength were apparent.

The original trader had also said the animals could become somewhat excitable at times, and they needed understanding and patience. If they got that, though, and behaved themselves, he believed no animal could be more useful to a farmer.

But the river trader who'd brought them to the valley people's kingdom hadn't been able to trade them to any of his own people's farmers. And until Green Field's father saw them, none of the valley people's potential buyers perceived any need to replace the reliability of oxen with the excitability and misbehavior of some beast they'd never seen before.

Green Field's father saw something else. He traded for the three animals, a male and two females—all unrelated, the trader promised—giving far less wheat and barley in exchange than any of the kingdom's farmers would've accepted for one of their oxen.

He was soon doing all his farm work with the animals and claiming their purchase was the best deal he'd ever made. He eventually traded some of their offspring to neighbors, as did Green Field after his father was killed in the war. But most of the farmers in the kingdom still scoffed at the idea that the animals might be superior in any way to their beloved oxen.

The word the river people used for the animals meant "horses" in the valley people's language. The valley people, like the hill people, only knew horses from their stories. They were an animal that once lived in the wild with the cattle, sheep, goats, deer, wolves, and bears.

The stories explained why humans never saw them anymore: they were so strong and beautiful the gods fell in love with them. Humans, though, rightly considering themselves the most beautiful creature in their world, vehemently objected to the gods' conspicuously bestowing favors upon another—and making fools of themselves as they did so.

But the gods refused to give in to the pleas of the humans to pay no further heed to their beloved horses. Instead, they simply removed them from the forest and hills and put them elsewhere— presumably so that their love-making could continue unseen by jealous and petty humans.

"Who can blame the gods?" Blue Sky once heard his mother ask. "Horses are beautiful. And no story says they fight wars with one another."

Chapter 9

Green Field appointed Fair Judge to be the first teller for the kingdom.

She'd once rebuked Law Keeper in open court for his refusal to leave an unnamed young teller alone. Most of the people present that day didn't know which young teller she was talking about. The king, the queen, and the tellers, though, knew she'd stood up for Spring Rain.

Many of the tellers believed Rainbow Evening, who publicly thanked Fair Judge for her "courageous" statement of the matter, had encouraged her to speak out. Later that day, Tall Oak privately delivered his threat to Law Keeper to remove him as the first teller.

Because the matter concerned Many Numbers and Spring Rain, Fair Judge asked the king and queen to keep it among themselves and the tellers.

Tall Oak and Rainbow Evening kept their word to the point of not letting even Green Field and Gentle Brook's family or the prince know about it.

But if those people had been told any such story about the two young tellers who sang with such feeling, they would've demanded that the king remove Law Keeper no matter what he promised he'd do in the future. They later proved they weren't above inciting the people to rebellion. Perhaps that's why they hadn't been told.

The women tellers and the male tellers too old to fight in the army, many of the latter being friends of the first teller who'd given up his life in the battle on the plain, had unanimously agreed to recommend to Green Field that he appoint Fair Judge to be the next first teller.

Green Field then appointed Many Numbers to be his chief warrior.

The two of them and Fair Judge conducted a brief ceremony for the men coming of age.

"The ceremony won't amount to much this year," Spring Rain had lamented.

"One sad song perfectly sung," Gentle Brook remarked, "would be enough for me."

She got her wish. Spring Rain did the singing.

*****

The men who came of age that day—together with Green Field, Many Numbers, Spring Rain, and Blue Sky—were now the valley people's army.

The new officials had declared Blue Sky of sound mind again—as if, he thought, there were such a thing as a sound mind in a world where the battle on the plain could be fought.

Early Harvest, Noon Breeze, and other survivors, their wounds healing, came to Green Field, insisting they were able-bodied enough to rejoin the army.

Green Field told them he appreciated their desire to help, but he wouldn't agree to rush them back into battle only to see them killed. They'd need to prove they were ready to be warriors again by practicing with those who were still able-bodied.

"We may need you more later on, when you're well," Green Field said to the survivors.

"Besides," Many Numbers agreed, repeating one of their people's favorite maxims regarding its army, "warriors who can't fight are only in the way of those who can."

So a number of survivors trained with the new army. Green Field and Many Numbers soon agreed Early Harvest, Noon Breeze, and a few of the others had healed enough to fight again, but they turned down most of those who'd offered their services.

"I'd rather you concentrated your efforts on healing," Green Field reiterated. "I meant what I said about your needing to stay alive."

"And there'll be other things you can do besides fighting," Many Numbers added.

For the final trek to the upper valley, Green Field promised there'd be room for all the wounded men in the ox carts and on the rafts. He didn't wish to see them walking.

Some of them, not surprisingly, insisted on walking anyway.

The new men of age, including Good Harvest, who'd have to do most of the fighting in the gorge could speak of little else. They paid attention to what Blue Sky, Early Harvest, Spring Rain, and Noon Breeze had to say, but when they heard those paragons of seriousness and caution, Green Field and Many Numbers, say the same things, they knew it was no longer just talk.

Blue Sky decided his father had chosen well. The warriors, from the recent boys through the healing wounded to the formerly disaffected, began to believe they could stop the hill warriors.

And that's what his people needed more than anything else.

*****

As the full moon approached, the people wasted no time emptying granaries, barns, houses, and storage pits and loading in ox carts and on rafts everything movable of value in the lower valley.

And as they worked, they couldn't keep from glancing in the direction of sunrise pass.

The day the wounded men and Blue Sky arrived home, they began telling the people what Wandering Star had told them: the hill people's army would come over the mountains through the pass. It was by far the closest and most convenient way for them to get into the valley.

And as soon as his people's warriors reached the encampments there, he'd also told them, their tellers would set the huts on fire. They believed the thieves' buildings were evil, even though their gods had never told them that. The hill people had to destroy those buildings, and only fire would rid the valley of their evil.

The rule applied, most particularly, to the encampment huts they could see from their side of the mountains. Lightning Spear ordered the tellers to set them on fire the first chance they got.

Once the valley people saw the smoke, they'd know the hill people's warriors had arrived. They'd also know how much time they had to prepare for battle.

Lightning Spear and Thunder Hunter didn't care if the valley people knew how long it would take their army to reach them. Whenever it happened, the valley people's old men, women, and children would be too paralyzed by fear to resist. The hill warriors wouldn't be making a sneak attack on the thieves. They'd be on their way to their enemy's final slaughter, and the valley people would be as helpless as newborn fawns and lambs.

After Green Field and Many Numbers let it be known that they believed Wandering Star's prediction made sense, the people kept glancing in the direction of sunrise pass.

The first sight of smoke there would've sent them on their way to the upper valley, no matter how many carts and rafts they had yet to load.

*****

"I wish I could be a warrior now," Gentle Brook said.

Green Field and Blue Sky looked at one another and silently agreed to remain silent.

Their house was empty. They'd loaded everything they had on carts and rafts: every hide and piece of pottery, every lentil and grain of wheat, every jar of wine and cup to drink it from. Their fire was out.

"Not when our army left our valley," Gentle Brook added, making no attempt to conceal her disgust, "to teach the hill people 'a damned good lesson.'"

She'd never disputed Blue Sky's youthful arguments that the hill people were no different from themselves. She'd seen what the bearded hill warriors had done in the last war. She'd seen what their king had ordered his warriors to do to Green Field and Tall Oak. But she'd also raised as her daughter the hill people's princess.

Their neighbors' oxen and carts were lined up on the path that would take them to the main path to the upper valley. Their family's horses were down by the river, where old men and boys were hitching them to raft chains.

All the valley people had to do was to lead the horses and oxen, and the animals would go wherever their leaders went. Humans were their gods—and probably made as much sense to them as the gods in heaven and hell did to the valley people.

"But stopping the hill people from taking our valley is something else," Gentle Brook said. "I wish I could help do that. Even if it meant thrusting a spear into another person's body. If it also meant shielding our children and our people, and holding their killers at bay, I'd do it."

She looked at the place where their table had stood and she, Green Field, Rose Leaf, and Blue Sky had eaten their meals and discussed affairs of the kingdom as well as spats among their neighbors, never knowing whether it was the large or the small that enlightened, amused, or appalled them the most.

Gentle Brook had watched Our Rose and Blue Sky simultaneously fall in love with Morning Sun. She'd recently admitted she'd known what was happening but opted to say nothing, hoping it would all somehow work itself out. Whatever Rose Leaf, Morning Sun, and Blue Sky chose, she would accept.

What they chose, though—assuming they ever really had a choice—had led her to declare her wish to become a warrior.

*****

One of Blue Sky's first memories was of his mother and father holding him and Rose Leaf on the backs of two of their most gentle horses. The animals didn't seem to mind walking around with children on top of them.

The valley people were aware they couldn't do that with an ox, which simply refused to move whenever anything was on its back.

They also knew a fully grown person's attempt to ride an ox could seriously injure the animal. It might even break its back and result in its untimely slaughter.

When Morning Sun came to visit them, Green Field and Gentle Brook would put him and Blue Sky on the same horse together. The prince was scared at first, but Blue Sky convinced him all he had to do was hold on to him really tight and he wouldn't fall off.

Blue Sky soon talked his parents into letting him take the halter in his hands. He'd realized he didn't need them to help him stay on a horse. One day when Morning Sun was on the horse with him, he proved it by making the horse go so fast even Green Field couldn't keep up with them.

Gentle Brook and Rose Leaf held one another and screamed, assuming the prince and Blue Sky were facing death. But after Blue Sky made the horse slow down, turn around, and go back to them with everybody safe and sound, they all began laughing.

From that day on, Rose Leaf, Morning Sun, and Blue Sky rode the horses by themselves, one to a horse, without needing anybody to keep them from falling off.

Green Field made them promise, though, that they'd stop riding the horses after they got bigger. He was certain the weight of an adult would injure a horse and render it useless. Maybe even a boy or girl within a few years of coming of age would be too heavy.

The three children assured Green Field they'd obey him. They didn't wish to hurt the horses. By then, they were convinced they loved them even more than the gods did.

*****

Green Field and Blue Sky went to the town to join the other warriors in the new army. They'd lead the oxen pulling the carts filled with the last of their people's bounty, bringing up the rear. As the army proceeded north from the town, not one person would remain behind it.

The river people had departed even before the old army had left for the battle on the plain. And they, like that army, hadn't come back.

"Who can blame them?" Spring Rain asked. "If my home were somewhere else, I'd certainly want to be there now—and not here."

"We'll have to get by without their tribute," Many Numbers said.

"The people will understand," the regent agreed. "They'll do whatever is necessary to defend the kingdom. Life will go on without the river people."

"Life will even go on," Blue Sky couldn't help adding, "without linen."

*****

Rainbow Evening and Fair Judge were the last to leave the court. Green Field, Gentle Brook, Blue Sky, Many Numbers, and Spring Rain met them in the courtyard.

The king and queen's oxen were hitched to the royal cart. Rainbow Evening had asked the court people, now mostly women, old men, and children, to give away the many hides she and Tall Oak had sat on whenever they rode in the cart.

"Somebody might need them this winter to keep warm," she said.

She also let it be known that she was glad she wouldn't be living in a court in the upper valley. She'd be hidden away, she said, in a village somewhere.

She had her arm around Spring Rain as if he were her son, perhaps even her lover.

Blue Sky had seen other women her age, including his mother, do that with the goddess of love, who'd come to the human world as a man.

All she had to think about, Rainbow Evening told them, was the day Morning Sun and Rose Leaf would come home together—and what a happy day that would be.

Full Harvest's family was already constructing two houses in the upper valley, one for Green Field and Gentle Brook to live in, and another for Rainbow Evening and Fair Judge. Neither dwelling would be a court—or a house "hidden away in a village." The surviving court people and tellers would be living in houses connected on either side of theirs the way they were outside the court in the town on the bluff.

When the time came to leave the courtyard, Rainbow Evening refused to ride in the cart.

"Give it to the first people who tire," she said to Green Field. "The old people. The sickly children. The wounded warriors. They get in the cart ahead of me. I haven't done anything for this kingdom. I've always only been in the way of the people who did the work."

Most of the individuals with her found it difficult to verbalize a response to that.

But not Blue Sky.

"You always quietly made it clear," he said, "you took the people's side against Sturdy Limb and Law Keeper. I'd say you did everything the people could ask their queen to do."

The others present had nothing to add to that, either.

"Do you suppose," Rainbow Evening asked Blue Sky, patting one of the oxen on his rump, "they miss Morning Sun as much as you and I do?"

Could an ox or a horse regret the loss of a human, especially a human who'd daily given it food, water, and new straw? Many Numbers said the animal couldn't, as did Sturdy Limb, Law Keeper, and most of the court people and tellers. Spring Rain, Morning Sun, and many of the farmers, on the other hand, insisted it could.

Blue Sky wondered if they might never know for certain one way or the other.

*****

Noon Breeze was staring at Blue Sky in the light of their torch.

The night being chilly, the people had found abandoned houses and barns to sleep in. The carts were scattered across the fields. The rafts were tethered to the same stakes the old men and boys had driven into the riverbanks during their first journey to the upper valley. The oxen and horses were grazing and sleeping in the closest pastures—it no longer mattered whose they were.

Many Numbers, Spring Rain, Noon Breeze, and Blue Sky had taken over a sheep barn to sleep in. The abandoned houses with their fireplaces were reserved for the wounded warriors, mothers and young children, and the elderly and ill.

The sheep barn was so small it didn't amount to much more than a large hut. Blue Sky and his comrades cleaned out the old straw and laid their hides on the dirt floor.

Noon Breeze had opened some wine and passed it around. Blue Sky hadn't had an opportunity to drink wine in a long while. It went straight to his head, too.

"You must miss Wandering Star," Noon Breeze decided to say to him at one point.

"Well, of course he does," Spring Rain said.

"Everybody saw you crying," Noon Breeze tried again, "the morning he left, up in the mountains. Early Harvest said he felt sorry for you."

"That was silly of Early Harvest," Blue Sky said. "Wandering Star thinks he can help us most if he's with his people. That's what's important. Not whether he and I are together."

Noon Breeze was just getting started. "Does he love you as much as you love him?"

"That's none of your business," Spring Rain retorted, again not waiting for Blue Sky to attempt a reply of his own. "That's between him and Wandering Star."

Like a hungry calf unwilling to let go of its mother's sore teats, Blue Sky drank more wine.

Noon Breeze persisted. "Before he met you, did he go with his people's tellers and apprentice tellers?"

"Why do you care?" Spring Rain asked. "Blue Sky doesn't have to answer that."

Many Numbers, though, had a smirk on his face as if he might welcome an answer.

"Wandering Star told me," Blue Sky replied, "there were a number of them he went with. Despite his exile, most of them were still quite happy to go with him."

"He told you that?" Spring Rain asked.

"He's sort of a prince," Blue Sky said. "They all know he's Lightning Spear's son."

Many Numbers studied Blue Sky's face as if he'd found something in it he'd never seen before.

Blue Sky and Spring Rain, though, had only themselves to blame for Noon Breeze's impertinent questions. They were sitting as close together as they could. But even without a fire other than the torch, it wasn't so chilly in the well-constructed sheep barn they could use that for an excuse.

Law Keeper's passion for Spring Rain never seemed unjustified to Blue Sky. Why wouldn't an old man want to go with him? As far as Blue Sky could see, Law Keeper's only mistake was his refusal to grant Spring Rain a choice in the matter, yes or no, and go on from there.

"Wandering Star is also pleasing to the eye," Spring Rain said. "Don't forget that. I'm sure going with him, having his body against your own—well, it must feel very good."

"Kissing his mouth, too," Many Numbers said, not without smirking again.

"Some of the men he's gone with prefer him beardless," Blue Sky said. "They can't let the other tellers know that, though."

Spring Rain turned to Blue Sky. "This is what you and he talk about?"

Many Numbers and Noon Breeze stared at Blue Sky, waiting for his response.

"When we're not talking about stopping a war," Blue Sky attempted. "A war he and I brought on, you know, all by ourselves. Some of those men he went with were killed in the battle on the plain. We watched as they buried several of them."

Blue Sky stared back at Noon Breeze.

"You would've gone with all of them. But maybe you killed them instead."

Noon Breeze grimaced. "All the men I've ever gone with were killed in that battle."

Spring Rain put an arm around his shoulders. Noon Breeze wasn't making that up.

"One after the other," Noon Breeze added. "I saw them lying on the ground, screaming in agony. It was a relief when you couldn't hear them anymore. You knew they were dead."

"Hell can't be worse than that," Spring Rain said. "And knowing you might be next."

"Almost hoping you'll be next," Noon Breeze agreed.

Spring Rain embraced him.

Noon Breeze liked that.

"We're all grateful you survived," Spring Rain said.

Noon Breeze, though, wasn't done with Blue Sky.

"I'm sorry to hear about Wandering Star's friends," he said. "I'm sorry if I might've killed any of them."

"No need to feel sorry," Blue Sky said. "You can't always choose the person you kill in a battle."

"Anyway," Noon Breeze went on, "Wandering Star admits he's been with other men. Well, that's good. He should go with any man he wants. Spring Rain's right. He's nice to look at. And yet, you've never gone with another man. Just him."

"That's right," Blue Sky agreed. "Just him. He's the only one."

Noon Breeze had his eyes fixed on Blue Sky's. "You might find you'd like going with somebody else for a change. It would be a chance not to think about the damned war for a while."

"I'm glad to know," Many Numbers remarked, putting his hand on Noon Breeze's shoulder, "your wounds are healing so quickly."

Spring Rain gave Noon Breeze another hug.

"Too bad," Many Numbers added, "you're not a prince."

*****

During their childhood visit to the upper valley, Blue Sky, Rose Leaf, and Morning Sun taught Early Harvest and Good Harvest how to ride a horse. Green Field had brought a young stallion to trade with Full Harvest for a promising young bull.

Before that, none of the farmers in the upper valley had horses.

"You pull the halter one way or the other," Blue Sky told Early Harvest and Good Harvest, "and that's the direction the horse will go. You have to hold yourself on the horse's back using your thighs. If you get them at the right angle and squeeze tightly, you won't slip off."

"The horse is so muscular and hard," Rose Leaf added, "it never seems to mind what you're doing."

Blue Sky and Rose Leaf somewhat tearfully told their upper-valley friends they'd miss the horse Green Field was giving them.

They knew many of their cattle, sheep, and goats as individuals, especially the oxen and the older cows, but they knew the horses even better. They seldom threw their arms around other livestock, but they often felt an urge to do that with horses. It wasn't difficult for Blue Sky, Rose Leaf, and Morning Sun to understand why the gods preferred horses to humans.

They explained to the cousins Early Harvest and Good Harvest—who might've been brothers, if the rumors were true—how much they enjoyed the smell of the horses and the sight of their glistening sweat in the summer sun. They didn't neglect to add that they loved leading them down to the river for a swim, with the humans as naked as the horses.

Early Harvest and Good Harvest stood next to the horses taking deep breaths.

"Cattle don't smell like that," Good Harvest said.

Blue Sky explained his father's rule against big children and adults riding horses.

"My father told me," Early Harvest said, "your father knows what he's talking about."

"Does your father think," Morning Sun asked him, "Green Field would be a better king than my father?"

The question, coming from the prince, left Early Harvest and Good Harvest speechless. People, especially children, weren't supposed to talk about the king in that manner.

"He never told me that," Early Harvest replied, pausing before going further than he otherwise would've. "He says he doesn't like your uncle, Sturdy Limb, and his deputies."

Morning Sun, Rose Leaf, and Blue Sky looked at one another and laughed.

"Who does?" Morning Sun asked.

Since that came from the prince, the cousins—or brothers—decided they might as well laugh too.

*****

Blue Sky and his three friends fell asleep together in the sheep barn.

When the people came again in his dream and confronted him with their shock, disbelief, and anger, he was glad he woke up next to Spring Rain.

The god of love knew what was happening, put his arm around Blue Sky, and comforted him.

Noon Breeze, though, slept through it, healing.

Blue Sky knew Noon Breeze wasn't in love with him. It was obvious the man would just as readily go with either Spring Rain or Many Numbers if they were available to him.

Noon Breeze was fortunate in one sense. The horror he'd been through didn't seem to disturb his sleep. Early Harvest and most of the other survivors said they often woke during the night terrified, after reliving in a dream the day the blood of their companions soaked the enemy's plain.

*****

The next day was their last in the lower valley. Word came back to those in the rear that quarrels had arisen among their people. At that moment, the rear guard included Green Field, Gentle Brook, Rainbow Evening, Many Numbers, Fair Judge, Early Harvest, Spring Rain, Good Harvest, and Blue Sky.

One family claimed their cow had wandered into a neighbor's herd, made the trip north with her new companions, and apparently decided to remain with them in the upper valley. The neighboring family dismissed the story as a fantasy and said the cow in question had always been theirs. Another family claimed a cartload of their wheat wound up in somebody else's barn.

Fair Judge and Green Field had asked a number of the tellers to remain in the upper valley after the first journey. They could both see what was coming.

Fair Judge once explained to Blue Sky how she attempted to find out which side cared less about the truth than the other regarding the crucial facts in a quarrel. She'd speak with each of the persons involved, but only out of the hearing of all the others. She'd let them go on as long as they wished.

"The more they tell me," she said, "the more I can find out what I need to know."

She needed to know which side had the more serious inconsistencies in its stories. That side wasn't telling the truth.

When she discovered which side that was, she could more confidently render a decision acceptable to both sides without needlessly accusing anyone of deliberate dishonesty.

"That family claiming the cow could use another one," Blue Sky said. 'You can hardly blame them for imagining a neighbor's cow is theirs."

Green Field didn't care for that remark, but what could he do?

"Maybe," he said, "we'll find them a cow somebody else doesn't need to waste feed on."

"That family lost two men," Spring Rain said.

Rainbow Evening closed her eyes.

Spring Rain put his arm around her shoulders.

"We lost a lot of men on that plain," Many Numbers said. "We must have more than enough cows to go around."

Green Field turned to Fair Judge. "Can the tellers make the cows go around?" he asked. "If they can, they'll be fighting the hill people's warriors just as much as the army will."

"That's another thing," Gentle Brook interjected. "Some of the women want to fight alongside the men in the army."

The remark of his mate brought the regent to a halt.

The rest of his party stopped as well.

"Two of them came to us," Fair Judge confirmed. "They're insisting on it."

Fair Judge, Rainbow Evening, and Gentle Brook had walked together the entire journey.

The two women insisting on fighting in the army were East Land's niece and her companion. They were speaking, they said, for a number of other women.

"I can't allow that," Green Field said.

"Those two women do the same work you and I do," Blue Sky reminded his father. "You've seen them. They're just as strong as many of our men."

Many Numbers, Early Harvest, and Good Harvest were shaking their heads.

"Never," Green Field repeated.

Gentle Brook, though, laughed.

"Men have the privilege of fighting to keep their people alive," she said. "Women don't. I'll have to try to figure out someday why that is. I should otherwise think children and grandchildren are as precious to women as they are to men."

Gentle Brook turned to Fair Judge.

"Do the gods deny that?" she asked.

Fair Judge shook her head.

"I've never heard a story in which they say that," she replied.

"There's a lot the gods don't say," Spring Rain added.

When he wasn't helping Many Numbers and Blue Sky repair carts, Spring Rain had spent a good part of the journey in the company of the three women.

After Fair Judge and Rainbow Evening had intervened on his behalf against Law Keeper's absurd demand to have him for himself, the four of them—Rainbow Evening, Fair Judge, Spring Rain, and Many Numbers—were often seen together, greatly annoying Sturdy Limb.

"Some women," Spring Rain added, "could be just as useful in a war as men."

Many Numbers looked at Spring Rain and Blue Sky amazed.

"We can't have women getting killed in a battle," he said.

Early Harvest agreed. "It's too terrible to think about."

"It's just as terrible to have men getting killed in a battle," Blue Sky said. "Everybody's had to think a lot about that lately whether they wanted to or not."

Green Field shook his head. "Women have never fought in our people's army."

"That might not be true," Fair Judge said. "Some of our stories describe women dying of spear wounds in wars. How did they get those wounds? Not all of them were running away. Some of them had wounds in their bellies just like the men."

"I suppose with their guts spilling out, too," Gentle Brook chose to say. "Spilling out onto the ground, just like the men's guts."

Fair Judge looked at Many Numbers. "You know those stories," she said.

"I've heard them," he agreed, reluctantly. "The gods don't say women can't fight in wars."

"Maybe," Fair Judge continued, "whenever women have been needed to fight, they've been accepted in the army. Maybe they'll never be as strong or fight as well as the biggest and strongest men. But maybe they can help anyway. Smaller men like Noon Breeze seem to do all right. They don't get sent home."

"He fought all day on the plain," Blue Sky said. "And he's still alive to tell us about it."

*****

Late that afternoon those in the rear caught up with the throng in the fields and pastures below the gorge waiting their turn to pass through it.

Suddenly, East Land's niece, who enjoyed eyesight as acute as Blue Sky's, looked back at the lower valley and loudly proclaimed the news their people least wanted to hear.

"The hill people's army," she cried, "is at sunrise pass!"

While others repeated her words for those further away, the people turned to see what they least wished to see.

Some insisted they saw nothing.

Blue Sky, though, could see what East Land's niece saw, low on the horizon and imperceptible at first to most of the crowd. But soon, as they watched, it billowed up from the top of the mountain ridge east of their town: smoke as dark as the final night itself in a dream of death.

The sunrise-pass encampment huts were on fire.

The rafts came to a halt so that the old men and boys could see the smoke. People already in the upper valley ran back to the gorge and up to the cliff-top above it to view the spectacle.

It was the last thing they could've imagined—prior to their army's leaving the valley to teach the hill people a lesson—they'd witness in their lifetimes.

Many of the valley people got down on their knees, pleading with their gods to save them.

A number of the people, though, remained standing, perhaps suspecting, as Blue Sky did, their gods were at least as foolish as humans and couldn't help them anyway.

Even if the gods felt as kindly toward them as the stories insisted, they might shed a few tears when the last of the valley people died off, but why would it matter to them beyond that? They'd still have the heaven they claimed was their home—and their horses, too.

Chapter 10

After all the valley people and their animals, carts, and rafts passed through the gorge into the upper valley, there was little time for amusement. Winter and the hill people's army, the valley people's two worst enemies, were both on their way.

Those who could do so began building houses for themselves and for those who couldn't. Full Harvest's relatives had already finished building one house for the regent and his mate, and another next to it for the queen and the first teller. They located the dwellings on the east side of the river on a gently sloping hillside its owners had previously used for pasture. As the court people and tellers put up houses and granaries on either side of those two buildings, and in rows parallel to that first one, all of the houses facing the gorge, the pasture began to resemble a town.

The chief warrior, the regent's son, and their comrades Spring Rain and Noon Breeze started constructing a house as close to the gorge as they could put it. They built it on a flat piece of land, also on the east side the river, and just above the line of rocks marking the highest level to which any of their people had seen the water rise in that area. They chose the site because it had an unobstructed view of the gorge and the lower valley beyond it.

East Land's niece and her mate chose to build a house directly across the river from them. Many of the other women who went with women in the lower valley decided to put up houses connected to theirs. They'd have to raft over the river to get to the passageway in the gorge, but they'd gladly do so, they said, if Green Field would let them fight with the army.

Just to the north of the place where the chief warrior, regent's son, and their friends were building their house, the men newly come of age, as well as the survivors of the battle on the plain who'd healed enough to help, were building two-man huts connected together in rectangles around an open fire, like the huts in the mountain encampments.

*****

The valley people's warriors who'd died on the plain had done most of the work raising and harvesting their crops and caring for their livestock. The old men, women, and older children were certainly capable of doing the same work, but the old people had aches and pains slowing them down, most of the women had other onerous duties to perform, and the older children still had their childhood to contend with.

The upper-valley people therefore opened their arms to the lower-valley newcomers with a reputation for hard work, and they gladly helped them build houses, granaries, and barns in their villages.

Green Field, the tellers, and the court people were attempting to settle the remaining lower-valley families, those not known for their diligence. Full Harvest's family and the other prosperous upper-valley farm families were letting themselves be talked into taking them in anyway.

The hard-to-place families, the regent's son went around saying, also had mates, sons, fathers, and brothers lying on the hill people's plain. He'd seen them there himself.

*****

Green Field ultimately ruled that women could participate in the coming battle. Neither he nor the people, though, would consent to their engaging in close combat with spears.

The regent admitted some of them, East Land's niece and her companion being prime examples, could probably train to the point where they'd be as effective in hand-to-hand combat as many of the male warriors. But he insisted he never wanted to see a woman die in battle.

Neither, as he well knew, did most of his people.

"I still can't imagine," the regent said to his son privately, "a woman thrusting a spear into another person's body, hoping to kill him."

"I still can't imagine," Blue Sky said, "doing that myself."

The one chance he'd had to kill an enemy was when he'd aimed his arrow at Wandering Star on sunrise pass, and he'd chosen not to let it go. He'd come to believe, though, it would've been a far better thing for both of their peoples if he'd murdered the man who later became his lover.

"But I'll do it," Blue Sky continued, to his father. "You did it. It has to be done."

Green Field had killed so many of the enemy in the last war with the hill people that his only son had assumed he could his spend his childhood and youth questioning anything he wished.

*****

A number of older men who'd fought in the last war with the hill people but were clearly unable to fight in the present one—and had since lost their mates as well—went to see the regent as a group. They volunteered to go to the upper-valley encampments to make certain no hill warriors were attempting to sneak up on their people by coming over the mountains.

It was something, they said, they could do.

Green Field accepted their offer, but not without insisting they take along oxen and carts filled with as much of the army's food, hides, and firewood as they'd need. They should avail themselves of enough carts to ride in whenever they got tired climbing the mountains.

It was as if he'd implored the wind to change its course.

The old men advised the regent they'd take their own oxen, carts, food, and hides. They'd gather firewood in the forest. And they wouldn't need any space in the carts for riding.

They'd found a good excuse to go back to the mountain-top encampments of their youth. Valley men often spoke of their encampment years as if nothing else in their lives mattered quite so much.

When the volunteers departed with their oxen and carts, their families gathered at the entrances to the forest to say goodbye. Their daughters and granddaughters, and not a few of their sons and grandsons, were in tears.

"Save your tears," one of the old men said, "for the hill people."

"And do whatever Green Field tells you to do," another thought to add.

*****

The new apprentice tellers were putting up their huts in a rectangle connected to the house the chief warrior, the regent's son, and their comrades were building.

They were working with their shirts off in the autumn sun.

Noon Breeze looked at them and laughed. "Spring Rain. He's the one they want."

Spring Rain and Many Numbers had gone to attempt to settle a dispute in a nearby village. Both sides had insisted the orphan boys hear them since Fair Judge was more than a day's journey away trying to resolve some other quarrel.

"I can't blame them," Blue Sky said, nodding toward the apprentice tellers. "Spring Rain is everybody's friend."

Noon Breeze's laughed. "They don't want him for a friend. They lust for his body."

Blue Sky felt his heart skip a beat.

"Spring Rain is pleasing to look at," he ventured.

Noon Breeze laughed again. "They think he's the most pleasing man in the kingdom to look at—even more beautiful than Morning Sun and Early Harvest. And those men don't go with men. Spring Rain does."

Blue Sky had overheard them engaging in that kind of idle talk.

"What good will it do them?" he asked. "Spring Rain isn't interested in going with anybody but Many Numbers."

Noon Breeze laughed again. "They can lust for him anyway. They can hope against hope some day he'll change his mind."

Blue Sky looked at them, sweating in the sun. They'd paired off as quickly as the previous year's apprentice tellers had. Some of them had apparently chosen each other even before they became apprentice tellers, as if they'd decided—reasonably, he'd have to say, after the battle on the plain—they had no time to lose. They seemed to be as happy with one another as one could expect of warriors who were awaiting their own and their people's massacre as soon as Lightning Spear's and Thunder Hunter's warriors broke through the upper gorge, as they were bound to do.

"And why shouldn't they hope against hope?" Noon Breeze asked. "No matter how foolish they make themselves look? That's what they see you doing."

Noon Breeze looked at Blue Sky, watching his last remark sink in, laughing as it did.

"And you're the regent's son," he added, twisting his blade to make it hurt even more.

"And should know better?" Blue Sky asked.

*****

When the valley people weren't building houses, barns, and huts, they had even harder work to do loading and unloading the carts the horses were pulling back and forth between the forest and the top of the cliff. At least the horses got to rest during the loading and unloading.

Late in the afternoon of the third day after all their people had left the lower valley, those doing the unloading on the cliff-top, Blue Sky among them, suddenly found reason to stop their work for a moment.

Somebody had spotted new smoke far to the south, too dark to be campfire smoke.

The hill people's army had reached East Land's village and set it on fire.

Eventually, more dark shafts of smoke began rising farther to the west. One of them rose above Blue Sky's village. He was quite certain he could tell which one it was.

Near the lower gorge that evening a huge cloud of smoke billowed upward with the grace and menace of a flock of ravens rising from a field. The town was on fire.

The valley people had three days, but likely no more, to finish their preparations.

*****

That same evening, Noon Breeze's mother and father arrived with his two brothers and two sisters. All of his siblings were younger than him. His mother had actually given birth to ten children, but the other five had died in their infancy.

Noon Breeze began wiping tears away with his sleeve when he saw his family coming down the path toward the gorge with ox carts filled with provisions for the army.

The night after the battle on the plain, under the influence of pod tea, Noon Breeze told Blue Sky of his worst fears while he was waiting for the hill warriors to finish him off. The foremost among them was that of his mother, father, sisters, and brothers hearing the news of his death.

A number of his younger cousins had come with them. It was apparent Noon Breeze was a hero to them. He'd made it back from the calamitous battle on the plain. And now he was living with the regent's son, the chief warrior, and Spring Rain.

The family lived in the northernmost tip of the valley. To get there, one had to paddle or pole a raft across the lake or take the long way and walk the path around it. Most of the valley people—even many who lived in the upper valley—had never seen their village.

During the last war with the hill people, Noon Breeze's father and uncles had fought in the lower valley defending the town. Otherwise, until Noon Breeze came of age, none of his family had been outside the upper valley. Once, when he was a child, they'd come far enough south to see the upper gorge. That was when Noon Breeze found out about the cliff-top.

Full Harvest had invited their family to the feast for Green Field's family and the prince during their visit, but Noon Breeze's mother was giving birth then, and they had to stay home.

Noon Breeze's family was considered one of the poorest in the kingdom. Too many children, the story went, and not enough land. Ordinarily in such a situation, Noon Breeze's becoming a teller would've been a blessing, especially since he had two brothers and two sisters. In Noon Breeze's case, though, it meant he'd be separated from his family for long periods of time, certainly if he chose to live in the town—and none of his encampment comrades could imagine he wouldn't.

During his last summer at home, he once told Blue Sky when they were drinking wine, his mother had only to look at him to begin weeping.

162

His family hadn't seen him for over a year, not since the day he'd started out on his own for the lower valley to attend the end-of-summer ceremony—the one where he officially came of age with the prince, Early Harvest, Solemn Promise, the apprentice tellers he went with in the encampment, and Blue Sky.

Noon Breeze's village had been the last to hear of the army's slaughter on the plain.

When Blue Sky and the survivors returned to the valley, they tried to get the messenger boys and girls to remember the names of the survivors whose families lived far from the town. That way, the families might find out as soon as they heard about the battle that their mate, son, father, or brother was still alive.

Blue Sky wasn't optimistic the scheme would work. Many of the children who usually served as messengers had just learned their own fathers or brothers were dead. There was no way they could be asked to do anything. Some of them volunteered nevertheless. Additionally, a number of sons, daughters, and siblings of survivors who lived nearby and in the town came to Blue Sky throughout that night, dutifully memorizing names before they set off.

The younger brother of Autumn Wine's injured grandson made it all the way to the remote meadows beyond the lake where Noon Breeze's family lived. He couldn't possibly reach them before the news of the army's defeat did, but they only had to wait another day before he showed up to let them know Noon Breeze was alive and had every reason to remain alive.

Many Numbers, Spring Rain, and Blue Sky prepared the evening meal. Green Field, Gentle Brook, Full Harvest, and Early Harvest came by to chat, drink, and eat with them.

The family stayed with Noon Breeze and his friends the next day as well. Noon Breeze's brothers and male cousins insisted on climbing to the top of the cliff to help the army prepare for the hill people. Noon Breeze, Spring Rain, and Blue Sky agreed the six boys could take their places. They stayed behind with Noon Breeze's parents and sisters, all of them helping, however they could, to finish building the huts for the army.

The regent had assured the family Noon Breeze had no obligation to serve in the new army. None of the survivors did, he explained. It was strictly each man's choice.

Noon Breeze's mother and sisters told Green Field they preferred that Noon Breeze not tempt fate again.

Noon Breeze wouldn't listen to them.

"Early Harvest is fighting again," he said.

They'd heard that was the case.

"And my wounds weren't as bad as his," he added.

Blue Sky would've said they were worse, but he wasn't about to correct his comrade.

"I didn't fight on that damned plain," Noon Breeze said, "I didn't watch my comrades get killed, I didn't stagger bleeding over those damned mountains, just to come home and give up."

His father turned to his mother and sisters. "It won't do any good to argue with him."

He himself had been wounded in the previous war. He walked with a pronounced limp, and one arm hung uselessly at his side. People wondered, Early Harvest told Blue Sky, how he got any work done.

There was one thing everybody remarked about that day near the gorge: the clouds of smoke above the lower valley heading their way. The hill people were systematically setting fire to every village.

The regent and his mate came again that evening. Fair Judge was with them. Ordinarily, when the apprentices became tellers, their people held a ceremony in the town. That year, though, Fair Judge simply told Noon Breeze and Blue Sky they had become tellers. The gods only required that she say it in front of the regent. And, with the year's other male apprentices lying dead, to a man, on the hill people's plain, that's all Noon Breeze and Blue Sky wanted.

Autumn Wine, her grandsons, Solemn Promise's sister, and the great-grandchildren, who were living in two houses in Full Harvest's village, joined them.

Autumn Wine jabbed her finger at Blue Sky. "Now you know what I told you about the hill people is true. They won't be happy until they've slaughtered every last one of us."

"At least two hill people," Spring Rain interjected, "don't want to see us slaughtered."

Autumn Wine turned to Spring Rain.

"You're dreaming just like him," she said, gesturing toward Blue Sky with her cup. "He's a bad influence on you. I hope you realize that."

Spring Rain, laughing, gave her a hug.

"Thank you for warning me," he said. "I promise you I'll never listen to him again."

After a day on the cliff-top, the older of Noon Breeze's brothers decided he'd remain near the gorge and do anything, short of actual fighting, the warriors needed him to do.

Green Field told him he could never allow him to do that. A boy in his position, the regent said, could best serve the people by going home with his family and taking good care of them.

Early Harvest, no less, assured the boy Green Field was right.

"Go home," he said. "Your turn to get killed will come soon enough."

Early the next morning, unwilling to assume their neighbors would care for their livestock any longer than they'd promised, Noon Breeze's family left for home.

His father was riding in an ox cart. The older of his brothers was seemingly—but most unhappily—in charge, barking orders to his siblings and cousins.

Full Harvest had given them some sheep he said his family would no longer need. The lambs were riding in the carts, several of them in the same cart with Noon Breeze's father. Sheep did well grazing the lower mountain slopes beyond the lake.

At the rear of the column, Noon Breeze walked with his mother and sisters until the path took them far enough away so that his comrades and the new apprentice tellers couldn't see the tears trickling down his face when he embraced them one last time.

*****

All that day the new army's warriors practiced in the gorge, while an auxiliary group of women, older children, and old men worked on the cliff-top.

All that day as well, the fires in the lower valley came closer. Before the end of the next day, the hill people's army would reach the gorge.

When their work was done, the warriors and auxiliaries enjoyed a feast the people had prepared for them.

One might've assumed the day's activities would've caused widespread exhaustion. The evening's drinking, dancing, and other forms of revelry laid to rest that fear.

Near sunset Many Numbers asked Blue Sky to come away from the festivities for a moment.

Blue Sky assumed the chief warrior had some lingering question as to how the regent's son thought the next battle with the hill people might best be fought.

"Noon Breeze is right," the chief warrior remarked instead. "You should have somebody to go with. This might be your last night alive."

Initially, Blue Sky couldn't think of any way to respond to what Many Numbers had said.

"The person I'd most like to go with," he finally blurted out, "isn't available."

Many Numbers smirked. "And I assume the person you have in mind now isn't a prince or at least a bastard kind of prince. I've often heard it said this person is more like a god."

He looked at Blue Sky closely, enjoying his comrade's obvious discomfort.

"No," Blue Sky agreed, "the person I have in mind isn't a prince of any kind. But he is a beautiful man. I wouldn't wish to cheapen him by comparing him to a god."

Many Numbers laughed. "I have good news for you. Spring Rain is available. To you."

Blue Sky eyed the chief warrior warily.

Many Numbers was seldom a party to a prank.

"Spring Rain has told you that?" Blue Sky asked.

"He's told me that. More than once he's told me that."

Blue Sky stared at Many Numbers.

"And you won't mind," Blue sky dared to ask, "if he and I go together?"

Many Numbers smiled at the regent's son as one would an exceptionally innocent child.

"I won't mind at all," the chief warrior replied.

He'd once, over wine, remarked on the friendship Green Field, Gentle Brook, and Full Harvest enjoyed, staring at Blue Sky as he said it.

"I'll be honest with you, though," Many Numbers added. "Noon Breeze asked me to go with him this evening. He said it's been much too long since he's gone with a man, and he's greatly in need. I promised him I'd try to help him out of his predicament."

As the enemy army drew closer, the chief warrior and the regent's son, fearing the untimely deaths of themselves and the persons they loved, not to mention the destruction of their people, embraced one another, laughing.

"Noon Breeze might be more deserving than I am," Blue Sky said. "But he isn't more in need."

*****

The four comrades hadn't wasted any time putting up walls separating sleeping areas in their house. Nor had they hung hides for that purpose—hides they or other people could better use keeping warm in the winter, assuming any of them were still alive when that season came again.

So they employed their fire that evening for more than heat and light. Many Numbers and Noon Breeze were on one side of it, Spring Rain and Blue Sky on the other.

"In that hut on sunrise pass," Blue Sky whispered in Spring Rain's ear, "you knew how much I wanted you."

Spring Rain chose not to argue the point.

The men who went with women among their people insisted the women they had children with shouldn't go with another man, to say nothing of falling in love with such a person. And they agreed it was only right that they shouldn't go, or fall in love with, another woman either.

It was also true, no matter what they said, some men and women did anyway.

The men would say they didn't want to toil on behalf of another man's child. Often, though, they raised nieces and nephews and even more distantly related neighbor children whose parents had abandoned them or died. And none of the men, tellers included, would ever say they wouldn't die in a war for the sake of all the children in the kingdom, related to them or not.

But the men who went with other men didn't have to worry about raising some other man's child. Many of the tellers felt free to go with as many other men as they pleased, and whether they loved them mattered not at all. On hearing that, young Blue Sky had assumed they'd become cynical after failing to find one person to spend the rest of their lives with, just the two of them, needing nobody else. As his two heroes, Spring Rain and Many Numbers, had.

In their stories, the gods often denounced lust, even though they often gave in to it themselves, sometimes going so far as to hunger for mere humans and horses. Their fulminations seemed justified in the case of an adult going with a child, or a person forcing himself upon an unwilling partner—even a Law Keeper placing his unwanted hands on Spring Rain's body.

That particular evening, though, Blue Sky couldn't imagine why any reasonable god could object to what he and Spring Rain were doing.

They were surrendering, Spring Rain reminded him, not to the enemy, but to a comrade.

That was a line a particularly promiscuous teller hero used on the eve of battle in a story the valley people's male tellers, as well as the hill people's, had taken delight in handing down through many generations.

Spring Rain, though, could've characterized going with Blue Sky any way he pleased, even as the greatest evil two humans had ever accomplished, and Blue Sky still would've done it.

Chapter 11

The next day the fires in the lower valley drew near.

Early in the afternoon the valley people's army assembled in the gorge.

The regent and his son chose to die, if that was to be their fate, next to each other in the center of the front line. As did Many Numbers and Spring Rain. As did Spring Rain and Blue Sky.

The warriors on either side of them in the line were the biggest, strongest, and most agile of the new men of age. If a first-rank warrior had chosen another warrior to fight and die next to, and if that comrade wasn't on either side of him in the front line, he'd be immediately behind him in the second line.

Early Harvest and Noon Breeze, along with the other survivors accepted into the new army, were several ranks back. Those two had grumbled all day that they'd healed so much, as their activities the previous evening had apparently confirmed, they should also be in the front line.

The army waited, watching the fires draw closer. Lower-valley people who'd lived near the gorge were naming for the rest of them the specific families whose villages were burning.

The day had reached the middle of its afternoon when the valley people saw flames and smoke rising from the lower-valley village closest to the gorge, which was hidden from them by the village orchard. The hill people had nothing left to set fire to.

Soon, on the main path below them, the valley people saw, coming from behind the orchard, the first hill warriors, all of them bearded, all of them with their hair to their shoulders.

Blue Sky knew who they were: Long Arm and his brothers and cousins—the autumn hunting party in the ravine, the abductors of Morning Sun and Rose Leaf, the warriors who'd openly sneered before the battle on the plain when War Cloud offered to kill Blue Sky and, without any say-so on the part of his king, drew his spear-tip across an unarmed man's belly.

Staring at the valley warriors in the gorge, Long Arm brought his party to a halt.

His brothers and cousins, pointing their spears in the direction of the gorge and the upper valley, yelled to their comrades behind them. "Here they are! The thieves! The farmers!"

Spring Rain translated those words in the valley people's language. Warriors behind him repeated them for the benefit of those farther back in the upper valley and on the cliff-top.

The hill people's army came on, spreading out on either side of the path. They were filling the harvested fields below the lower-valley entrance to the gorge.

Blue Sky and the survivors of the battle on the plain had attempted to prepare their people for their first sight of the hill people's army. They predicted that the hill warriors would fill the fields, and there still might not be enough room for them all. The sight of that happening, though, created a far more powerful impression than their verbal warnings ever could.

Blue Sky could also see that the oldest boys who'd carried back the injured and dead on the plain had become warriors. Now Blue Sky would have to do everything in his power to kill them.

The valley army, and the people on the hillsides behind it, stared at their enemy in silence.

The hill people's army parted near its center, making way for a contingent led by their king, Lightning Spear. Behind him, a warrior carried a chair. In both peoples' stories there were references to kings who were seated when they faced their enemies. The valley people always understood those remarks to mean the king was too elderly, or had been too grievously wounded in a prior battle, to remain standing. Neither of those conditions seemed to apply in the present case.

The warrior with the chair placed it on the stubble, and Lightning Spear sat down on it as if he were ready to hear arguments in court.

Green Field drew a breath so deep Blue Sky could hear it.

"That's him," Blue Sky murmured.

Lightning Spear and some of the other hill people had probably figured out by then who the older man standing next to Blue Sky was, and where and why they'd seen him before.

Wandering Star had undoubtedly told them Green Field was the regent of the farmers' kingdom as long as Morning Sun was in captivity and unable to rule himself.

"Do you know who the others are?" the regent asked his son.

As they were before the battle on the plain, Thunder Hunter and his sons, Dark Storm and War Cloud, along with the lesser chieftains, were on one side of Lightning Spear. Long Arm and the first teller, Heaven's Voice, along with his high tellers, were on the other side.

True Hunter, Thunder Hunter's teller nephew who'd fought all day in the battle on the plain, the survivors had told Blue Sky, and killed many valley warriors, was in the second rank behind Dark Storm and War Cloud.

True Hunter, War Cloud, and Long Arm were three powerful reasons why all of the valley people's tellers, all but one of their apprentice tellers, and most of their court people who'd fought in that battle were dead.

True Hunter killed Tall Oak and Sturdy Limb. Long Arm killed Solemn Promise. War Cloud killed Valley Defender's brothers and gave Valley Defender the wounds that killed him. The three of them alone made Green Field the valley people's regent.

"Tell the army and our people who they are," Green Field said. "They should know."

Blue Sky did so, shouting out their names and identities: "their king," "their second most powerful tribal chieftain," "his older son, promised to Rose Leaf," "his younger son," "their first teller," "the spy who took Morning Sun and Rose Leaf at spear-point and is now the king's chief warrior," "their finest warrior, I've been told, although War Cloud and Long Arm might disagree."

Blue Sky didn't leave out that Thunder Hunter was the chieftain whose warriors had killed a grandmother for nothing more than lamenting the death of her son.

Warriors behind Blue Sky repeated his remarks for the benefit of those farther back.

Long Arm was also restating Blue Sky's comments, in the hill people's language, for the benefit of Lightning Spear and Thunder Hunter. Other hill warriors were freely passing Blue Sky's remarks out to their flanks and back to their rear.

When the repeaters fell silent, Thunder Hunter turned to Lightning Spear.

"You should've let us kill him," he said, loudly enough for the valley warriors in the front lines to hear, "when we had the chance."

The hill warriors also repeated that observation.

Spring Rain gave the valley people a translation, which soon echoed in the gorge.

Blue Sky's people knew what Thunder Hunter was referring to.

And Noon Breeze couldn't resist.

"You're damned right you should've," he yelled back at Thunder Hunter, using the words of the hill people's language he'd picked up from Wandering Star, Spring Rain, and Blue Sky. "You would've done us a big favor."

The hill people's warriors repeated those remarks, too.

Spring Rain, laughing, told the valley warriors near them what Noon Breeze had said. They passed it on to the people in the rear, the laughter going with it.

"I'll punish him for that," Many Numbers, the chief warrior who'd gone with the offender the previous evening, promised the regent.

A number of the hill warriors, realizing Noon Breeze's remarks were in jest, even in the face of battle, began laughing themselves.

Lightning Spear, Thunder Hunter, and the others on either side of them, though, were in no mood for sarcasm, even if its only possible purpose was to amuse people who were about to die.

Long Arm was peering as far into the gorge and upper valley as he could.

Blue Sky assumed he was attempting to determine how many of the people he was facing were warriors and how many were noncombatants.

Lightning Spear looked up at him and said something the valley people couldn't hear.

Long Arm turned to the valley people again.

"These words are from Lightning Spear, our people's king," he shouted across the empty space between them, first in the valley people's language and then in his own.

The words once again echoed in two directions and two tongues.

"This valley is ours," Long Arm continued. "You must leave it immediately. Otherwise, we'll kill you."

Lightning Spear said something else to him the valley people couldn't hear.

"We'll kill you all," Long Arm added. "Every last one of you."

Green Field chose to make no response to that.

Thunder Hunter turned to Long Arm, apparently making his own request.

"Including," Long Arm said, "your women, old men, and children."

Green Field stared at Lightning Spear in the last light of that early autumn day, listening to the echoes, remaining as silent and defiant as stone.

Once again, Noon Breeze took it upon himself to break the silence.

"Lightning Spear," he shouted, "you can go to hell!"

The valley people and army repeated that reply with gusto, yelling it again and again in unison until it became a deafening roar.

The hill warriors didn't dare repeat it on their side.

Nor did they need to. As Noon Breeze well knew from his nights drinking wine with Wandering Star, the words "go to hell" were the same in both tongues, and he'd used the hill people's pronunciation of Lightning Spear's name, which many valley people recognized.

Through it all, Long Arm was still attempting to figure out how many warriors the valley people had in the gorge.

Lightning Spear stared at Green Field and Blue Sky.

He'd had both of them in his grasp, and both had slipped away.

"We'll attack them in the morning," Lightning Spear pronounced. "Tomorrow they all die."

His promise went out to both armies.

Green Field turned to his chief warrior and spoke so quietly only that official, Spring Rain, and Blue Sky could hear him.

"I don't think you'll need to punish Noon Breeze for anything he said today."

*****

The hill warriors withdrew to the orchard and beyond, where they pitched their tents. They were far enough away from the gorge to ensure the valley army couldn't launch an attack while they slept.

Their distance also guaranteed that the valley warriors wouldn't be the victims of a surprise attack by the hill army.

To make certain no such thing happened, the valley people kept guards on the cliff-top. Many Numbers chose volunteers among the auxiliaries who were free to agree upon their coming and going themselves—so long as there was no moment during the night when at least three of them weren't fully awake, keeping watch over the enormous hill warriors' encampment beneath them. They were to sound the alarm if they saw any hill warriors moving toward the gorge.

That evening the apprentice tellers loudly sang and danced around the fire at the center of the rectangle their huts and the house of the four comrades enclosed.

They enjoyed watching the chief warrior serve Noon Breeze his food and wine.

"Green Field himself told him to do that," one of them remarked, exaggerating a bit.

Their excitement kept giving way to displays of affection, with Noon Breeze receiving, and returning, many of them.

"Bring on Lightning Spear's army!" he grew fond of shouting when he wasn't kissing the apprentice tellers or touching them under their loincloths.

That morning Blue Sky had heard him letting them know what had happened the previous night.

The moon was rising above the mountains. The evening was warm for autumn.

From several directions they could hear the singing and laughter of the other new men of age, the survivors of the battle on the plain, and the women who'd come to visit them. They could hear more singing and laughter from the women across the river.

Noon Breeze and one of the apprentice tellers he was kissing began removing their clothes. Other apprentice tellers, pairing off, followed their example, some in the shadows near the huts, some like Noon Breeze and his friend in the full glare of the fire.

Blue Sky had seen Noon Breeze do that on full-moon nights in the encampment on sunrise pass. Noon Breeze was almost always the one who "got things started," as they liked to say.

One new apprentice teller, having remained apart from the others, was exchanging glances with the chief warrior almost as if Noon Breeze had taught him how to do it.

Spring Rain said something to Many Numbers Blue Sky couldn't hear.

Many Numbers left them and approached the apprentice teller near the fire.

Blue Sky turned to Spring Rain. "It must be the war," he said.

Spring Rain was staring at Many Numbers and the apprentice teller, who were kissing.

Spring Rain turned to Blue Sky and smiled. "If I die tomorrow, I hope you and Many Numbers will always remember I loved you both."

Many Numbers and the apprentice teller disappeared inside the young man's hut.

"You won't die tomorrow," Blue Sky said. "Even the wicked hill people won't kill a person as pleasing to look at as you are."

"I didn't hear that silly remark," Spring Rain said, putting his hand over Blue Sky's mouth. "I told Autumn Wine I'd never listen to you again. Maybe this time I should keep my promise."

Blue Sky ever so slightly licked the inside of his hand.

Spring Rain withdrew his hand from Blue Sky's mouth and replaced it with his lips.

It was time for them to disappear inside their house.

Blue Sky imagined he was renewing the hope of every apprentice teller that he might be the next to disappear, for a while at least, with Spring Rain.

*****

"You knew this would happen," Blue Sky said.

The campfire was dying. Noon Breeze and Blue Sky were the last to sit by it.

"You saw it happen before," Blue Sky persisted.

"Yes," Noon Breeze admitted, "I did."

"The night before the battle on the plain."

"Yes. Except then, there weren't any women around. Some of the men who wanted women let the tellers do favors for them instead."

Autumn Wine's older grandson, drinking pod tea during his return to the valley, had informed Blue Sky he was one such man. And Noon Breeze himself had done the favoring.

Noon Breeze took Blue Sky's cup and drank from it. Earlier in the festivities, he'd mislaid his own and had taken to drinking out of the cup of whichever person he was with.

"Do you remember," he suddenly asked, "when you first told me about Morning Sun?"

"First told you what about Morning Sun?"

Noon Breeze laughed. "He was the only man you'd ever love. That's what you told me. You said you'd never go with anybody except Morning Sun. That's what you told me. And since you couldn't do that, you'd never go with anybody. That's what you told me."

Blue Sky took his cup back and drank from it.

"You've had a lot of fun at that silly farmer boy's expense," he said. "You should be grateful you have somebody around who amuses you so much."

The fire was almost out.

Noon Breeze would have to find his clothes in the morning, before the battle.

*****

The warning came down from the cliff-top shortly after dawn.

The valley warriors and auxiliaries took up their positions.

Green Field sought out Early Harvest and Noon Breeze.

The warriors surrounding them fell silent and made way.

The people had sided with the two upper-valley warriors. It was true their wounds weren't completely healed yet, but in practice it was clear their fighting abilities weren't impaired.

Green Field accordingly told Early Harvest and Noon Breeze they could fight wherever they pleased. If they wished to fight in the front line, he'd ask Many Numbers to make room for them. The choice was theirs.

The front line made room for them.

*****

Below the gorge the early sunlight sparkled on the river like fire. The gods had decreed another excellent day for a battle between eternal enemies.

If two opposing armies weren't present, their warriors facing death, a passerby would've heard people singing hopeful songs as they began their day's work, maybe even those with lyrics thanking the gods for the gift of human life itself.

That morning, though, as Lightning Spear sat in his chair, and Thunder Hunter, Heaven's Voice, and the chieftains of the lesser tribes stood on either side of him on a grassy knoll halfway between the orchard and the lower-valley entrance to the gorge, their warriors— Long Arm, Dark Storm, War Cloud, and True Hunter among them— approached the gorge.

They were holding their shields somewhat higher than they usually would've.

Many Numbers explained: "They think we should have archers on the cliff-top trying to pick some of them off."

Ordinarily, that's what the valley people would've done.

Archers firing down from such a position always had an advantage over an enemy on the ground below. The cliff itself was shield enough for warriors at its top. They could poke their heads above the edge of it, get off a quick shot and crouch back down before an enemy warrior could take aim at them.

The trick was guiding the cliff-top warriors to fire randomly so their opponents would never know who'd pop up next. The warriors had to have somebody calling out the order of firing for every six or seven archers on the line, and that person had to resist any tendency to follow a pattern their opponents could detect.

In order to shoot back arrows of their own, the enemy warriors would have to stand exposed. The warriors up above, after firing a shot, would tell their comrades which enemy warriors were doing that—which they should aim for.

And any postponement of the outcome of the battle could only work to the valley people's advantage. In another day or two, Wandering Star had explained, the hill warriors would have to start hunting for their next meal. The valley warriors' supplies were right behind them, along with the people who'd see to it they got everything they needed to keep fighting.

177

Lightning Spear, Thunder Hunter, and the other men on the knoll were pointing at the cliff-top and laughing.

They were no doubt assuming, correctly, their enemy was so lacking in warriors they'd put them all in the gorge and had none left over for archery duty where it could've done some good.

The valley people also had too few warriors in the gorge to fight the enemy with arrows. The hill warriors could've remained spread out in a wide line just below the gorge but close enough for the valley warriors to be within range of their arrows. Every time one of the front-line valley warriors dropped his shield and took a shot, he'd be exposed to the fire of four or five opponents. All the valley warriors would be fatally wounded long before the hill warriors were.

So, without hindrance, and in near silence except for the tromping of their feet on the valley people's beloved fields, the bearded hill warriors marched into the lower end of the gorge.

Reaching the steepest stretch of the passageway just below the valley army's front line, they dropped their shields and bows and arrows and came forward with their spears, relentlessly closing the gap between the armies.

The valley people's front-line warriors handed their shields to their comrades behind them. And, having no bows and arrows to discard, each of them soon found his man.

The hill warriors swung their spears above their heads.

The valley warriors swung theirs below their knees.

On first clash, a number of the hill warriors' spears went flying.

Blue Sky's opponent, the teller cousin called True Hunter, kept his but briefly stumbled. His comrades on either side of him quickly grabbed his arms and pulled him to safety before Blue Sky could thrust his spear into his belly.

Long Arm gave the order, and the hill army's front line fell back to regroup and take on replacements for their warriors who'd lost their spears.

That order was what the valley people were waiting for.

If the hill warriors had looked to the cliff-top then, they would've seen survivors of the last battle, younger women, and older boys at the edge of it. Obeying Green Field's strictest order, to keep them from falling into the gorge, they had vine and leather ropes looped around their waists, with the other ends securely tied to the few stunted trees that grew up there.

And they were sending down a barrage of tree limbs and boulders the valley people had collected in the forest and loaded in carts for their horses to pull to the cliff-top.

The hill warriors looked up and screamed in terror.

A second line of auxiliaries—Full Harvest, Gentle Brook, Rainbow Evening, and Fair Judge among them—were rolling forward more tree parts and rocks from the huge piles of missiles the horses had hauled up there.

Even after the battle had commenced, some of their people, Autumn Wine included, were leading horses pulling carts loaded with still more limbs and boulders up the path to the cliff-top.

The older of Noon Breeze's brothers had convinced his sisters and younger brother they could provide feed and water and otherwise care for their family's livestock without him. He'd blatantly disobeyed the regent and come back to the gorge. Now he was on the cliff-top with Autumn Wine's grandsons rolling rocks and tree limbs over the edge of the cliff.

A tree stump hit Blue Sky's new opponent on his spear-thrusting shoulder. He cried out, dropped his spear, turned his back on Blue Sky, and ran.

So did his comrades, running into more missiles from above.

Many Numbers raised his spear as a signal to the auxiliaries to stop the bombardment.

As soon as they did so, the valley army's front line ran forward.

Blue Sky ran with them, thrusting his spear between his retreating opponent's shoulder blades. Holding on to his spear stuck in his adversary's ribs, Blue Sky rode him as he staggered and stumbled down.

At the lower entrance to the gorge a whole tree was falling over the cliff-top and onto the hill people's army.

Holding his opponent down with one foot, Blue Sky yanked his spear from the hill man's body, pulling out flesh and bones, as blood spurted around it.

Spring Rain, who had his opponent on his back, was removing his spear from the man's belly, pulling out guts with his weapon.

Blue Sky swung his spear and slit the throat of Spring Rain's opponent.

With his foot, Blue Sky rolled his own opponent over onto his back.

Spring Rain swung his spear and slit his throat.

Blue Sky swung his spear in the other direction and slit the throat of his father's opponent.

The missiles from above and the carnage at the front sent the other hill warriors fleeing.

The fallen tree, though, was blocking their exit from the gorge.

Those in the valley front line ran forward together, thrusting their spears into the backs of their opponents, pulling them out, swinging them again, and slitting their throats.

Their comrades in the next rank ran through their line, catching up with the fleeing hill warriors, most of them injured, many of them getting themselves entangled in the tree with their comrades it had fallen on.

Line after line taking the lead, all the valley warriors moved forward, killing the hill warriors who'd killed so many of their comrades on that plain—warriors who'd bragged they'd come to kill every last one of the valley people's old men, women, and children.

Blue Sky discovered, once he'd started, he couldn't kill enough.

He caught up with the lead line time after time and found ever more opponents to sink his spear into, some of them cowering among the limbs of the fallen tree.

He kept his comrades occupied finishing off his opponents.

A survivor of the plain ended up doing nothing more than retrieving Blue Sky's spear from a fatally wounded hill warrior and handing him another one for his next kill.

Blue Sky couldn't help himself. He did what he did without seeming to think what needed to be done.

He loudly shouted orders to his comrades, even the regent and chief warrior.

And all of them obeyed him. They understood he could see more than they could.

It was the first time he became fully aware that something had happened to his mind.

Whenever he met the eyes of his father, Spring Rain, or any of his other comrades, he could see they could see it. He could even see his adversaries could see it before he killed them.

The night after the battle on the plain, only a few of the wounded men could climb into the carts on their own. Often, when Wandering Star was helping one of them, Blue Sky simply picked up the next injured warrior who needed assistance, found a cart for him, and gently laid him in it. Some of the wounded were at least as big as he was. But lifting them one after the other, and being obsessively careful not to reopen or worsen their wounds, seemed as if it took no effort at all.

He hadn't imagined doing what he did. The wounded men told the story to the people, but Blue Sky, who couldn't account for what he'd done, refused to speak of it.

And so it was in the gorge. He could never explain how he did what he did that day.

Finally, Many Numbers ordered the valley warriors to fall back.

As they did, they soon found themselves imitating Blue Sky, who was attempting to make certain, with an extra swing of his spear, every fallen hill warrior on his way was dead or would soon die.

The entire passageway between the tree and the valley army's front line was red and wet with blood.

And so were Blue Sky and his comrades, from head to toe.

A few of the valley warriors had nasty cuts of their own, but none of them, they could soon tell, was seriously wounded.

Lightning Spear and Thunder Hunter and their companions on the knoll were staring at the cliff-top.

There was no way they could've imagined the valley people's horses—the hard, strong, muscular creatures in both of their peoples' stories their gods had fallen in love with—pulling cart-loads of tree limbs and boulders up to such a place.

Spring Rain and Noon Breeze pointed out for Blue Sky a lone man standing on a rise near the orchard, quite apart from the hill people's army.

"That's him," Noon Breeze said.

The man had no beard.

181

He was staring at the gorge. He could see what Blue Sky saw: the hill people had lost a great number of warriors, but all of the valley warriors were still standing.

Lightning Spear was issuing orders to his army. He was commanding the warriors to remove the tree and their dead comrades from the passageway and prepare for another attack.

There was no cheering on the valley people's side.

Some of their enemy's dying warriors were still writhing in pain.

Blue Sky and his comrades stood gaping at one another, covered with the blood of their opponents, each having killed humans, most for the first time.

And there were so many more of them to kill.

When Lightning Spear finished barking his orders, all the valley warriors could hear was an occasional exchange among the women, boys, and survivors on the cliff-top directing the continual coming and going of horses and carts and the piling of limbs and rocks in just the right places—Many Numbers and Spring Rain had seen to that—for the boys, young women, and survivors who might be called upon soon again to launch them over the edge of the cliff onto human beings below, maiming and killing them.

Whatever other persons might've been thinking then, Blue Sky knew there was no reason why the hill people and his people couldn't live together peacefully. Yet there his beloved people were, killing other human beings for no lesser, or greater, excuse than their own wish to stay alive.

And there he was, crimson as a setting sun, killing people who probably no more deserved an early and horrific death than he did, depriving children of their fathers and lovers of the men who loved them. He knew what he was doing was evil. He was the one who'd set in motion the events that forced upon him the need to kill humans.

Could gods who were good-hearted, Blue Sky wondered, no matter whose gods they were, allow humans to go to war with one another? And if they could, why would they? But if they, like humans, had no choice in the matter, why did humans call them gods?

*****

182

Having risen from his chair, Lightning Spear was in a heated discussion with Thunder Hunter, the lesser chieftains, and their chief warriors.

This time, though, they were careful, despite their agitation, not to speak loudly enough to let the valley people know what they were saying.

Heaven's Voice was staying out of the debate, choosing instead to study the valley people's warriors.

Blue Sky wondered if perhaps he found Spring Rain, even covered with gore, as enchanting as the valley people's former first teller had. Or maybe it was the tall, left-handed Early Harvest, just as bloody, who'd caught his eye.

Blue Sky looked at Wandering Star, who was staring back at him.

Some of the blood smearing Blue Sky's body might've spurted from the throats, breasts, and bellies of men Wandering Star had been friends with, even men he'd gone with.

Blue Sky might've been the evil farmer warrior who'd killed them, all for the purpose of clinging to a valley his people had no right to, a valley that once belonged to the ancestors of the people he was killing—Wandering Star's ancestors.

One might've thought Wandering Star was fortunate. He got to survey battles without fighting in them. He didn't have to kill other human beings in order not to be killed himself.

One might've imagined the sons of kings in general were lucky.

Blue Sky later learned that another king's son had nothing better—or worse—to do that day than sit outside a tent in the autumn sun, chat with his elderly guards in their language, and play endless games with their grandchildren.

Morning Sun was charming them and the children's mothers, aunts, and grandmothers as much as he had the valley people. He'd figured out how to do it.

And yet Blue Sky was certain both those sons of kings would've gladly exchanged places with him, no matter how caked with dust and blood he was, waiting in the upper gorge with his comrades for another onslaught. It would be their next excuse, coming down from heaven itself, to brutally kill other human beings in defense of their own—their next excuse to prove to the gods that they, when called upon, would be heroes who deserved to be remembered forever.

*****

A number of unarmed hill warriors came running toward the gorge dragging vine ropes, intending to tie them to the nearest limbs of the fallen tree as quickly as they could and run back to their comrades, who'd be pulling on the ropes, dragging the tree from the mouth of the gorge.

When the hill warriors came well within range, a line of valley people consisting of survivors, younger women, and older boys rose to their feet at the edge of the cliff-top, took aim, and fired off a hail of arrows, dropping more than half the rope-draggers with their first shots.

The hill people—their king and their most brutal chieftain included—screamed in shock.

Their first teller, heeding the prompt, added his wail, heavenly or not, to the chorus.

The valley people had tricked them into believing there were no archers on the cliff-top.

That was Autumn Wine's older grandson's idea. The auxiliary handing him his arrows was Solemn Promise's sister, the mother of their two children, both of them planted in her when she was still married to another man, who died on the plain with the other court warriors.

The archers fired arrow after arrow until all the hill people's vine-draggers had fallen, with at least two arrows piercing each of their bodies, most of the projectiles sticking out of their backs. The cliff-top archers had foiled their attempts to turn and run out of range to safety.

The rope-draggers' comrades came rushing forward behind shields, armed with bows and arrows of their own.

The valley people's archers on the cliff-top crouched down, took cover, and remained there.

Most of them had argued during their practices that after they pulled off their cruel trick, they should engage in the usual kind of bow-and-arrow fight with the hill warriors, citing their obvious advantage on the cliff-top.

Green Field and Many Numbers, though, wishing to take no chances with the lives of boys, healing warriors, and women, some of them mothers of young children, refused to consider it.

The valley people's warriors in the gorge were pleased to see that none of the auxiliaries popped up to take some shots anyway—not so much because Green Field and Many Numbers were right and the outspoken auxiliaries were wrong, but because their people were fighting a war, and obeying their leaders was mandatory.

People could make their own rules in a war, as Green Field and Tall Oak had in the last one, only when it was clear that their leaders no longer deserved their respect.

The cliff-top auxiliaries had other tasks to perform anyway. They laid down their bows.

Behind their shields, the hill warriors eventually pulled the tree out of the gorge and carried their rope-dragging comrades, who were either dead or dying, back behind their lines.

Then they came, still behind their shields, for their dead comrades from their first attack.

The valley warriors in the gorge and the auxiliaries on the cliff-top watched.

They knew this moment would arrive. Speaking of it, in fact, had revealed another difference of opinion among their people as to what their response should be.

Fair Judge said their people had always allowed enemy warriors to take their dead comrades off a battlefield. She could think of no story in which their people had prevented an enemy from doing that. The gods were sometimes heard to say dead warriors could no longer harm anyone, and even enemy warriors deserved a proper burial.

After she spoke, a number of valley people, Gentle Brook and Spring Rain most conspicuously among them, nodded their heads in agreement.

Early Harvest, Noon Breeze, and the other survivors of the battle on the plain, though, reminded everybody present that their people's many warriors who'd died on the hill people's plain had gone unburied, "a feast for vultures, ravens, and wolves," they kept repeating.

"And Wandering Star told us," Early Harvest said, "his people will never bury them."

Gentle Brook, who was standing next to him, embraced her lover's son despite their apparent disagreement on the matter at hand.

"The hill people," Blue Sky offered, "didn't prevent us from burying our dead. Our people simply never had the opportunity to do it. Our gods don't say we have to bury the enemy dead for them. I'm sure the hill people's gods don't say that either."

He got the same quizzical looks he so often encountered when he tried to make a point.

"Do you agree with Fair Judge?" his father asked him.

"No," Blue Sky replied, "I agree with Many Numbers and Early Harvest."

Early Harvest pointed out that they could make it costly for the hill warriors if they attempted to retrieve their dead. On the other hand, if the valley warriors let them take their dead away, they'd be removing obstacles to their next charge into the gorge. Why go along with that?

In all the stories Fair Judge and Spring Rain could cite, Many Numbers noted that letting the enemy remove their dead didn't have any effect on the outcome of the battle—and did give the valley warriors a chance to repair their weaponry, slake their thirst, tend their wounds, and rest their bodies.

"But in our case," Early Harvest insisted, "it damned well could effect the outcome."

That moment of truth was on its way. The hill warriors were coming for their dead. Half of them carried both shields and spears. The other half came with just their shields so they could grasp a dead comrade's hand or foot and drag him away.

The valley warriors stood silent and watched as the hill warriors filled the lower end of the gorge, some of them coming within the length of two spears from the valley people's front line.

Many Numbers quietly raised his spear once more, giving the signal.

Like a torrent of water plunging over a falls, rocks and tree limbs hailed down on the hill warriors. Another tree rolled off the cliff-top, trapping the hill warriors on the wrong side of it.

As they'd done before, the hill people's army screamed as one.

Warriors dreaded the unexpected more than anything.

As Tall Oak and Sturdy Limb had discovered on the plain, surprise won battles.

Many Numbers raised his spear again. The bombardment from above ceased.

The valley warriors ran forward, as they'd practiced repeatedly, impaling their shocked and confused opponents. The hill warriors who'd come without spears, as well as those felled by a rock or limb, were easy to kill.

The valley warriors surrounded the few hill warriors on their side of the tree who were still standing and holding onto a spear. One valley warrior, swinging his spear, would send the opponent's spear flying, a second would thrust his into the man's belly, a third would drive his between the man's shoulder blades and turn him over, a fourth would swing his to slash the man's throat. And they could all claim equal credit for killing an opponent.

Through it, Blue Sky was shouting his instructions to them, up and down the line.

When the hill warriors withdrew, the valley warriors could once again see that every hill warrior on their side of the fallen tree was dead or dying.

And all their own warriors, soaked in the blood of their enemies, were standing.

None of the valley people, not even those on the cliff-top, possessed the temerity to speak.

The only sound they could hear was the moaning of enemy warriors in the final moments of their lives.

The gods had made what seemed to Blue Sky to be a fatal mistake. It was as if they didn't wish to exist in his mind—where they'd become human hopes and dreams but nothing more, and every story they'd told was yet another all-too-human concoction.

Chapter 12

While their leaders conferred again, sometimes raising their voices, often gesturing with their spears for emphasis, the hill warriors dragged the second fallen tree out of their end of the gorge. Those not pulling on the vines stared at their fallen comrades on the passageway between them and the valley warriors. Many of the dead lay body to body.

Their leaders still had sense enough not to let the valley people hear anything important they had to say. The valley people who understood their language could only pick out the insults they were flinging at one another, "cowardly" being the one Thunder Hunter and his sons Dark Storm and War Cloud seemed to prefer, "stupid" being the favorite of Long Arm and his men.

Wandering Star, standing apart but close enough to hear, appeared to be following the discussion as if nothing else could matter so much.

When it was over and Lightning Spear was giving orders to the warriors nearest him, Wandering Star was vigorously shaking his head.

*****

The day having reached early afternoon, the hill warriors chosen to lead the next attack glared across the passageway at their valley adversaries.

Gazing at True Hunter, Blue Sky realized why the stories said warriors shouldn't let their eyes rest on an enemy for long. Without his beard, True Hunter could've been with him at the fire the previous evening. And if Blue Sky thought of him as such a person, he might never bring himself to kill him. It was the mistake Blue Sky had made with Wandering Star on sunrise pass—the error that launched the most devastating war the valley people had ever fought.

The hill warriors marched up the gorge toward the valley warriors. Reaching the place where the trees had fallen, they broke into a run.

Lightning Spear had chosen to send his warriors sprinting through the bombardment from the cliff-top, hoping to get enough of them to the valley people's front line to kill at least some of their warriors, even if the lopsidedness of the number of the dead hill warriors to those of the valley warriors was as extreme as it had been on the plain.

The missile throwers on the cliff-top quickly put that hope in serious doubt.

The valley warriors had noticed the number of tree limbs and rocks in the second bombardment substantially exceeded those in the first.

The auxiliaries' third barrage was even more intense.

It was difficult to imagine so many limbs and rocks could be piled so close to the edge of the cliff and so easily made to fall over it. Of course, the valley people up there had the advantage of not having to kill individual enemy warriors. They were only protecting their blood-covered mates, lovers, and brothers in the gorge. They could kill as many unseen humans as they wished.

The charging hill warriors, stumbling over their own dead, had no chance of success. The valley people's bombardment felled all but a few of them. A third whole tree came down, trapping, as the cliff-top auxiliaries had done twice before, a significant portion of the hill people's army.

Blue Sky and his comrades quickly surrounded and slaughtered the few hill warriors who'd made it through the onslaught from above but hadn't retreated quickly enough to escape the tree.

After the valley warriors accomplished that task, they swarmed over, and "finished off," as they put it, the other hill warriors who'd been knocked down and maimed by tree limbs and rocks.

And when the valley warriors were done again, they were all still alive.

And ready for more blood, more war, more killing, as if they'd just gotten started.

Then, standing silent, having nothing to say, they heard one of the wounded hill warriors, not yet dead, weeping.

*****

Once again, the valley warriors and their opponents stared at the dead and dying men in the passageway between them, their congealed blood attracting flies.

Wandering Star, having thrown his spear to the ground in an evident display of disgust, was making his way through the hill people's army.

His father's warriors were stepping aside to let him pass. Many of them seemed to be urging him on, but their comrades were noticeably choosing not to repeat their remarks, whatever they were, either for the benefit of the whole army or the king and his retinue on the knoll.

Straining to catch what the warriors were saying, Spring Rain and Blue Sky heard one plead with Wandering Star to "stop the slaughter." Then they heard others repeating his request.

Blue Sky and Spring Rain passed that on, in their words, to their people.

Long Arm stared at them. He, knowing the valley people's language, realized they'd heard what they weren't supposed to hear.

Spring Rain and Blue Sky yelled out the request again, this time using the hill people's words for "stop the slaughter." The valley people echoed those words, too, taking sides with the enemy warriors who shared their most deeply felt desire that afternoon.

As Wandering Star approached Lightning Spear and Thunder Hunter, the valley people fell silent again, bystanders at a spectacle none of them could've imagined they'd see.

Dark Storm and War Cloud left their own comrades and, raising their spears and yelling "Halt!" over and over, ran to intercept Wandering Star, as if they were needed to protect their king and their chieftain father from an unarmed exile.

"Don't touch him!" a hill warrior screamed at the brothers.

Other hill warriors took up the cry: "Don't touch him!"

Spring Rain and Blue Sky quickly passed that on to their people.

Dark Storm had his spear pointed toward Wandering Star's belly. War Cloud's was aimed at his throat.

"Touch him and die!" the nearest hill warriors were yelling, their own spears raised.

"Touch him and die!" Spring Rain and Blue Sky repeated, first in their people's words, then in the hill people's.

The valley people again took them up on that, echoing the warning in both people's words.

They were letting the hill warriors know they understood what was happening. They were speaking to them, over the dead and dying humans lying between them, about what really mattered.

Wandering Star moved forward until he was standing closer than the length of a spear from Dark Storm and War Cloud.

"The blood you wear honors you both," he said to them. "I'll never question your courage. And our people should never forget what you've done today."

Dark Storm and War Cloud were as thoroughly soaked in blood as Blue Sky and his comrades were. So were Long Arm, True Hunter, and the few others who'd fought in and yet survived all three of the valley people's cliff-top bombardments.

But the blood covering the hill warriors was that of their comrades.

Somehow, they'd been able to evade the valley people's boulders and limbs and clamber over three trees to safety. Luck could've played a part in that. Blue Sky was of the opinion, though, that their strength and agility—the very qualities he and his comrades who went with men found so appealing in them—had much more to do with it.

"It's a pity," Wandering Star said to the brothers, looking up at their fathers on the knoll, "your fighting had no good purpose, and your bravery was shamelessly wasted."

Then he turned fully around, faced the dead warriors in the passageway and pointed his finger at them.

"As were the lives of those men!" he yelled.

Dark Storm and War Cloud stared at Wandering Star while their people and the valley people repeated the remarks of their king's bastard son, who wore no blood at all.

He turned around again and, stepping forward, pushed aside the shaft of Dark Storm's spear with one hand and War Cloud's with the other.

The brothers glanced at the warriors surrounding them and made no attempt to push back.

When Wandering Star reached the base of the knoll the king and his chieftains and highest tellers were standing on, he came to a halt and looked up at his father.

"You can't win this battle," he shouted. "Stop it now. For your own sake, keep the warriors you've still got."

Hill warriors repeated his words.

Spring Rain shouted a translation. The valley warriors passed it back and could hear the people behind them and up on the cliff-top gladly repeating it.

Lightning Spear shook his head. "We either fight them here, or we go over the mountains. And you told me it'll be hell going over the mountains."

Thunder Hunter shook his head derisively.

"It will be," Wandering Star said.

"Then we go through this gorge," Lightning Spear said.

"You can't," Wandering Star countered. "You can see you can't. Those people on the cliff-top will kill all your warriors. If you keep trying, they'll kill them all."

"Traitor!" Thunder Hunter yelled, pointing his spear, which he hadn't yet seen fit to use in the battle, at Wandering Star. "Traitor!"

"Liar!" some of the hill warriors began shouting back at Thunder Hunter.

"Liar!" others echoed, as did the valley people, using the hill people's word.

Despite the furor, Lightning Spear rather calmly turned to Wandering Star.

"What would you do?" he asked the supposedly disgraced exile he denied was his son.

Wandering Star, making a half-turn this time, glanced at the valley people.

"Let them have the upper valley," he replied, turning back to face his father. "Make it a gift to them. A king can always do that. A great king, a king who lives on in his people's stories, would do that."

"Never!" Thunder Hunter screamed.

Lightning Spear stared at Wandering Star, as his son's remarks went out to both peoples, along with the mighty chieftain's "never!"— another of those few words needing no translation.

193

"He's a traitor!" Thunder Hunter bellowed in the direction of his sons. "Kill him!"

Dark Storm and War Cloud repositioned their spears.

"You'll get all your warriors killed for nothing," Wandering Star shouted at Lightning Spear. "The farmers will kill every one of them. And they'll still have their upper valley."

"Kill him!" Thunder Hunter repeated, shouting at his sons.

"Don't touch him!" came Long Arm's response to that command.

As two peoples repeated those remarks, Lightning Spear, Thunder Hunter, Wandering Star, and Long Arm stared at one another. This was to have been the day the hill people finally defeated their enemy. Instead, their own kingdom was cracking apart like a poorly fired pot.

Dark Storm and his younger brother War Cloud had a decision to make. War Cloud had killed a great number of the valley people's warriors on the plain, almost as many as his teller cousin, True Hunter, who fought on the other side of Dark Storm, had slaughtered.

War Cloud, Dark Storm, True Hunter, and Long Arm had been in the front line in both of the hill people's attacks in the gorge that day, and they were among the warriors who'd attempted to retrieve the bodies of their comrades when the valley people bombarded them with stones and limbs from the cliff-top.

They hadn't had a chance to kill any of the enemy warriors in the gorge. The passageway incline above which the valley people had chosen to make their stand was too steep, even for them.

They'd gotten away, though. Blue Sky, who'd desperately wished, with good reason, to see those four men dead, couldn't hope to catch them. They were too fast, too nimble.

In any event, it was time for blood-soaked Dark Storm and War Cloud to decide what they should do: kill the king's bastard son, or defy their father?

"Don't touch him!" the hill warriors around Long Arm yelled, more of them approaching Dark Storm and War Cloud with their spears raised.

"Long Arm," Lightning Spear suddenly declared, "have your men take Wandering Star away. I've heard enough from him."

194

"Kill him!" Thunder Hunter implored his sons. "Kill that traitor!"

"But don't hurt him," Lightning Spear added, raising his voice above Thunder Hunter's. "Don't let your spears touch him. I don't want to see a scratch on his body."

Wandering Star looked at Thunder Hunter and laughed.

"I'll see you in your grave," he said. "I'll throw dirt on your face and bury you. And I'll dance on your grave after I've finished and you're rotting in hell."

The hill and valley people both knew he was twisting the promise a younger male member of a royal family might make to a well-respected older person—selecting just the right words, speaking in a proper tone of voice, exercising care as to his demeanor, and choosing an appropriate occasion, say the person lay dying. Both peoples considered it a high honor for the dead to have a prince shovel earth into their graves.

The valley people loudly repeated Wandering Star's remarks. The boys on the cliff-top gleefully hurled them at one another, some of them using the hill people's words for "grave," "dirt," "bury," and "rotting," pronouncing them just as Wandering Star had, making them sting.

Thunder Hunter could hear the valley people—and not a few of his own—laughing at him.

Wandering Star chose to make his exit as he had his entrance. He approached Dark Storm and War Cloud, daring them to kill him on the spot, face the warriors who'd come to save him, and know their people had fallen into a civil war on the very day they'd assumed they'd achieve their final victory over the thieves who'd long ago chased them from their sacred valley.

The brothers, not having anticipated the sudden skirmish, had thoughtlessly become separated from their own tribe's warriors just to appease their father. They knew that if they even raised their spears to kill Wandering Star, Long Arm's men would instantly slay them.

They exercised the restraint Long Arm, who was a hero in the eyes of their tribe just as much as he was among the other tribes, had asked of them. They chose not to touch Wandering Star. He passed between them, once again praising them for their bravery in battle.

The bastard son of the hill people's king clearly wasn't lacking in courage. In order to see what Long Arm and his deer-hunting comrades were doing on sunrise pass the previous autumn, he'd deliberately left himself open to Blue Sky's arrow. He later told Blue Sky he hadn't thought he was taking much of a chance. He'd already figured out, from watching and hearing Blue Sky in the guard post in conversation with Spring Rain, he'd never let his arrow go.

Blue Sky still believed Wandering Star had taken a substantial risk and knew it. Being human, Blue Sky made serious mistakes in his life, and he could've committed another such blunder that day and killed Wandering Star.

If he'd done so, he would've been following the orders he'd been given. His cold-blooded murder wouldn't have been regarded as an error at all—except whenever Blue Sky remembered the look on the dying hill man's face. And that would've happened every day for the rest of his life.

"Prepare for another attack!" Lightning Spear ordered his army, ignoring the man whose life Blue Sky had unwisely—but gladly, selfishly—refused to take.

*****

The sun in its cloudless sky had reached the fourth quarter of its arc that early autumn day.

The valley warriors remained steadfast in their positions in the gorge, heedless of the blood and dirt caking their skin, clothes, and weapons, heedless even of their exhaustion after their three encounters with the enemy. Every eye was on the lower-valley fields beyond the gorge.

The hill warriors had ignored Lightning Spear's last order.

At first, they appeared to be racing about aimlessly. Then the valley people could tell they were separating themselves into two groups.

Some of them were taking up positions with the warriors who'd sought to protect Wandering Star. The others were rushing to the side of Dark Storm and War Cloud.

Blue Sky could see the warriors favoring Wandering Star were Lightning Spear's and those of the lesser chieftains. They were still

196

significantly more numerous than their opponents, Thunder Hunter's warriors, and they were rapidly surrounding them.

Not one of Thunder Hunter's warriors was attempting to make a run for it. Each of them was choosing instead to make a stand with his tribal comrades. The choices guaranteed them their safety, at least for the moment—as well as their encirclement.

Blue Sky pitied them, but no more than he admired them.

"Prepare to fight the enemy!" Lightning Spear bellowed.

The hill warriors paid no more attention to that than they had the king's preceding command.

The valley people, gratefully reduced to spectators, watched and listened in total silence, as at a particularly enthralling performance by the tellers.

Lightning Spear and Thunder Hunter began arguing, their voices growing louder and louder. From what the valley people could hear, above the rumbling of the warriors, Thunder Hunter was once again describing Lightning Spear's warriors as "cowards."

Lightning Spear, on the other hand, was complaining that his warriors and those of the lesser chieftains were doing the fighting and dying, while most of Thunder Hunter's weren't doing "a damned thing." It was the battle on the plain all over again.

Thunder Hunter sharply responded to that. If his warriors all joined the battle, he said, Lightning Spear's and those of the lesser chieftains, being cowards, would simply run away.

Even as their leaders' argument raged on, and without any orders being given, Lightning Spear's warriors and those of the lesser chieftains completed their encirclement of Thunder Hunter's. The factions, their spears raised, were ready to fight one another—not the enemy warriors in the gorge their leaders wanted them to fight.

Thunder Hunter's warriors, though outnumbered, stood shoulder to shoulder, and could've forced their adversaries to fight them one-on-one, as Tall Oak and Sturdy Limb's warriors had in the battle on the plain. And the result could only be another slaughter.

Lightning Spear and Thunder Hunter broke off their argument and stared down at their warriors. Both of them were apparently too shaken by what they saw to verbalize a sensible order.

They watched as the valley people did—in silence as if in a spell—as Long Arm entered the no man's land separating the encircling warriors from those encircled.

He strode between them with his spear raised over his head, inviting any warrior brave enough to deliver a fatal thrust into his gut to do it.

The warriors on both sides stared at the blood-covered man who'd returned their princess, abducted the farmer-thieves' prince, and fought all day on the plain, as well as that day in the gorge, without suffering a wound.

"Get back!" he yelled at Lightning Spear's warriors and those of the lesser chieftains. "Get back!"

He was the chief warrior of Lightning Spear's tribe. Their warriors were supposed to obey him, and they did. He wasn't the chief warrior of the tribes of the lesser chieftains, but their warriors also obeyed his order, moving back a step or two as Lightning Spear's did, but without taking their eyes off their adversaries.

Long Arm turned to Thunder Hunter's warriors.

"Stay where you are!" he yelled. "Don't move!"

Although he wasn't their chief warrior either—Dark Storm was—they obeyed him.

Long Arm turned again to the encircling warriors.

"Get back!" he repeated, at the top of his voice. "Get back!"

The first two ranks took a few more steps backward.

Without being told a second time, Thunder Hunter's warriors stood frozen.

Many of the encircling warriors, having by then had a chance to consider what would happen if fighting broke out, were stepping back as much as Long Arm wanted them to do, enlarging the no-man's land, some of them repeating his command over their shoulders to their comrades: "Get back!"

Thunder Hunter's reciprocated, shouting to one another: "Don't move!"

Long Arm wasn't done. At the orchard end of the hill people's army, he walked toward the front line of Lightning Spear's warriors and those of the lesser chieftains.

Approaching the line, he pointed with his spear toward the space between two warriors.

"Separate," he said. "Make a path."

The warriors closest to him did as they were told.

Long Arm began striding in the direction of the orchard, repeating the order.

The warriors again took up his command: "Separate! Make a path!"

An escape route for Thunder Hunter's encircled warriors began to form.

Lightning Spear, Thunder Hunter, and their retinue on their knoll, not unlike the valley people in and above their upper gorge, chose to remain silent, barely breathing.

When the route of escape was sufficiently wide, Long Arm ordered Thunder Hunter's warriors to pass through it.

They obeyed him again, scrupulously heeding his specifications as to how wide their column could be—wide enough to provide them with a sense of safety, yet narrow enough to keep a margin on either side of them guaranteeing no surprise attack by either faction.

Long Arm ordered Thunder Hunter's men to move beyond the "woods." The hill people had no word in their language for "orchard."

Late-afternoon shadows lengthened across the precious fields enemy warriors occupied.

After Thunder Hunter's warriors completed their passage, Long Arm ordered Lightning Spear's and those of the lesser chieftains to withdraw beyond the orchard as well.

As they did so, Long Arm looked up at the rise where Lightning Spear, Thunder Hunter, the lesser chieftains, Heaven's Voice, and the high tellers were standing, apparently as mesmerized into silence by what the chief warrior had done as the valley people were.

He shouted at those above him, surely knowing the valley people were taking great interest in every word he said. "There'll be no more fighting this day," he announced.

*****

The odor of death was beginning to rise from the dead hill warriors in the gorge.

Green Field summoned Fair Judge, who brought with her Rainbow Evening, Gentle Brook, Full Harvest, and the high tellers, who were mostly women now. The regent explained to them what he and Many Numbers wished to order their people's warriors to do.

While they considered the issue, the people who'd been hauling tree limbs and rocks made their way to the gorge with their horses and carts. They'd come to reclaim the missiles the auxiliaries on the cliff had thrown down. They intended to cart the missiles, many of them splattered with the blood of hill warriors, back to the cliff-top, for use in the next day's fighting.

But so many valley people were attempting to enter the gorge to help load the carts, Many Numbers had to order the army to allow only the most able-bodied to pass through. They, of course, were the same younger women, survivors of the plain, and older boys and girls who'd been up on the cliff-top launching tree limbs and boulders and firing lethal arrows.

The warriors didn't just let the auxiliaries enter the gorge. They cheered and embraced them, one after the other, the warriors' caked blood and dirt be damned.

Early Harvest lifted Noon Breeze's brother off his feet, conceding his and the regent's advice to the boy to go home and stay there might've been a mistake.

After Fair Judge and the other tellers gave their assent to the army's plan for the enemy dead, the warriors proceeded to carry it out. Working in pairs, one taking a dead hill man's feet, the other his hands, they carried the bodies to the edge of the river and flung them into it.

What they were doing might've seemed utterly lacking in sympathy, but the truth was to the contrary. Both factions of the hill people's army had pitched their tents the previous evening near the river downstream from the gorge. That's where they were now, with Long Arm no doubt keeping them at a safe distance from one another.

The valley people knew the hill warriors would notice what they were doing and see the bodies of their dead comrades floating toward them. The river that time of the year in their vicinity was languid and low. Without too much effort, even if some of the bodies were sinking before reaching them, they'd be able to retrieve and bury their dead.

200

And, it soon appeared, that's what they were doing.

It's also true there were so many bodies they colored a long stretch of the river, bank to bank, between the gorge and the still-living hill warriors, scarlet.

The valley people saw it, but it gave them no pleasure. They were casting humans into the river as if they were useless dead animals. But it was human blood turning the river red.

*****

The valley people's warriors made the river run red a second time that day. Where it passed the encampments above the gorge, it was also slow, but wide and deep. And that's where they all ended up, washing blood as well as the day's sweat and dirt from their clothing and bodies.

Climbing out of the water, Blue Sky found Autumn Wine waiting for him on the bank.

He was wet and naked, but that didn't stop her from embracing him.

After all, she reminded his snickering comrades, shaking her finger at them, she'd seen him naked in his mother's arms.

"Wandering Star," she began, "even if he is one of them, he's a damned good man."

She pointed her finger in the direction of the hill people's army.

"He told their king the truth," she said. "He split their army. He knew what he was doing. He stopped the battle."

The warriors in the river and the people up and down the bank had turned to hear what she had to say.

"And that Long Arm," she continued. "The one who started this, taking Morning Sun and Rose Leaf from us. When he tells those people what to do, they do it. It's a shame he isn't on our side."

Many of the valley people were saying that.

Having engaged in a prolonged embrace with a wet and naked man in front of a host of curious people, including the man's father and mother, Autumn Wine bade him goodbye and went on her way.

Her grandsons and the mother of her great-grandchildren had spent the day on top of the cliff. They and their comrades, having finished reloading the carts with limbs and rocks for the next day's battle, were coming up from the gorge leading the horses.

Autumn Wine was going to meet them.

They'd surely wish to know how she'd gotten herself so soaked.

They'd just as surely laugh when she told them she was only kissing the regent's son.

And who could blame her for doing it?

He'd killed an astonishing number of hill warriors that day.

Chapter 13

Around the fire that evening, Blue Sky's comrades didn't need any instigation on the part of Noon Breeze. Their revel and those of the warriors and auxiliaries in the encampments on both sides of the river were louder and went on longer than the previous night's.

They'd stopped the hill people in the gorge without losing a single person of their own. They thought the previous night could've been their last, the present night the first of many more.

*****

Many Numbers and Blue Sky were the final two at the fire that evening.

Sometimes in the apprentice tellers' encampment on sunrise pass, Many Numbers and Wandering Star had talked late into the night, long after Blue Sky and Spring Rain had fallen asleep in their hut.

Blue Sky had a question for the chief warrior: "Did you and Wandering Star go together?"

Many Numbers looked at Blue Sky and smiled. "I told him I'd like to go with him."

"What did he say?"

"He said he was quite certain he'd enjoy that."

"So did you? That's what I asked. Did you?"

"No."

"Why not? If you liked one another so much, why didn't you?"

"You. Spring Rain."

Blue Sky laughed. "Those weren't good reasons. You saw us touching one another every chance we got."

"You were both pretty blatant about that. But you hadn't gone together."

"Only because we were fools."

Many Numbers laughed and placed his arm around Blue Sky's shoulders.

"Only because you were in your youth," he said. "The blissful innocence of your youth."

"The blissful ignorance of my youth. You must've had the same problem."

"You could say that."

The chief warrior was looking at Blue Sky again.

"Until you came along," he added.

"Until that day I accosted Spring Rain in the courtyard."

"Until that day."

*****

Even Noon Breeze admitted he'd once fallen in love. As a boy two years shy of his manhood, he'd become enamored of a young teller who regularly visited his family's part of the upper valley. The teller seemed to be as taken as he was. But when Noon Breeze insisted they go together, the teller had, for obvious reasons—not the least of which was the tendency of boys to engage in idle boasting chatter with their friends—turned him down. Instead of considering that the teller might be doing the right thing, Noon Breeze took the refusal as a rejection.

He still hadn't gone with the man until the night before the battle on the plain. The next day, after seeing his friend take a fatal thrust from a hill warrior, Noon Breeze gave him the last of his own water trying to keep him alive. Later, whenever anybody mentioned the man in his presence, Noon Breeze would turn away in tears.

*****

"Now we know better," Blue Sky said.

The campfire was dying. Their comrades were sleeping.

All the supervising and apprentice tellers who'd been in the encampment with Many Numbers and Spring Rain and had helped them evade Law Keeper's preposterous decree keeping them apart were dead now, thanks to the punitive expedition Tall Oak and Sturdy Limb had led to the hill people's plain.

"Now we know better," Many Numbers agreed.

The teller who was willing to let Spring Rain take his place and spend a year on sunrise pass with Blue Sky might've been too old, in the opinion of some people, for another grueling year in the mountains with the apprentice tellers. But he wasn't too old to die on the plain.

"First we suffer youthful infatuations," Blue Sky said, "and then we become Law Keepers."

Many Numbers laughed. "But there's no reason why we can't enjoy the part in between."

*****

In the morning, the people on the cliff-top reported seeing groups of hill warriors leaving their encampments for the forest.

"Hunting parties," Many Numbers was the first to remark.

While Blue Sky and Spring Rain were working on the cliff-top that afternoon, they saw one party bringing back two wild sheep and a deer they'd killed.

A number of hill warriors were wading in the river, spearing fish.

No warning came down from the cliff-top that day. There was no battle to fight.

*****

But shortly after dawn the next day, other news came down.

The valley people ran to the gorge to see for themselves: the hill warriors were striking their tents and assembling near the river.

"There he is," Noon Breeze said, pointing with his spear.

High on a hill on the west side of the river, almost as high as the cliff-top above the gorge, Wandering Star was shielding his eyes from the sun, observing his people's warriors.

"He was right, too," Early Harvest said.

The hill warriors began crossing the river. As low as it was, they still had to swim across most of it. Getting to the other side of the river was much more difficult for them than it would've been for the valley people. Since the hill people didn't build rafts, their warriors couldn't just swim it once. They had to go back and forth, each time taking only as many of their weapons, shields, tents, hides, food, and cooking and eating utensils as they could without drowning.

Many Numbers turned to Green Field. "Wandering Star was right."

*****

Guiding the valley survivors out of his people's land, Wandering Star had questioned them relentlessly, despite their injuries and Blue Sky's imploring him to let them rest. In the apprentice tellers' encampment Wandering Star had heard them speaking of the upper valley. Now he was demanding that Early Harvest, Noon Breeze, and others describe it for him in detail.

After they did, Wandering Star said their people should retreat to the upper valley.

He wasn't lying to his father. He'd rambled all over his people's sides of the mountains surrounding the upper valley as well as the lower valley. So had Long Arm. They both knew how steep the upper-valley mountains were.

"You've got to stop my people's army at the upper gorge," he told the survivors.

He spoke to groups of them stretched out along the path they were taking to get home, explaining, over and over, why that was so important.

"If you can't," he whispered to Blue Sky so the others couldn't hear, "you're all dead."

From many of Wandering Star's questions for Early Harvest, Noon Breeze, and the other upper-valley survivors, Blue Sky concluded he was trying to figure out where the gorge was in relation to the mountains he knew outside the valley. He made them describe the terrain on his people's side of the mountain as they saw it from the encampments. Then he wanted to know how that particular encampment was situated relative to the rest of the valley.

"Oh, I see," he sometimes said, suddenly, in the middle of one of their answers. "I see."

That the valley people had to stop his people in the gorge was the first lesson they needed to learn. The second concerned what would come next if they did stop them in the gorge.

"There's only one place where they might come at you over the mountains," he said. "Long Arm knows where it is. If you stop them in the gorge, they'll go there next."

That was the second place where the valley people would have to stop his father's army. The approach to the valley on the hill people's side in that location was still steep but hardly as precipitous and forbidding as the mountains were elsewhere outside the upper valley.

The valley people had an encampment there. It was on a ridge between two of the higher mountains at the southern end of the western upper-valley forest. They called it "sunset pass."

Reaching it from inside the valley wasn't difficult. The path to it began across the river from the pasture where the valley people had built their new town. Most people could walk up there between dawn and dusk on a long summer day.

On the other hand, if an army were outside the upper valley, say near the gorge, it would take its warriors at least three days, most of that time spent going around the mountains, to get near the same place. It might take a good part of another day for the warriors to crawl to the top.

"What happens then is anybody's guess," Wandering Star said. "You'll have a day to get your warriors up there. You'll have a few more days to prepare for the battle. Think about it."

At first, many of the valley survivors hadn't wanted to think about it. Wandering Star had nevertheless shamed them into doing so. His people had just inflicted severe injuries on them, and yet he dared to bully them with his many questions and insistent conclusions.

Fortunately, his pod tea rendered the survivors as docile as cows, ewes, and nannies when they weren't in heat or defending a threatened calf, lamb, or kid.

"You'll have to stop them there, too," he said. "You'll have to plan for that along with the gorge. You'll have to stop them both places."

They stared at him, dazed by what they'd seen on the plain, by their injuries, by the tea.

"But if you do, your people might survive. Some of you might live to tell about it. You're already heroes. But what good will that do you if all your people die?"

By the end of the second day coming home, they were listening to him.

"If you stop them in the gorge," he said, "you'll be able to tell where they're going next."

He stared at them to make certain they were listening, despite the tea. He drank it himself once and knew what it did to a person.

"The first thing they'll do," he added, almost shouting at the men who'd somehow survived the plain, "they'll cross to the western side of the river."

Alone with him again, Blue Sky was angry. "Why do you need to yell at them?"

And Wandering Star let him know, his eyes flashing, how much that question irked him.

"Why do I have to explain this to you?" he asked. "They're heroes. They survived a horrific battle with my people. Your people will listen to them. That's why I yell at them."

*****

Lightning Spear left a contingent of warriors below the gorge, presumably to keep the enemy warriors from coming out of the upper valley and attacking his army in the rear.

The valley people, though, had no wish to attempt anything of the sort. They'd decided to move their entire army, including the auxiliaries, to sunset pass, taking with them all their horses, their best and strongest oxen, and as many carts as the animals could pull up the mountainside.

A number of the people the army would leave behind—Fair Judge, Gentle Brook, Full Harvest, and Autumn Wine included—would spend most of their days on the cliff-top and in or near the gorge. They were to make themselves visible to the men the hill people had left behind. They'd carry spears taken from dead hill warriors. They'd do their best to strut like warriors who'd killed other humans and could only marvel at the pleasure they'd taken in doing it.

The hill people below the gorge would have to assume, at their distance, the enemy army hadn't moved. In this situation the valley people's partiality for shaven men proved fortuitous, allowing women and young boys as well as old men to pose as warriors.

Their task wasn't trivial. If the contingent of hill warriors below the gorge were to discover all the real warriors and missile-throwers had left to go up the mountains, they could be tempted to launch a surprise attack through the gorge, which could end in the victory they believed the gods had promised them: every farmer dead and the whole promised valley, at long last, theirs again.

*****

The valley people decided Green Field shouldn't fight in any more battles with the hill people. His age and physical condition had nothing to do with their decision. They were saying he was too valuable as the regent of the kingdom. He'd overwhelmingly won the battle at the upper gorge. The valley people didn't want to take any chance he'd be killed.

Noon Breeze said the people simply didn't want to take a chance that Blue Sky, next in the line of succession, would become their regent.

Blue Sky agreed, happily conceding the people had made a wise decision.

It fell to Full Harvest to make known to Green Field, with the whole army present, the people's view of the matter.

"I'm as responsible for this war as anybody," Green Field began his response.

Blue Sky wasn't sure what his father meant by that remark. Green Field and Tall Oak had needlessly abducted Rose Leaf? Green Field had refused to become the kingdom's chief warrior? He and Gentle Brook had raised two spoiled, defiant, and rebellious children?

"Our kings and regents have always fought in our wars," Green Field insisted. "I don't wish to be known in our people's stories as the regent who thought he was too valuable to fight."

"You've earned enough glory as a warrior," Full Harvest countered. "You don't need any more. It's time for you to give up fighting."

The day after Green Field and Tall Oak had returned with Rose Leaf in the last war, they'd tied sheepskins over their wounds and resumed fighting alongside their former comrades.

Green Field had two answers to that: "I don't believe the leader of our people is entitled to less risk of death than anyone else is. But I do believe a kingdom with a coward for a leader is doomed to fail."

Gentle Brook shook her head as if she'd heard a person arguing that the sun rose in the west. "You've killed hill people in two wars now," she loudly declared. "Nobody in their right mind would say you're a coward. If I heard someone call you that, I'd make them eat their words."

The growing crowd wildly cheered those remarks.

The truth was, the last person the people wanted to see die was Green Field. He never would've led the army to the hill people's plain. He'd acceded to his son's and the survivors' pleas to retreat to the upper valley. Everybody could see he'd made all the right decisions.

"Here's how it is," Blue Sky said to his father and the throng. "Many Numbers, Early Harvest, and I have spoken with all the warriors and auxiliaries. They've agreed with us not to let you fight. We're following the will of the people, not yours, on this single point."

And Blue Sky was the one person among his people, as Long Arm was among his, who could say what needed to be said.

"I thank the gods," Gentle Brook addressed the crowd, "for giving me a sensible son."

Spring Rain, standing next to her throughout the proceeding as if she and he were lovers, took her hand.

The crowd once again cheered without restraint.

Green Field stared at his son. "How do you intend to stop me from fighting?" he asked.

"We'll physically restrain you," Blue Sky replied. "Early Harvest and his cousins have offered to tie you to a tree. They'll do it gently, of course. Unless you struggle, you'll feel no pain."

"I thank the gods again," Gentle Brook said to Full Harvest, "for the son they gave you."

Fair Judge, shrugging her shoulders, looked at Green Field.

"I told your son, our chief warrior, and Early Harvest our laws don't allow them to physically restrain a king or regent," she said. "They told me it doesn't matter what our laws let them do. They'll do it anyway."

Green Field glared at Blue Sky, knowing his son had him trapped.

"I realize," he finally said, "it would be selfish of me to find my own son and his allies guilty of treason. Therefore, because any one of their lives is more precious to our people than any personal wish I might have, I'll agree with them and you and no longer fight with the warriors."

What the regent got for that decision was a cheer so loud and sustained the hill people's contingent below the gorge, if not the gods in heaven themselves, surely heard it.

"But as long as I'm able," he clarified, after the cheering had subsided, "I'll fight in all the battles to come in this war."

No cheer, no response of any kind, followed that statement.

Green Field answered the question he couldn't help but see on the face of every person present: "From now on, I'll do my fighting with the auxiliaries."

The people responded to that with their loudest roar of the day.

As Blue Sky and his warrior comrades prepared and served the meal that evening, it was possible every auxiliary came by to personally welcome his father into their ranks, each of them embracing him as they did so.

*****

Early the next morning, the valley warriors and auxiliaries, together with their horses, oxen, and carts, crossed the river on a wide bridge they'd constructed by tying together all the rafts the valley people had. As soon as they made the crossing, they began climbing the path going up the mountainside.

The hill warriors in the contingent below the gorge couldn't see what they were doing.

Reaching their destination late that night, they had no opportunity for sleep before sundown of the next day. They had no choice but to continue their preparations for the arrival of the hill people's army.

It was just as well they had so much to do. In the valley the autumn nights had turned chilly. But on the pass, which was just above the tree line, a cold wind blew after the sun went down. And the valley people had to get by without making a single fire. Wherever the hill warriors were, they might've been able to see the smoke.

When the valley warriors and auxiliaries did get a chance to sleep at the end of their first day on the pass, the wounded men who still had the most healing to do slept in the encampment huts, as Green Field had said they would before they started up the mountainside. The rest of the army slept on and under as many hides as they could find, as close to their comrades as they could get—boys with boys, girls with girls, women with women, men with men, and men with women. Despite the cold, they were physically exhausted, and sleep came quickly.

*****

At the end of their third day on sunset pass, the news sped from the encampment guard post and throughout the army: there was no longer any reason to doubt Wandering Star's prediction.

Far below, the hill people's warriors were coming into view.

Many Numbers went to the guard post, crawling most of the way on his hands and knees.

The guard post was near the center of the pass where the ridge line suddenly jutted toward the hill people's side. If a warrior approached it standing up, persons on that side could see him.

Ordinarily, the valley people's guards on the pass would hope they could be seen, the better to serve as a warning to any hill people in the vicinity not to come near. But the valley people now wished to make it appear as if their army was still resting at the upper gorge.

Accordingly, Green Field and Many Numbers gave strict orders to the warriors and auxiliaries to resist curiosity and not let any part of themselves, not even the tops of their heads, be observed above the ridge. The warriors had piled rocks on the hill people's side of the guard post in such a manner as to create a number of peepholes where their guards could observe the slope below without being seen themselves.

Many Numbers crawled back from the guard post.

The hill warriors were where they'd expected to see them first, based upon what Wandering Star had predicted. They were pitching their tents in a meadow, where they'd undoubtedly remain for the night. They had a long hard climb ahead of them the next day.

Despite their losses on the plain and in the gorge, though, their warriors still greatly outnumbered the valley people's. Many Numbers estimated that if only half of them were able to make it over the top, they'd surely be able to do with the valley people whatever they wished.

The valley people's army resumed their work.

*****

At dawn the next day, the hill people's army started moving up their side of the mountain.

Valley warriors took turns crawling on their hands and knees to the guard post to retrieve the latest information on the enemy's advance.

Several of the warriors waiting to set out for the guard post took exception to the inordinate amount of time their predecessors were wasting at the post, and upon their return, loudly made them aware of their transgressions. At least twice, so far as Blue Sky could see, the angry words led to an exchange of blows and a need for comrades to impose a physical separation.

Noon Breeze blamed the acrimony on their army's not having had a single opportunity for a revel since they started up the mountains.

"It's too damned cold up here at night," he complained, "and there's too damned much work to be done during the day."

"If we get this work done and live," Blue Sky said, "we'll be glad we sacrificed revels."

"If we get this work done and live," Spring Rain added, "we might have some damned good revels—revels we'll never forget."

Noon Breeze turned to Spring Rain.

"I'm going to hold you to that," he said, before turning back to Blue Sky. "And you're not going to stop us, either. I don't care if you are the regent's son. You're nobody special to me."

Blue Sky laughed. "Maybe we should ask Lightning Spear to do to you what he did to Green Field and Tall Oak in the last war."

"Oh, no," Spring Rain moaned, grabbing Noon Breeze and hugging him tightly. "Not Noon Breeze. Not that."

213

Brazenly regarding Blue Sky across the tree they were working on, Noon Breeze smirked.

Blue Sky had put him right where he most wanted to be.

*****

On the other side of the ridge, though, the hill warriors were steadily climbing closer.

To many of the valley people, it was disturbing not to be able to see the enemy with their own eyes. Nevertheless, they could only finish their work, dreaming of their next revel or not.

It was one time Blue Sky was glad his father had become the regent, and the other warriors would let him have his way, as if he were a prince, whether he deserved it or not.

He chose to be the last person to crawl on hands and knees to the guard post, but with ropes tied around his waist. He took his spear with him, too. He wouldn't need to come back for it.

*****

Blue Sky saw what the other observers had seen: the hill people's warriors were climbing the rocky slope as a disciplined army would, keeping themselves tightly together, the strongest and ablest among them giving their comrades a hand whenever they needed it.

The slope on the hill people's side of sunset pass began far below in the meadow where their army had spent the night. Coming up from the meadow, the warriors soon encountered a jumbled landscape in which only a few scraggly shrubs had taken root, and through which there was no continuous path. In many places they had to jump from rock to rock. Sometimes they had to boost one of their warriors to the top of a crevice so that he could reach down and help lift the next one up, each warrior in turn assisting his preceding and following comrades in the same way.

The last tenth of the slope nearest the ridge, though, was hard unbroken rock without boulders or shrubs, as if the gods themselves had swept it clean with brooms.

Soon after Blue Sky arrived at the guard post, the hill people's vanguard started climbing out of the rough terrain onto the bare upper part of the slope. Assembling in at least two times ten ranks across the breadth of the pass from the mountain wall on the north to the similar straight-up-and-down wall on the south, they advanced toward the ridge behind their shields.

They'd left their bows and arrows in the meadow below. Wandering Star had assumed they wouldn't bother exchanging volleys of arrows with the valley people. They'd only need their spears for close fighting to overpower and finally defeat their enemy.

Two days previously, before the hill warriors arrived, Many Numbers had his warriors practicing on the featureless slope. They were on it all afternoon and into the evening as late as the light of the waning moon and the stars allowed. He'd insisted they imagine, and never stop imagining, how it would be when the hill people attacked them, and what they should do.

Starting out with a great many opinions as to what would happen and what should be done, they quickly saw most of them fall by the wayside, and others grow more and more dubious. The few that survived seemed solid enough, but who except a god could say they were certainly right?

Then, too, all the valley army could do was practice and hope for the best. No actual hill warriors were present for the countless fatal wounds the valley warriors were inflicting.

Some of Blue Sky's predecessor lookouts had gotten the impression that, however cautiously the hill warriors were approaching the ridge, they seemed to be assuming nobody was on the other side of it. If so, the valley army's efforts to conceal its presence hadn't been wasted.

Blue Sky could hear the hill warriors.

They were exchanging the usual remarks questioning the manhood of their adversaries. Maybe they'd failed to notice that in the battle in the gorge a number of the valley army's most lethal fighters— those on the cliff-top—weren't claiming anything in that regard.

The hill warriors guffawed at a comrade's suggestion that Thunder Hunter could soon have his way with the mangled and lifeless body of the son of the thieves' regent. They had good reason to be cheerful. They believed they were about to enter the upper valley unopposed.

The hill people didn't have oxen and horses. They couldn't imagine carefully looping one end of a vine and leather rope around an animal and the other end around the felled trunk of a tall and sturdy evergreen, which grew plentifully not too far below on the valley people's side of sunset pass. They couldn't imagine expecting a log to go anywhere they didn't drag it themselves, certainly not up the side of a mountain, certainly not in fearsome numbers piled end to end just below the valley people's side of the ridge.

The hill warriors were as human as the valley people, Blue Sky knew, and so their joyful anticipation of an easy entry to the valley and their ultimate victory thereafter was pleasant to hear.

But it was also true they were coming to kill the valley people. And not only the valley warriors, their king had vowed, but their old men, women, and children as well.

Therefore, at the appointed time, when the front line of the hill warriors came within two house-lengths of the ridge, Blue Sky pulled on one of the ropes he'd dragged down to the post.

At his end of it, Many Numbers pulled back.

Blue Sky yanked on it again, confirming it was the signal his people were waiting for.

*****

As evergreen trunks came thundering over the ridge, the front ranks of the hill warriors froze.

A moment later, screaming in panic, they turned and ran, many of them colliding with their comrades in the ranks behind them.

Some had already fallen when the first volley of trees hit them.

Some were lucky, and the trees hit on the rocky surface and bounced over them.

The second volley, though, flattened a number of those who'd been spared, even as the first volley caught up with the panicked warriors farther down the slope fighting their comrades to escape.

The valley army sent a third volley over the ridge, felling every hill warrior left standing or kneeling on the upper slope.

Behind the third volley, all the valley warriors scrambled over the ridge.

Blue Sky leapt out of the guard-post. Spring Rain, Many Numbers, and the apprentice tellers were on one side of him. Noon Breeze, Early Harvest, Good Harvest, and the upper-valley cousins were on the other. They were the center of a rank of valley warriors between the mountain walls defining the pass. And that single rank included every warrior the valley army had.

Moving down the slope as they'd practiced, they finished off the fallen hill warriors. The trees killed very few of them outright, but left many maimed and immobile.

The first warrior Blue Sky reached, lying flat on his back and apparently unable to move either his arms or his legs, was begging, in the hill people's language, for death.

Blue Sky obliged him, swinging his spear and slitting the man's throat.

The rolling trees had only stunned some of the hill warriors. The valley warriors surrounded them as they struggled to their feet, picking them off one by one.

The valley warriors worked their way down the slope, thrusting and slashing, soaking themselves once again in the plentiful blood of hill warriors.

Spring Rain and Blue Sky would kill one warrior, Noon Breeze and Blue Sky the next.

From one end of their line to the other, the valley warriors methodically slaughtered their adversaries. Many Numbers had told them they wouldn't be fighting on the slope just to keep their enemy out of the upper valley.

They needed also, he insisted, yelling at them as Wandering Star would, to make the battle so costly the hill people would never consider attacking them on sunset pass again.

The surviving hill warriors, though, were regrouping in the rough terrain where they'd fled to safety.

The valley people had anticipated a large number of them would be able to reach that part of the slope, jump into its many fissures, and watch the timbers bounce over them.

Finishing off the last of the fallen hill warriors, the valley warriors drew so near to the surviving hill warriors in the crevices at the boundary between the upper slope and the rough lower slope they could hear what their opponents were saying.

The valley warriors who understood the hill people's language shushed their comrades and listened.

The hill warriors were noting that even if the thieves did hold the higher ground, they obviously didn't have enough warriors to keep the valley's rightful owners from getting over the ridge. The thieves had also ventured much too far down the slope. They were hopelessly exposed.

The only thing that bothered the hill warriors was the line of people at the top of the ridge.

"They're women, children, old men," one of them pointed out.

"They haven't got spears," another noted.

"What good will the ropes do them?" one asked.

The valley warriors had no more fallen hill warriors to dispatch. They stood in one unbroken line just above and facing the rough terrain. Nobody in their line spoke.

Nor did any of the auxiliaries on the ridge.

The hill warriors themselves stopped talking, out loud at least.

The valley warriors could no longer hear them.

Suddenly, one of the hill warriors near their center gave the command: "Attack!"

That was Long Arm. His order echoed on either side of him to his comrades.

Hill warriors began climbing out of their crevices.

Many Numbers gave the signal for his side: "Retreat!"

The valley people had imagined the surviving hill warriors would hope to chase them up the slope and over the ridge; easily slaughter the outnumbered valley warriors as they lost the advantage of higher ground on the other side; massacre the valley women, old men, and children; take the upper valley in the name of Lightning Spear; and never need to fight a war with the thieves again.

The valley warriors therefore turned their vulnerable backs to their opponents, and the auxiliaries drew taut the ropes tied around their waists.

Green Field had decreed that each warrior had to have at least two ropes in case one of them snapped. Auxiliaries on the ridge, in groups of three to six, depending upon their size and strength and the size of the warrior they were assisting, held the other ends of the ropes.

This is what they'd endlessly practiced two days before—climbing back up the steep slope and staying ahead of the hill warriors, and out of harm's way, with the aid of the ropes.

The auxiliaries needed to keep the ropes tight enough to give the warriors the advantage of their pulling, but loose enough not to pull the warriors off their feet.

In their first attempts, many warriors stumbled and ended up on their bellies, a few of the harder falls resulting in loud expressions of anger.

But the people controlling a warrior's lines tended to be his mate, lover, brothers, sisters, cousins, and neighbors—even in some cases, including Blue Sky's, fathers. They plainly didn't wish to be responsible for letting the hill people subject their lovers, kin, and friends to a horrific death for all of them to see.

Blue Sky heard no one grumble about the lateness of the practice or Many Numbers' loud and relentless insistence on caution.

It soon became apparent in practice that some of the auxiliaries had the right combination of strength and feel for the job, but they weren't evenly dispersed along the line.

Blue Sky asked Autumn Wine's grandsons, who'd insisted on pulling his ropes, to help two other warriors whose auxiliaries didn't include any pullers with their ability. Blue Sky assured them the regent and the two remaining boys from their village were more than sufficient for him.

The other warriors with a surfeit of talented auxiliaries did likewise.

Eventually, Many Numbers was satisfied all their warriors had, as Green Field had insisted upon, "a fairly equivalent chance to live or die."

That's the way it had to be, the army agreed, knowing they had no warriors to squander.

Now the auxiliaries were pulling the warriors up the slope once again, but this time it was no practice, and the hill warriors were in fact pursuing them.

This time, too, the valley warriors occasionally had to scramble over the bodies of dead and dying hill warriors. In order to practice that aspect of the battle, the auxiliaries had taken turns lying on the slope, pretending they were dead hill warriors.

The warriors learned they had to keep their eyes fixed on the slope directly in front of them.

The other thing they needed to do, using their peripheral vision, was to stay in line with their comrades.

Despite their panicked response to the valley army's onslaught of trees, the hill warriors who'd survived them had regained their initial discipline, maintaining a coherent front. A number of them might've been able to scramble up the slope ahead of the rest and plant their spears in some enemy backs. They were resisting, though, any temptation they might've had to do that.

That was what renewed confidence in the inevitability of ultimate victory could do for an army. When an enemy's warriors turned their backs and ran, rendering their spears useless for defense, victory was almost always near.

In the eyes of the hill people, the farmers had left their warriors—all of them at one time—defenseless to a counterattack. The people up on the ridge pulling on the ropes must've been engaged in some equally absurd enterprise. The ropes no doubt helped their warriors climb the slope faster than the hill warriors could, but they were only prolonging their certain defeat.

This, in the eyes of the hill warriors, was a rout.

The valley warriors could run as fast, and with as much assistance of the ropes, as they wished. The far more numerous hill warriors would eventually catch up to, overwhelm, and kill them all.

And that's how the valley army had hoped the hill army would envision it.

Out of the corners of his eyes, Blue Sky could see their supposedly retreating warriors were moving up the slope as they'd finally mastered it in their practices. They were keeping the remaining distance at any point between their line and the ridge ahead approximately the same, even as they were everywhere increasing the distance between their line and the hill warriors behind them.

But, like all their warriors, Blue Sky was mostly keeping his eyes on the slope in front of him. A warrior might stumble now and then, but he didn't want to fall.

Tumbling to the ground without quickly regaining an upright posture could get him killed.

220

If he got too far behind his neighboring comrades, they were required to keep moving up the slope with the line and not come back to help him. But no warrior wanted to put his comrades through that. They'd lament his gruesome death, and their own inability to help him, until the end of their days.

As the valley warriors had meticulously practiced, they reached the ridge simultaneously, and their rope pullers made way for them by moving down their side of the ridge.

The valley warriors climbed over a fourth row of evergreen trunks now lying where their first row had lain, just over the top of the valley people's side of the ridge—and just out of sight of the hill warriors.

Valley warriors and auxiliaries pushed against the timbers, rolling them over the ridge top.

Without looking down the other side but hearing the renewed screams of hill warriors they'd hoped for, they got behind a fifth row of trees and rolled them to the top of the ridge.

When they had them balanced on the ridge in a line—and they could see hill warriors lying maimed on their side of the mountain and others panicked again, crowded together, vying with one another for position—they gave the trees, on their chief warrior's command, a push.

After helping the auxiliaries roll a sixth and final row of trees over the ridge, the valley people's warriors started down the slope as they'd done before.

Once again, no hill warrior was left standing on the upper part of the slope. All the hill warriors who could still maintain an upright position were in the rough lower terrain.

"There he is," Spring Rain said to Blue Sky, pointing toward the southern mountain wall.

Wandering Star was standing on a ledge alone—it was difficult to see how he'd gotten there—staring at them.

The valley people looked back at him but hardly knew what to think. They were repaying his obvious affection for them by killing and maiming a great many of his kinsmen.

Why, Blue Sky couldn't help but wonder, would benevolent gods put humans in a position where they had to kill people they could love as if they were their own?

221

Chapter 14

As the valley warriors had done before, they ran down the slope from one fallen hill warrior to the next, finishing them off.

It wasn't so simple this time. The newly fallen were lying among the hill warriors the valley warriors had finished off after the first assault. The valley warriors had to turn a great many of them over to get a better look, and determine whether they were dead or about to die.

The battles in the stories their gods had given the valley people—and the hill people, Blue Sky had discovered—never described parts such as these. The gods must've realized very few of their human underlings, after hearing what actually happened in a battle, would wish to fight another one.

Unless they were under some dire threat to kill their entire people, how could humans examine other humans for a sign of life—a pulse or a breath—only to snuff it out?

*****

Another instruction Many Numbers enjoined his warriors not to forget that day concerned the extent of their battlefield. They were not, under any circumstances, to pursue the hill people beyond the featureless upper part of the slope.

The reason for the rule was clear. The valley people could see it from the ridge. The rugged lower slope had too many uncertainties—too many washes and gullies for an adversary to hide in, too many boulders and blind corners for him to conceal himself behind.

When the valley warriors got near that border, though, a fallen hill warrior suddenly stood up and confronted Noon Breeze, striking his spear against Noon Breeze's with such force that Noon Breeze fell to his knee.

Early Harvest from his side of Noon Breeze, and Blue Sky from his, charged the hill warrior, who quickly realized he couldn't possibly defend against them both.

He turned and ran.

He fled toward the nearest drop-off into the lower slope. Noon Breeze, having righted himself, with Early Harvest and Blue Sky close behind, gave chase.

Just as the man reached the cleft, and leapt, Noon Breeze thrust his spear, sinking it into his opponent's back.

Noon Breeze, whose agility often made up for his lack of brawn but not for his lack of good judgment and his overabundance of daring, clung to his spear and flew over the edge of the cleft on top of the hill warrior, his feet on the man's buttocks, riding him down.

The nearest valley comrades on the slope, as well as those on the ridge behind them, sent up a shrill cry of alarm.

Reaching the crevice themselves, Blue Sky and Early Harvest could fully appreciate the wisdom of Many Numbers' instruction. Other wounded hill warriors were cowering there.

Three of them confronted the sudden intruder, Noon Breeze, in their sanctuary.

Blue Sky and Early Harvest jumped over the edge, as did Good Harvest.

"No!" Many Numbers screamed. "No!"

Blue Sky landed awkwardly on a big rock, taking the blow with his left arm.

As if the day's battle and the sudden turn of events had addled him, one of the hill warriors wildly thrust his spear in the direction of Good Harvest.

"No!" Many Numbers and Spring Rain were screaming. "No! No! No!"

Noon Breeze withdrew his spear from his opponent's back. He and his comrades had the hill warriors outnumbered four to three.

The two comrades of the wild-eyed hill warrior pulled him back, and the three of them wisely made no further attempt to attack their adversaries.

Blue Sky could see why Many Numbers was screaming. Others of their people's warriors, having witnessed the regent's son, Early Harvest, and his cousin jumping over the edge into the treacherous lower slope, were following suit.

They were also encountering hill warriors, some of whom, believing they were cornered and had nothing to lose, were choosing to stand and fight.

The valley warriors were still badly outnumbered. If they attempted to fight their opponents in the crevices, they could quickly and easily turn victory into total defeat.

"Let them go!" Blue Sky yelled as loudly as he could in the hill people's language. "Let them go!" he repeated in his people's language.

Early Harvest, realizing what Blue Sky was doing, promptly echoed him.

Their people's warriors on both sides of them repeated what they'd said.

"Retreat!" Blue Sky shouted in the hill people's language. "Retreat!" he repeated, using his own people's words.

That plea, cast as an order, also sped out to both ends of the valley people's line.

"Go!" he yelled in the hill people's language to the three warriors who'd come to confront Noon Breeze. "Go!"

That, as well, went out to the comrades.

"Let them go!" he yelled in the hill people's language. "Let them go!" he yelled in his.

Up and down the line, the hill warriors were backing away from the valley warriors.

Up and down the line, the valley warriors were choosing not to pursue them.

As their opponents disappeared deeper into the lower-slope labyrinth, the valley warriors climbed out of it and back onto the upper slope, where nobody could hide and surprise them.

Having called for a cease-fire themselves, and the hill warriors having accepted it, Early Harvest, Good Harvest, and Noon Breeze quickly agreed with Blue Sky they couldn't finish off the hill warrior Noon Breeze had chased over the edge.

He looked as if he might survive. Noon Breeze's spear had left an ugly wound in his back, but there was no blood coming out of his nose or mouth.

Blue Sky and his comrades gave the man water and sat him up against the rock Blue Sky had landed on. They hoped the wounded hill man's comrades would come back for him.

Blue Sky also hoped the wounded hill man would survive the battle on sunset pass. Despite the valley people's killing trees, he came much too close to winning the battle for his people.

And he would've accomplished that heroic feat by doing nothing more than making an unexceptional attempt to save his own life.

*****

Early Harvest, Good Harvest, Noon Breeze, and Blue Sky climbed out of the crevice into which they'd unwisely leapt. Spring Rain and Early Harvest's cousins helped pull them up.

"Report missing warriors!" Many Numbers yelled.

As their warriors duly repeated his order to those away from the center of the line, Blue Sky caught the chief warrior with his good arm and clung to him.

The order required their warriors to look to their left and right to ascertain whether their nearest neighbors on either side of them were present. If they were, a warrior said and did nothing. Only if a neighbor was missing, was he to call out that person's name.

As was proper, the two farthest echoes of the order, the last, were voiced simultaneously.

Then came a fearful pause.

The only thing the valley people wanted to hear in response to the command was silence. But in view of what had happened, it was impossible not to dread hearing names of comrades.

A persistent silence—a silence that grew more joyful the longer it lasted—is what they got in lieu of names.

Many Numbers nodded his head, and a roar went up from the warriors.

"This renews my faith in the gods," Spring Rain said, embracing Many Numbers and Blue Sky at the same time. "They do love us after all. I've always said that."

*****

Using his right arm only, Blue Sky carefully pulled Many Numbers away from the others.

226

"I'm begging you," he whispered. "Don't punish Noon Breeze."

"He disobeyed the most important order of them all," Many Numbers said, holding his voice down, gritting his teeth. "For that, I'm throwing him out of the army."

"I'm begging you not to."

"That was a crucial order. You saw what happened. If we'd started fighting them down there, and if the retreating hill warriors had come back, they would've wiped us out."

"But that didn't happen," Blue Sky countered.

"Only because you and Early Harvest didn't let it happen."

"Early Harvest and I also disobeyed your order. Will you punish us, too?"

The second part of the order required their warriors to utterly forsake anybody who foolishly chose to disobey the first part of it.

"But what were we supposed to do?" Blue Sky asked. "Watch the hill warriors kill him?"

Many Numbers looked at Blue Sky, scowling.

"Good Harvest and all those other warriors violated the order, too," Blue Sky said. "They thought they were supposed to do it. They saw Early Harvest and the regent's son do it."

The warriors and auxiliaries knew what was going on between Many Numbers and Noon Breeze. They'd made up jokes they passed around about the strange relationship between the most serious person in the kingdom and the least.

"Are you going to punish all of them, too?" Blue Sky asked.

Many Numbers took a deep breath.

"No," he replied. "Of course not."

"Then don't punish Noon Breeze, either."

The cheering among the valley warriors and auxiliaries had faded away to silence. They'd taken notice of the discussion between the chief warrior and the regent's son. They stared at them, straining to hear what they were saying, attempting to read their lips. Some of them could.

"All the army love him," Blue Sky said. "All the people, too. They love him. He left his family to become a teller. He survived the battle on the plain. They need to continue loving him."

227

Noon Breeze was standing between Early Harvest and Spring Rain, staring at Many Numbers and Blue Sky. He damned well knew he was the subject of their discussion.

"He only did what my father and Tall Oak did in the last war," Blue Sky pleaded. "They disobeyed the king's order, but that's never stopped the people from insisting they were heroes."

Many Numbers glanced up at Green Field, standing on the ridge with the auxiliaries, all of them waiting in silence like their warrior comrades to hear what came next.

"Everybody will know Noon Breeze disobeyed your order," Blue Sky said. "Those who saw what happened will tell the others. They'll also know we could've traded victory for defeat, thanks to him. Noon Breeze already knows that. What's the point of punishment?"

"You want me to do nothing about it?" Many Numbers asked.

"We won anyway," Blue Sky replied. "All our warriors survived."

Many Numbers looked at the warriors. A few of them were injured.

Good Harvest, who'd come of age that autumn, appeared to have suffered a severe wound in his thigh from the confused hill warrior's thrashing about in the crevice.

"More than anything else, the people need a victory," Blue Sky said. "A clear, unsullied victory. They don't need punishment. No matter how much Noon Breeze might deserve it, the people don't need it."

Many Numbers straightened himself up and faced the warriors.

"Move back to the ridge," he ordered, first to his left and then to his right.

Noon Breeze approached Blue Sky, knowing the regent's son had successfully argued his case.

"You hurt your arm," he said.

With his other arm, Blue Sky pulled Noon Breeze toward him until their faces touched.

"Just promise me one thing," the regent's son whispered. "Promise me you'll behave yourself from now on."

The pain coursing through his injured arm that moment brought tears to his eyes.

"I'm sorry I caused your injury," Noon Breeze apologized. He had as many tears in his eyes as Blue Sky had in his.

*****

Those of the valley warriors who could make it up the slope on their own took off their ropes. They looped Blue Sky's around Early Harvest and Noon Breeze, who were carrying Good Harvest on a hastily improvised sling made of spears and garments. Other warriors likewise lent their ropes and pullers to those who needed them most.

The valley warriors were more than halfway to the ridge when the auxiliaries began shouting and pointing toward the slope behind them.

Turning, Blue Sky saw what the commotion was all about.

Long Arm stood alone, facing the valley warriors, above the crevice at the boundary between the upper slope and the rough terrain. He carried neither weapons nor shield.

"I'll go speak with him," Blue Sky said to Many Numbers, handing his spear to Spring Rain and starting down the slope before the chief warrior had a chance to say no.

As he approached Long Arm, the man remained motionless, observing him.

Standing alone, in the open, without a shield, he was taking a chance one or more of the valley people on the ridge might fire arrows that found their mark. Blue Sky assumed he was aware by then the valley people weren't so foolish as to wish to kill Lightning Spear's admirable chief warrior—unless they had to, in a battle. Still, Long Arm's doing what he did required uncommon courage, and both his people and Blue Sky's knew it.

As Blue Sky drew closer, he saw intense sorrow unblemished by tears on Long Arm's face.

"We wish to retrieve our dead comrades," Long Arm said, speaking the valley people's language.

There was no reason except malice itself why the valley people would attempt to stop the hill people from doing that.

"Have your people come up here without their spears," Blue Sky said, speaking the hill people's language.

Long Arm glanced up at the valley people's warriors on the slope.

All of them, and all the auxiliaries behind them, were staring at him and Blue Sky.

"How will we know they won't attack us?" he asked, in the valley people's language.

"They'll withdraw to the ridge," Blue Sky replied.

Long Arm examined the slope above them.

"They'll still be close enough to attack us," he said.

"I'll stay here with you," Blue Sky offered. "You know my father is our people's regent. If my people attack your people, you can kill me."

Long Arm allowed himself the slightest possibility of a smile. He understood Blue Sky wasn't putting his life at risk. He knew there would be no attack.

*****

Hill warriors, having come up the slope without their spears, were dragging their dead comrades away.

Late in the afternoon that early autumn day, the valley people's warriors and auxiliaries stood in a line on the ridge, watching and waiting in silence.

Blue Sky mentioned to Long Arm the injured hill warrior he and his warriors had left propped up against a rock.

Long Arm ordered his warriors to find the man and carry him down the mountain.

Long Arm still had a question. "Why didn't you finish him off?"

"There was no point to it," Blue Sky replied. "The battle was over."

Long Arm asked to see Blue Sky's arm.

Blue Sky took off his shirt and showed it to him. Any other time Blue Sky would've enjoyed feeling the autumn sun on his body.

"You broke a bone," Long Arm said in the matter-of-fact way he spoke. "It needs to be set. I'll do it for you."

Long Arm was speaking the valley people's language.

Then Blue Sky realized why he was doing it. Long Arm didn't want his people to know what he and Blue Sky were talking about.

From then on, Blue Sky spoke in the valley people's language as well.

Using the head of a spear one of his slain comrades had dropped, Long Arm cut several leather strips from the garments of the same comrade, and fashioned splints from the spear shaft. He fetched a cup of Wandering Star's pod tea from a comrade, and gave it to Blue Sky to drink.

He held Blue Sky's arm against the hard surface of the slope.

Blue Sky's comrades stood shoulder-to-shoulder on the ridge with his father, viewing a scene they'd had no reason to believe they'd see in their lifetimes. A hill warrior they initially abhorred but then came to admire was caring for their regent's injured son.

When Blue Sky thought he was ready, he told Long Arm to do what he needed to do.

Long Arm did so, pressing Blue Sky's arm back into its proper shape.

Blue Sky screamed.

Holding Blue Sky's arm in place with his foot, Long Arm tied the leather strips around the splints.

When Long Arm was done, Blue Sky lay on the ground, whimpering like a child.

Some of the nearby hill warriors snickered.

Blue Sky could scarcely blame them. He was still alive to sob over a mere injured arm, quite unlike the throat-slit comrades they'd come to retrieve.

Long Arm wrapped Blue Sky's shirt around him. Because Blue Sky was still shivering, Long Arm took a bloody deerskin shirt from the body of another of his dead comrades and wrapped that as well around the son of the regent of his people's eternal enemy.

*****

Blue Sky sat up. He thought he must've fallen asleep. He blinked his eyes.

"You passed out," Long Arm said. "From the pain."

He held the cup of pod tea to the regent's son's lips.

231

"Morning Sun, your prince," he said, suddenly, "he claims you're his best friend."

"Do you see him?" Blue Sky asked.

"Every day," Long Arm replied. "He lives with my family. He frequently speaks of you. He knows what happened to your people's army. He knows you and your father are still alive. He knows his own father, his uncle, and his cousins are dead. He knows your father is the regent in his absence. Wandering Star told him all of that."

"Is he well?" Blue Sky asked.

"He's very well," Long Arm replied stiffly, almost as if Blue Sky's inquiry offended him. "My family treats him as if he's one of our own."

Lightning Spear's chief warrior watched the tears run down Blue Sky's face.

"They've grown fond of your people's prince," he added. "Quite fond of him."

Blue Sky could've guessed—but hadn't—that might happen.

"Your princess?" Blue Sky asked. "We called her Rose Leaf. Do you see her?"

"She insists we call her Rose Leaf, too. She also lives with my family. Our people were surprised to find out she and your prince could speak our language—thanks to you and Wandering Star."

The sun was making its first contact with the western horizon, and Long Arm's men were still dragging away their dead.

"She thought you were her brother," Long Arm said. "She often talks about you and your father and mother. She misses you, but she's glad to know you're all still alive. She's convinced my family that you and some of the other farmers aren't really our enemies. Nor is your prince."

"I wish all your people knew that."

"Maybe someday they will."

The pod tea might have been responsible for Blue Sky's next question: "Do Rose Leaf and Morning Sun spend time together alone?"

Long Arm glanced at his comrades. "Lightning Spear is adamant on that point. He says we can never let it happen."

Even though they were speaking in the valley people's language, Blue Sky whispered his response: "I imagine it would be best then if Lightning Spear didn't know."

"My family and I realize what we did to your prince and our princess was wrong," Long Arm said. "We attempt to make it up to them however we can. We no longer view them as enemies. They've become part of our family. We didn't intend for that to happen. But it did."

So Blue Sky sat in the dying autumn sun in the company of the man the hill people considered the greatest hero their people had ever known—because of the enormous wrong he'd done to the valley people's prince and their own princess.

And Blue Sky was openly weeping.

Long Arm stared at him unblinking. "I apologize for spying on you and Wandering Star. I never should've done that. If I hadn't, none of this would've happened."

Blue Sky shook his head. "You didn't know what would happen. None of us did."

"What I did was wrong," Long Arm insisted. "I spied on you. I spied on two people who had every reason to believe they were alone and nobody could hear them. My people's tellers say it wasn't wrong. Wandering Star was an exile, they say, and you were a farmer. But I know that can't make it right. You were two humans talking about what mattered to you most. Using what you said, I abducted your best friend and the woman you thought was your sister. I stole them from their homeland. Neither of them had done anything to deserve what I did to them. I have a lot to answer for."

He nodded toward his people's warriors, carrying away the last of their dead comrades.

"And look what good it's done my people," he said.

*****

The valley people had fires that evening, lots of them. Hot water, too. Spring Rain helped Blue Sky wash the hill people's blood off his body.

Noon Breeze came to tell Blue Sky the oxen and drivers were ready. They were taking the injured warriors down to the valley. All

Blue Sky had to do was climb into a cart. His comrades would see to it that his hides, weapons, and other possessions got into the cart with him.

Blue Sky was lying on and under hides near a big fire the apprentice tellers had made.

"I'm not going down to the valley," he told Noon Breeze.

Green Field and Many Numbers had decided the army should remain at the pass for at least two more nights. They assumed the hill people wouldn't attempt another attack the next day, but they couldn't be certain.

Blue Sky had informed Long Arm, in passing, that his people had "many more" volleys of trees ready at the ridge. In truth, they only had six.

Blue Sky had also told Long Arm the valley people had a particularly good reason for hoping the hill people wouldn't attack them again at the upper gorge or sunset pass: they didn't wish to see Long Arm or his brothers and cousins killed.

"Many Numbers insists you go," Spring Rain said.

Blue Sky shook his head. "If the army stays here, I stay here."

"I'll get Many Numbers," Noon Breeze said. "He isn't going to like this."

"He's busy," Blue Sky said. "Don't bother him. He has a kingdom to run. My father and Fair Judge can't do it all by themselves. Just tell the drivers to leave without me."

"They won't," Spring Rain said. "Many Numbers said you had to go with them."

"Then they'll have to take me by force," Blue Sky insisted. "I won't give up without a fight. I'm not the reasonable man my father is. I'm stubborn and proud."

The apprentice tellers, eating their evening meal and drinking wine, snickered.

"Get Many Numbers," Spring Rain said to Noon Breeze.

Autumn Wine's younger grandson, who was one of the drivers, had promised Blue Sky he'd go see Rainbow Evening and Gentle Brook as soon as he returned to the valley. He was to tell them Long Arm's family were taking good care of Morning Sun and Rose Leaf, who were so far from the battles fought to determine their fate they

234

probably couldn't imagine, outside a horrific dream, what had happened in them.

Autumn Wine's younger grandson told Blue Sky he understood why it would be important for Rainbow Evening and Gentle Brook to hear his message. He also said he was pleased Blue Sky had chosen him to deliver it.

"You'll be a lot more comfortable in the valley," one of the apprentice tellers said to Blue Sky. "Warmer, for sure. You can recuperate inside a house."

"You can stay with your mother," Spring Rain offered.

Blue Sky pointed his cup in the direction of the apprentice tellers.

"Could I have a bit more of your wine?" he asked them. "I seem to be empty. I don't know why I'm so thirsty this evening."

One of them brought over their jug and refilled his cup, not for the first time that evening.

Many Numbers and Noon Breeze soon came to the fire.

"I told you to get into a cart," Many Numbers said to the regent's son.

Blue Sky laughed. "And I, chief warrior, am refusing to get into a cart."

The apprentice tellers resumed snickering.

"No," Blue Sky continued, "I won't go voluntarily. I'm afraid you'll have to order your warriors here to tie me up and throw me into the cart."

"We'll do it, too," Noon Breeze loudly promised.

Blue Sky and the apprentice tellers guffawed at that.

At the moment, though, Spring Rain seemed to have no sense of humor whatsoever. Done with Blue Sky, he was washing the blood and dirt off his own body with clean hot water.

"This man broke his arm," he said, pointing his finger at Blue Sky and glaring at Noon Breeze, "in order to save your life. And that was the second time he saved your life, too."

"You can't blame Noon Breeze for that," Blue Sky interjected, softly. "I'm supposed to save lives. My own misbehavior brought this war on. What else can I do? Noon Breeze isn't responsible. He's innocent. And I really have no choice in the matter. It must be what your gods want me to do. When they tell me to jump into a crevice, I do it. I don't think about it."

The apprentice tellers seemed much more interested right then in the unclothed Spring Rain, washing himself, than either the roast beef, onions, and cheese sauce they were eating or the nonsense Blue Sky was spouting.

"Here's what I think," one of them had the temerity to say, taking advantage of Blue Sky's intoxication on wine and pod tea. "He just wants to spend the night with Spring Rain."

Blue Sky and the apprentice tellers laughed.

"Who doesn't want that?" one of them asked.

Many Numbers, as if saddened to see wine drooling from Blue Sky's lips, shook his head.

"Are you telling me you aren't injured severely enough to ride in a cart?" he asked. "If you aren't, you'll have to stay up here and go home when the army goes home. You'll walk down the mountain with the other warriors, too. No carts will be available to carry you. Nobody will help you. If you pass out again, the other warriors will walk around you. They'll leave you where you fall. Is that what you want?"

"Very much so," Blue Sky affirmed.

"I won't be walking around him," Spring Rain snapped.

Spring Rain, of course, could talk back to the chief warrior as much as he pleased, but he rarely took this liberty in front of others.

"Fine," Many Numbers replied. "I'll let you stop for him. I'll also hold you personally responsible for his safe return to the valley."

"Oh, hell," an apprentice teller said, "we'll get him back to the valley."

"That's fine, too," Many Numbers quickly responded. "You apprentice tellers will also be exempt from my order to step around him. You'll have to pick him up if need be and carry him. I'll hold each of you responsible for making certain the regent's son, of all people, gets back to the valley alive."

"Let's hear it," another apprentice teller said, "for the regent's son."

His comrades, laughing, sent up a loud cheer.

Blue Sky thought he was seeing and hearing the reason for his existence. The gods could never give him more than what his comrades had.

236

Even living in a fertile valley wasn't a greater gift than being a comrade. The old men who'd gone to the guard posts knew that.

Many Numbers turned to Noon Breeze. "Tell the drivers to go without him."

"Thank you," Blue Sky said to Many Numbers. "That's very good of you. So thoughtful. You're a kind-hearted chief warrior. The one before you wasn't like that, I'm sorry to say."

The apprentice tellers sent up another cheer, this time for the current chief warrior.

They'd heard all the dark stories condemning Sturdy Limb, who was no longer around to defend himself—to explain in particular why he'd had ample cause one spring day in the courtyard to attempt to impose order on an unruly, unthinking mob, and to arrest Green Field's son, the impulsive, loudmouth fool who'd fancied himself to be that mob's leader.

The cheeky apprentice teller had guessed one of the reasons Blue Sky had insisted on staying in the mountains. He did wish to sleep next to Spring Rain.

He also wanted to share a fire with his comrades, all of them still alive after another day of bloody battle—and hear them laugh.

*****

The sentries called the valley army to the ridge the next morning.

Behind them, the sun was breaking over the eastern mountains.

The meadow far below on the hill people's side of the pass was still in the twilight before dawn, but the valley people could make out what their warriors were doing.

They were taking down their tents and putting out their fires.

It soon became apparent they were leaving the way they'd come.

*****

After setting Blue Sky's arm the previous evening on the slope, Long Arm, staring at the valley people's warriors and auxiliaries on the ridge line, startled the regent's son.

"You don't have enough warriors to break out of your upper valley," Long Arm said. "And you won't have enough to do that for at least another generation."

"Enough, though," Blue Sky said, "to keep your warriors out of it for another generation."

"More than enough for that," Long Arm agreed.

Long Arm's comrades were carrying the last of their dead down the mountain.

"And neither you nor I," Long Arm added, "wants to see one more warrior killed."

"Neither of us," Blue Sky agreed. "Not one more."

In the evening shadows at the end of a summer day in a ravine on a mountain pass, the two of them had begun the hostilities between their peoples.

Then, in the evening at the close of an autumn day on another mountain pass, the hill people's rightful hero helped the son of the valley people's regent, despite his pod-tea intoxication, to his feet.

They embraced—in sight of all the people who'd taken part in the fighting that day and survived it—and brought the killing to an end.

CHARACTER LIST

Spoiler alert: some of the information in this list gives away the plot of the first Promised Valley novel, *Promised Valley Rebellion.* If you wish to read about the rebellion before you read about the war, you shouldn't peruse this list until you've enjoyed all the surprises and reversals in the rebellion story.

Valley People

Autumn Wine: Green Field and Gentle Brook's elderly neighbor. Her two grandsons, orphaned in the last war with the hill people, live with her. Despite the unusual number of years she's lived, she's remained vital in both her body and mind. Having suffered profoundly in the last war with the hill people, she finds it difficult to think well of them. Her older grandson's lover is a young woman whose family and undesirable husband are wealthy and influential town people.

Blue Sky: Green Field and Gentle Brook's son and Rose Leaf's brother. He's also the best friend of the prince, Morning Sun. When Rose Leaf, Blue Sky, and Morning Sun came of age, the king, Tall Oak, refused to permit Morning Sun and Rose Leaf to marry and have children together. He also refused to explain his incomprehensible decree. That provoked Blue Sky into leading a rebellion against the king and the officials he'd appointed to run the kingdom, many of whom the far more numerous hardworking farmers despised. After meeting and consorting with a hill man, Wandering Star—each committing treason by simply befriending an enemy of his people—Blue Sky learned the truth. Taking the chance that he might grievously fail, he led the way in making it known to the valley people.

Early Harvest: Morning Sun's chief competitor in their coming-of-age games as well as in his pursuit of Rose Leaf's consent to be his mate. Although Rose Leaf chose the prince, at a crucial moment Early Harvest implored the people not to stand in the way of Rose Leaf's marriage to his rival.

East Land: an outspoken farmer who fought alongside Green Field, Tall Oak, and Full Harvest in the last war with the hill people.

239

Like Autumn Wine, he finds it difficult to think kindly of the hill people.

Fair Judge: a special friend of the queen, Rainbow Evening. She's also the teller who was in charge of the education of the prince, Morning Sun, as well as the orphanage where Spring Rain and Many Numbers grew up. To show their respect, the people insist upon calling her Fair Judge. She openly castigates the first teller, Law Keeper, for his corruption and cronyism.

Full Harvest: Early Harvest's father, who fought alongside Green Field and Tall Oak in the last war with the hill people. He's now a wealthy upper-valley farmer and the apparent father of a large number of children born to mates of his brothers, who died in the war. Late in *Promised Valley Rebellion* Blue Sky discovered how it came about that Full Harvest and Gentle Brook—the wife of Full Harvest's best friend, Green Field—are lovers.

Gentle Brook: wife of Green Field, mother of Blue Sky and Rose Leaf, and cousin of the queen, Rainbow Evening. She and Full Harvest, her husband's compatriot, cousin, and friend, are lovers. She insists that valley women have the right to join the fight to defend against the hill people, whose leaders proclaim their intent to exterminate the valley people.

Good Harvest: said to be a younger cousin of his best friend, Early Harvest, but more likely his half-brother. He comes of age in *Promised Valley War*.

Green Field: Gentle Brook's mate and Blue Sky and Rose Leaf's father. He's a farmer hero who saved the life of his best friend, Tall Oak, then a prince, in the last war with the hill people. At the end of the recent rebellion, he convinced the farmers to approve the marriage of the current prince, Morning Sun, to Rose Leaf. He and Gentle Brook had led the people to believe Rose Leaf was their daughter, but Blue Sky forced his parents and the king and queen to reveal she's actually the daughter and sole heir of the hill people's king. Blue Sky took a gamble that the people would do whatever his father asked them to do. He believed his father was a far more gifted leader than Tall Oak, whom heredity alone had made king.

Law Keeper: the kingdom's first teller and Sturdy Limb's submissive ally. The farmers openly laugh at his awkward attempts to impress them with his authority. He used his position to attempt to separate the physically attractive Spring Rain from Many Numbers and have him for himself. Blue Sky not only mocked and ridiculed Law Keeper but also revealed his scheming to the farmers, who, adoring Spring Rain, expressed their outrage.

Many Numbers: a young teller who lives with his mate, Spring Rain, in an ivy-covered house. Many Numbers was the first to join Blue Sky's rebellion on behalf of the prince and Rose Leaf. Many Numbers had good reasons to wish to see the downfall of the ill-chosen Law Keeper and Sturdy Limb and their corrupt regime.

Morning Sun: the prince, the only living child of Tall Oak and Rainbow Evening. He's also Blue Sky and Rose Leaf's best childhood friend. Perhaps as a result of that, he tends to side with the farmers against his father's officials.

Noon Breeze: a scrawny, boyish, no-apologies, pleasure-loving son of poor farmers. He became an unlikely friend of Blue Sky's in the apprentice tellers' encampment.

Rainbow Evening: the queen, Morning Sun's mother, and Gentle Brook's cousin. She despises Sturdy Limb and Law Keeper and spends a good deal of her time with Fair Judge.

Solemn Promise: a son of a wealthy court family and a friend of the prince, Morning Sun.

Spring Rain: Many Numbers' mate, a young teller the people favor for his lovely tenor voice, patience in hearing their arguments, and pleasing looks. As a supervising teller, he shared a hut with Blue Sky in the apprentice teller's encampment. Spring Rain was the second man—Morning Sun was the first—Blue Sky fell in love with but couldn't have.

Sturdy Limb: Tall Oak's brother and chief warrior. Most of the farmers would be pleased to see him dead, with no chance of his ever becoming their king.

Tall Oak: the king, Rainbow Evening's mate, and Morning Sun's father. At the end of the last war with the hill people, he appointed his brother, Sturdy Limb, to be chief warrior, after Green Field, the people's choice, turned down the position. The rebellion that Blue Sky led resulted in Tall Oak's permitting Green Field to tell the people the truth regarding Rose Leaf.

Valley Defender: the oldest of Sturdy Limb's three sons and Morning Sun's first cousin. He also wished to be Rose Leaf's mate.

Hill People

Dancing Song: Wandering Star's mother.

Dark Storm: the older son of Thunder Hunter, the hill people's second most powerful chieftain.

Heaven's Voice: the hill people's first teller.

Lightning Spear: the hill people's king. Rose Leaf, abducted by Green Field and Tall Oak in the last war with the valley people, is his only legitimate child.

Long Arm: a skillful hunter who spies on Wandering Star and Blue Sky, commits the act that starts a war with the valley people, and immediately becomes a hero among his people.

Rose Leaf: she grew up believing she was Green Field and Gentle Brook's daughter and Blue Sky's sister. Morning Sun, Early Harvest, Valley Defender, and many other young valley men wished to be her mate. The king, queen, and her parents warned her she couldn't choose Morning Sun. But she isn't Green Field and Gentle Brook's daughter or Blue Sky's sister. In the last war with the valley people, Green Field and Tall Oak, escaping from their captors and correctly guessing she was Lightning Spear's only child, abducted her, intending to kill her. When they realized they couldn't kill a child, they took her back to the valley with them. Upon seeing her, Gentle Brook wished to raise her as her daughter.

Thistle Dew: the hill people's queen. After her daughter Rose Leaf's abduction, she refused to appear in public.

Thunder Hunter: the hill people's second most powerful chieftain, after his cousin, their king, Lightning Spear. He's known for his exceptional brutality. His sons are Dark Storm and War Cloud.

True Hunter: a cousin of Dark Storm and War Cloud. He's also a physically attractive teller and exceptional warrior.

Wandering Star: a hill man who became Blue Sky's friend, both of them aware they were committing treason every moment they were together. Wandering Star informed Blue Sky who Rose Leaf was. He won over the valley people when he apologized for what Lightning Spear, the hill people's king, had done in the last war.

War Cloud: Thunder Hunter's younger son. He's as physically seductive as True Hunter, and True Hunter's and Long Arm's only rival as a warrior. He begs his father and Lightning Spear to carry out executions

www.ingramcontent.com/pod-product-compliance
Lightning Source LLC
Chambersburg PA
CBHW071146170626
46809CB00002B/788